Blood Born

RENEE LAKE

To my mom Carmen. Who thinks I am weird, but has always encouraged it. It's not easy having a daughter who'd rather be a vampire than a princess.

CHAPTER ONE

Jolene Harper
Yesterday at 2:55 pm
Just got done registering for classes! Scored a great house to rent and a prime place in Ms. Dulcara's Eastern European Studies Class!

Comments:

Madeline West
Lucky! I'd have given anything to get into that class. I got stuck with anthropology instead. Can't wait to see you when classes start. This summer away from you has been too long!
Lucca West
Ugh, can you two please not flirt where I can see it? I will be in your class Jo. Hopefully you guys will have some cute roommates you can hook me up with!

Allison Hastings
@princessallie
Nothing like transferring schools a year in to make you feel insecure. Hope the new roomies have some class.

Oh, hell no.

Madeline West stared at the large, rambling house in front of her and thought, not for the first time, that maybe she should have just gotten a dorm room. The place was made of dark wood, with large windows, a pointed roof, and the first floor had a wraparound porch. It had to be at least three stories tall.

"It looks intense," her mother said, standing next to her.

"Looks haunted," her father teased, nudging her shoulder. He was carrying a box full of her stuff.

"The price was great. Off campus housing isn't usually cheap," Mom said.

"It does look kind of old," Madeline, or Maddie, to everyone who knew her, said. *I can't live here; what kind of person would live here?*

"Let's go inside and check it out. We can always try to find you somewhere else if this place is awful." Dad gave her a friendly push. Maddie went up the five creaking stairs and walked across the porch. The front door matched the house: big, dark, and made from some sort of heavy wood.

"I wish Lucca was here." Maddie bit her lip after she said it. She hadn't wanted to go to the same college as Lucca, but it was the only way her parents would let him go to college at all. *Ghosts...no vampires...I know, serial killers.*

They dropped off Maddie's twin brother, Lucca, at the boys' dorm on campus first. Lucca wanted a true college experience, full of parties, late nights, girls, and living in a dorm room.

Maddie just wanted to not worry about him for once, but she knew that wasn't likely to happen.

"No one would be comfortable with your brother living in a house full of girls." Mom tried the door handle, but it was locked.

"But we do wish he would have wanted to room with you too," Dad said, looking concerned. Lucca was born with a heart condition; idiopathic cardiomyopathy. Which basically meant eventually he would experience complete heart failure. Everyone tended to fret over him.

"Huh, thought the landlord said it would be unlocked?" Mom frowned and took out her phone from the pocket of her blazer. Maddie looked just like her mother; long, chestnut brown hair, pale skin with the bare hint of freckles across her nose and large, green eyes.

There were only two major differences between Maddie and her mom. The first being two red birth marks below Maddie's ear, like a vampire's bite mark, each a dime in size. Maddie hated them, she'd been born with them and teased as a child.

The second was their skin color, her mother was about five shades darker than Maddie. Maddie hoped college would be different; in their small home town the birth marks weren't the only reason Maddie had been teased. You couldn't tell by looking at her, but Maddie was half Puerto Rican. Though, if one more person asked her if she spoke Spanish, she might flip her shit.

It was a matter of personal shame that her mother spoke it fluently, but Maddie did not. She didn't even like to talk about her heritage or check the Hispanic box on forms. The only real way you could tell Maddie wasn't all the way white was the thick and rich texture of her dark brown hair.

"Lucca will be fine," Maddie commented, wishing, again, that she hadn't said anything at all.

"Is it locked? Should we call the landlord?" Dad asked. He was tall, getting soft around the middle, and his blond hair was thinning out. He and Lucca had matching blue eyes.

"Ah, the landlord sent an email. The key is in the flower pot." Mom knelt next to a rust colored pot with nothing but soil in it and pulled out a large, brass key. With a twist in the lock and a shove against the door, it opened into a spacious front hall.

The place smelled like pine trees, and sunlight filled the rooms. A mahogany and yellow flowered rug covered the wood floor in the entryway. There was a light on above them, shining brightly and a small table that had a land line phone and five sets of keys. Who even used a land line anymore?

"Okay, this is much better," Maddie said, relieved. The place was old, but everything seemed to be updated and clean. *Okay, I can do this. I can't let my imagination run away with me.*

"Very nice!" her dad exclaimed, shifting the box. Must have been filled with her books.

"Your room is on the third floor, number five." Mom was reading paperwork from the landlord. She grabbed a set of keys that had the number five attached to it with paper, placing the dirt covered key on the table.

"Well, these boxes won't unpack themselves," Dad joked and started up the stairs first. The third floor had dark purple carpets and smooth wood paneled walls, there were only two bedrooms and a shared bathroom, each door was a deep brown with purple trim that had the room number in bright lavender paint.

Mom gave Maddie her keys and they went into her room. "Oh yes, this is great!" Maddie felt happy. She'd never lived outside of her parents' house before and had worried about the living conditions. A queen-sized bed filled one corner, a desk, internet and cable hook ups, and a decent sized closet took up the other. The windows looked out over the yard and you could see an old mansion in the distance. Everything outside was starting to turn rust colored, as fall made her slow entrance into the world, pushing summer away.

As she looked out the window at the Dulcara Mansion, a shiver of something, not quite fear, ran up her spine. Foreboding maybe? Or just nerves? Closing her eyes and counting to ten, Maddie pushed the feelings aside. Her parents had told her a dozen times not to let her imagination get the better of her.

"That's a historical landmark, apparently this house and the mansion used to be on the same property before the family sold the acres in between to the city," Dad said, setting a box down, as mom went to get some more.

"Yeah?"

"Yup, looked up some things about this town when you decided to come here. This house and the Dulcara Mansion are still owned by the family. They give tours of the mansion. You and Jo should check it out."

"Dulcara? Like the professor?"

"One and the same." Dad gave her a smile and headed down the stairs. Maddie was about to follow, it was all her junk after all, when she heard a familiar laugh; Jo!

Taking a deep breath, she quelled the negative thoughts in her mind. She should be ecstatic Jo had decided to go to college with her. A few times over the summer, Maddie had wished Jo hadn't been so eager for them to be together forever. How would she have any adventures with Jo watching her every step? She loved her girlfriend, she did...Jo was just exhausting.

Maddie straightened her white off the shoulder dress and quickly left the room. Jo would be irritated if Maddie didn't come greet her. She wondered if Jo had changed over the summer, grown her hair out, pierced her nose, or maybe started wearing colored contacts.

Taking the stairs as fast as she could, Maddie almost collided with Jo on the second floor. The girls embraced and Jo pressed her lips, warm and dry, against Maddie's.

"I missed you so much!" Jo told her.

Jo and Maddie started dating their junior year of high school, they'd spent the last summer apart with nothing but emails and phone calls to keep their love from dwindling.

Jo's dad hadn't been happy about his daughter's school choice or Maddie, to be honest. He wanted Jo to marry well and give him Ivy League bound grand babies. In fact, one of the stipulations to him agreeing to pay for school was that Jo and Maddie have separate rooms and not take any classes together.

Maddie's mom and dad loved Jo, they were more down to earth than Jo's rich dad. Not that Maddie's family was poor, but while Maddie grew up in a cozy ranch style house on five acres, Jo lived in a two-story modern home where everything was clean, white, and brand new.

"I missed you, too," Maddie said.

"This is going to be a fun year. We get to live in the same house and be treated like grownups," Jo told her. Jo was a lot taller than Maddie. She had a handsome face with short brown hair, skin that was forever tanned, and dark eyes. Where Maddie was curvy, Jo was broad shouldered and narrow hipped. Jo wore pin striped pants, combat boots, and a black t-shirt, she called the outfit her lesbian uniform.

"Grownups help schlep their own boxes!" Maddie's dad called from the front door. "You need help with your stuff, Jolene?"

"No, thanks, Mr. West, I got it covered!"

The two girls laughed and, arm in arm, went down the stairs.

Sooner than Maddie was ready for, all her boxes were in her room, and it was time for her parents to leave.

"Remember, we're only a few hours' drive away if you need anything." Mom kissed Maddie and Jo goodbye, sniffling.

"Alright kiddos, behave yourselves." Dad gave a friendly salute and they were out the door. It shut loudly behind them. Jo and Maddie stood in the foyer and didn't speak until they heard the car pull away.

"So, your dad didn't come?" Maddie asked, as they began to explore the first floor. *Who lived here before us? Did they have slaves? That would be awful. I don't think I could live here with that history.*

"Nope, I packed up and drove myself. Thankfully the job with Dad all summer made sure the Jo-mobile was in tip top condition for the drive." Jo spent the summer at her dad's law firm, basically running errands and acting as a receptionist. It was another condition for paying for college at Humboldt State. Jo wanted to be a lawyer too, but she didn't want to go to Stanford, like her dad.

Walking into the living room, Maddie noticed the built-in shelves full of books first while Jo gave an appreciative whistle at the large, flat screen, HD TV. The room had a deep blue carpet and two comfy, if a bit worn looking, brown, leather couches. Warm light came in through the large, bay window, blue curtains hung loosely around the delicate frame.

Maddie pictured her and Jo curled up in the window together reading their favorite book, *Nightmare Abbey* by Thomas Love Peacock. That was how they met, they both went to the library for a book to do a report on and chose the same novel. There was only one copy, and since neither wanted a different book, they decided to share. Jo got the better grade as she usually did. It had been quite the meet-cute. They both loved the novel and had spent hours talking to each other about it, leading to their first date.

"I wish they'd put you on the third floor with me," Maddie told her, focusing on Jo; she had a bad habit of letting her mind wander.

"Me too, then it would be easier to sneak into each other's rooms." Jo tickled Maddie and gave her another kiss, as they moved on to check out the kitchen and dining area.

"Well, as long as you didn't lose any of your skills over the summer, the distance won't matter," Maddie teased. Jo was not her first girlfriend, but she was her first lover, and Maddie missed the intimacy of their relationship while they had been apart.

"Nope, nor did I use those skills on anyone but myself." Jo laughed, as

Maddie blushed. The kitchen was very modern with polished concrete counters, stainless steel appliances, and brand-new cabinets. There was a breakfast nook with a cream-colored bench and small table next to a window that overlooked the side yard.

"How was Puerto Rico?" Jo asked.

"I sent you half a dozen emails and several letters," Maddie responded, not that Jo had answered any of them. Maddie's grandma had engulfed Lucca and her in the culture, she'd taken so many pictures of the food she worried her Instagram would break.

"I know, but they were kind of dull, and you weren't much better on the phone," Jo said, leading the way into the dining room.

"I have pictures. It was amazing, and my grandma says hi."

The dining room connected to the kitchen, and a large oak table that sat eight held prominent place in the center of the room. Walls with gold wallpaper and a matching rug under the table and a low hanging chandelier gave the room a decadent feel. A vase full of orange speckled Humboldt lilies sat on the table. A portrait of a woman hung on one wall, but neither girl paid attention to it.

"Wow, pretty room," Maddie said.

"That we'll most likely never use."

"We might. We can have romantic dinners here."

"Are you going to cook?" Jo asked, raising an eyebrow.

"Maybe, you never know. I could develop a passion for it." Maddie felt a little irritated. Just because she didn't cook didn't mean she couldn't learn. *Maybe I should take a cooking class, I could make elaborate meals like paella or lobster Thermador.*

"Right, I'll believe it when I see it. We are more take out type people," Jo said dismissively. Maddie opened her mouth to argue but stopped as a new voice broke up their almost fight.

"Hello!"

Jo took Maddie's hand and they rushed to the front hall. Maddie's heart rate leapt. The prospect of new people meant new friends and hopefully new experiences. Maybe the other roommates would be unique and fun. A dred-wearing surfer girl who only spoke in clichés, or someone from a foreign country and Maddie could take French or Chinese and ace it! Or maybe they'd be horrible, and she could write a book about what it was like to live with a heroin addict from Idaho or a bad-tempered gang member.

The door was wide open, and a girl stood in it, framed by the sunlight. She was quite short with large breasts and hips. Maddie was envious, while she was pale and kind of pink, this new girl had a beautiful ivory complexion, the kind found in makeup ads. Her eyes were a brilliant blue and the hair she had wound into an elaborate French twist was red. She wore a white mini skirt with matching sandals and a cerulean tank top.

"Glad to see I'm not the first to arrive," she said, in a voice heavily laced with a southern accent. She held a vase full of fresh, white roses.

"Hi! I'm Jo, room three, and this is Maddie, room five." Jo thrust out her large hand, and the new girl seemed to study it for a moment and then placed her well-manicured hand in Jo's.

"I'm Allison Hastings, I believe I am in room one."

"Flowers?" Maddie asked. *Should I have brought something? Maybe a fancy fruit or cheese?*

"One always brings a gift into someone else's house." She set the flowers down on the table next to the rest of the keys. Reaching into her fancy purse, she pulled out a letter, pursing glossy lips, she quickly read a few lines and nodded. Folding it back up, she grabbed the keys on the table with the number one.

"Okay, bring it in!" she called behind her. All three girls moved to the side, as several muscular men began to bring in boxes.

"Where to, Miss Hastings?" A burly looking guy with a beard asked.

"Second floor, room one," Allison said, then she turned her attention back to Jo and Maddie.

"So, where are you from?" Jo asked, looking amused.

"Houston, you?"

"Maddie and I are from a town a few hours from here, actually."

"Freshmen?" Allison inquired.

"Yes," Maddie jumped in, if she didn't talk now, she wouldn't at all. Jo was a big personality and sometimes overshadowed her. "I'm in Women's Studies, and Jo is doing her generals before moving on to law."

"I'm a sophomore. I heard this college had a better business program so my father made a few calls, and here I am!" Allison exclaimed, her smile large.

"Oh, that's cool, my brother is majoring in Business Administration," Maddie said. Allison's eyes seemed to grow brighter.

"A brother? Is he cute?"

"Most girls think so," Jo said, snorting back a laugh.

"You'll have to introduce me. Now if you'll excuse me, I need to tell the movers where to put my things." Allison went up the stairs, pulling out the newest iPhone.

"She'll take some getting used to," Jo muttered.

"Seemed nice."

"You think everyone seems nice." Jo leaned over and kissed her cheek. Their almost fight seemed forgotten.

"My dad said this house is owned by the Dulcara family," Maddie said, as they went into the living room and sat together, close, limbs intertwining.

"Yeah, that's what I read online. The family is rich. I can't wait to meet Professor Dulcara, everyone says that she is an amazing teacher." Jo reached up and twirled a lock of Maddie's hair, giving her goosebumps.

"Why are you taking an Eastern European class anyway?"

"I hate history, you know that. I have to fulfill a history requirement though, so this seemed like a fun option."

"Doesn't hurt that if you score a coveted TA position it sets you for life." A new voice entered the conversation. Jo and Maddie looked up, Maddie couldn't believe they hadn't heard the door open again.

There was a black girl leaning against the doorway. She had on jeans with ripped knees, a bright red crop top that had a black outline of Angela Davis on it, matching Doc Martins, and her hair was short, ebony, and natural. She was very beautiful, like classically, her brown eyes framed by long thick lashes.

"Excuse me, who are you?" Jo asked, standing up.

"I'm going to live here with you. I'm Scarlet Jones," she said, without smiling.

Jo and Maddie quickly introduced themselves.

"Looks like I'm in room two, second floor."

"In between Jo and Allison then, Allison is already here," Maddie explained.

"She own the fancy car out front?"

"I guess so." Maddie didn't think Scarlet could be talking about Jo's car. Jo's car was nice, but not fancy. Jo was given a BMW when she turned sixteen and wrecked it within a week, so her dad made her pay for the next one.

"Look, my best friend is right behind me, I gotta warn you ahead of time. She has psoriasis and is self-conscious about it. It's not contagious and if you say anything to her I'll be really pissed," Scarlet spoke fast, eyes narrowing at the two of them.

"We would never, I mean...we're not stupid, no need to threaten us," Maddie said, not wanting to get off to a rough start with her new roommates. *I don't even know what psoriasis is. I better look it up.* She took out her phone, trying to be nonchalant and did a google search.

"If we're clear, Queenie is...a little different. We're rooming outside the dorms this year hoping it will make a difference," Scarlet said.

"Oh, you're not a freshman?" Jo asked.

"No, Queenie and I are juniors. So, if you want booze, ask. We both turned twenty-one this summer," Scarlet said, laughing.

"Scarlet?" A soft voice called from the front porch.

"In here, Queenie!" Scarlet called back. She turned around and gave the first genuine smile to a girl slowly entering the room. The smile softened Scarlet's face and made Maddie realize she probably wasn't as tough as she came across.

Their last roommate was a sun kissed blonde with hazel eyes. She had a sincere looking face, not pretty, with a large nose and forehead. Her neck was long, and she was very tall and very thin. She wore jeans and a green peasant blouse. A hemp bag that said, "Save the Trees" was slung over her left shoulder, and Maddie could see faded red splotches on her arms.

Maddie took a liking to her instantly. "Hi! I'm Maddie, and this is Jo."

"I'm Queenie, Queenie Myles," she said, voice soft, timid, but friendly.

"Scarlet was just telling us about Professor Dulcara's class, something about the teaching assistants?" Maddie focused on Scarlet. She was interested in this professor. She sure seemed to own a lot of land in Arcata, and the way they talked about her made it sound like she was a prominent member of society.

"You have Professor Dulcara?" Queenie asked.

"I do," Jo said.

"She's weird. My uncle doesn't like her, and he has good reason."

"Reasons you won't share with me," Scarlet huffed, looking offended.

"Sorry Scarlet, family secret."

"Your uncle?" Maddie changed the subject.

"Queenie's uncle is an anthropology professor here. It's true Professor Dulcara is kind of strange, but I had her last year and her class is amazing," Scarlet said.

"She picks a TA every few years to help with all her classes, sometimes undergraduates," Queenie informed them.

"Why's that strange'?" Maddie asked.

"Teachers usually pick grad students, however the amount of money the Dulcara Foundation pumps into the community and school allows her special privileges. Sometimes she will choose an undergraduate," Scarlet answered.

"Her TAs do very well in life. She uses her connections when they graduate to get them whatever they want; a job, internship...even a spouse. Sometimes the TAs become her lovers." Queenie's eyes got larger with every word.

Her lovers? What would that be like, to be in bed with an older, experienced woman? Maddie's thoughts weren't running away from her, they were sprinting.

"Oh, those are just rumors, Queenie, don't scare the freshmen," Scarlet chuckled, slinging an arm around Queenie.

"There's a portrait of her in the dining room, if you're curious," Queenie said.

"Good job snagging that class so early on. You won't regret it," Scarlet said. "Come on, Queenie, let's get our stuff." They turned and went back outside, heads together whispering.

"Whatcha think of that?" Jo asked after they left.

"I think I want to see that painting." Maddie stood up, leaving Jo in the living room, trying to figure out the remote controls.

She entered the dining room and this time focused on the portrait of the woman hanging on the back wall. It was an oil painting on canvas with a gold frame. Maddie felt shock go through her system as she gazed upon it.

The woman sat in an ornate, wooden chair, black hair wound around her hair in an old-fashioned elaborate style. Later Maddie couldn't tell you what she was wearing or if she was outside or in the middle of the circus.

"I know those eyes," Maddie said to the empty room. She knew the shape, the black pools surrounded by long lashes.

Collapsing into a dining room chair, Maddie's heart raced out of control.

Those eyes had been in her dreams.

CHAPTER TWO

9:00 am TTH and 11:00 am MWF Eastern European Studies Class

From: Professor Valora Dulcara

Welcome to Humboldt State University. If you are receiving this email, you have received a spot in my coveted freshmen/sophomore class of the semester. You should have already received the syllabus and purchased a copy of <u>Hungarian Myth and Legend</u> *as well as* <u>The Turkish Invasion.</u> *These are the books I have assigned this year. I am very much looking forward to getting to know each of you and am excited by the areas of study we shall be pursuing.*

Please be prompt to class and come prepared, participation is 15%.

This year I am pleased to announce there are two extra credit activities instead of just one. The Dulcara Mansion is releasing historical family documents to the local museum, and I will require ten students to assist in cataloguing them. I have been informed an English credit will be given upon completion. I will begin taking applications the second week of September. Next, my Yuletide trip to Romania: this year we are bringing back soil and sapling samples for the science and forestry department. This trip takes place over winter break and will earn the students selected a science credit. I will select students for this trip based on enthusiasm and grades.

A reminder—no intense food smells, perfumes or lotions are allowed in my class.

If you are caught caring more about your hair or makeup than the material, you will also be asked to leave.

Cordially,
  Valora Dulcara

*M*addie and Jo spent their last free day before classes started making sure they had all their books and knew the fastest way to get to all their classes. It seemed most freshmen were doing the same, though their older roommates rolled their eyes or laughed at the girls' enthusiasm.

"I got an email from Professor Dulcara about the extra credit she is offering this year," Jo said, perched on the end of Maddie's bed. "She's doing a family historical project at her house."

"Are you going to participate?" Maddie asked, as she watched the sun begin to set. She loved the view from her room. *How many feet is it to the ground? Would I die if I jumped? Wait, what kind of question is that?*

"Well, I have to submit a resume and application, so I don't know."

"It would look great on your resume, so you should do it. All your resume has is community service and your dad's job. You've been looking for something else, what did you say, something to make you seem more rounded?"

"True, maybe I will."

Maddie's phone went off, the sound of birds filled the room.

"I hate that ring tone, either change it or tell Lucca to stop calling."

Maddie hit ignore. She'd call him back later. Jo didn't like it if she picked up while they were together.

"I like birds. There was a get together today for those students majoring in Business Administration. I told him to call me after. I hope he enjoyed himself." She tried to hide the worry in her voice.

"Don't stress about him! Lucca has been fine on his new medication for years now. Didn't the doctors okay him coming to school and acting like a normal boy?" Jo raised her eyebrows. Maddie hated it when she did that, it always followed a statement that meant Jo thought she was being foolish.

"I can't help but worry," Maddie said. "Come on, let's go downstairs and get some dinner."

"Sounds like a plan." Jo grabbed her hand and whisked her down the stairs. They were the only ones home; the others were all out and about enjoying their last day of freedom.

"What should we order?" Jo asked, they hadn't gone shopping yet, though shopping would mainly consist of things they could heat up like pizza rolls, chicken pot pies, and ramen noodles.

"Pizza."

"Pepperoni?"

"Let's do one pepperoni and one cheese. I think Queenie is a vegetarian. If they come home, I want her to feel like she can eat with us."

"I am not buying pizza for the whole house."

"It would be a nice gesture."

"That I'd be paying for."

"I'd pitch in, you know that," Maddie said, defensively.

"No, no, I'll do it." Jo took out her cell phone to search for the nearest pizza place and within ten minutes, two large pizzas were on their way.

"I hate that picture. It stares at you," Jo said, as they walked into the dining room.

"I like it, can't wait to meet her in person." It was a truth and a lie. She did like the picture, but she feared meeting Valora Dulcara. Why did Maddie feel like she knew her?

They sat down at the elaborate table, both girls getting their phones out.

"See, we will use this room!" Maddie exclaimed, mischief in her voice.

"Fine, though technically checking social media and playing dumb games isn't what this room is for." Jo flashed Maddie her phone screen showing Facebook's blue and white coloring. Maddie decided not to say anything else and opened a game on her phone.

About ten minutes later, Allison came in the room looking sharp in a pale pink sheath dress. "Hello! I'm back!"

"Hi, we ordered pizza if you want any," Maddie said.

"Oh no, I don't eat any fast food, but thanks anyway." Allison sat down near Maddie. "I met your brother today."

"You did?" Maddie asked. She shouldn't have been surprised, Allison did tell her she was majoring in Business Administration too.

"He is so good looking, and sweet! Do you mind if I ask him out some time? It's rare I come across a gentleman this far west," Allison said.

Maddie paused, not sure how to answer. She'd never been asked if someone could date her brother before. *If they get married, she'll be my sister. If they break up will she hate me too?*

"Go for it, Lucca is great," Jo quickly said, covering Maddie's hesitation.

"Are you sure?" Allison looked at Maddie again.

"Yes, of course, that's fine. I don't care," Maddie stammered.

"It doesn't sound like it's alright," Allison said, she sounded less friendly than before.

"No...I mean, yes, it really is fine. I just wasn't prepared for the question." Maddie tried for damage control.

"Okay, thanks!" Allison said, smiling, and left the room.

"What's the matter with you?" Jo asked.

"I was just taken aback by it, that's all." Maddie felt embarrassed. The doorbell rang and Jo got up. Maddie heard the hushed tones of conversation and realized it was probably not the pizza. She followed the sounds into the hallway. Jo was talking to another woman.

The woman was older than Jo and Maddie, but Maddie couldn't tell by how much. She was exquisite to look at. She had olive skin and a voluptuous figure. Her hair was thick, and midnight colored, starting at a widow's peak at her forehead and flowing straight down her back. She wore a dark purple suit and matching heels.

"Maddie!" Jo exclaimed, meeting her eyes over the woman's shoulder. "Sorry, Professor Dulcara, this is Maddie West, my best friend."

Maddie paused. Best friend? She'd ask about that introduction later.

The professor turned and Maddie saw sharp beautiful features and those large black eyes. The ones Maddie would know anywhere. She wanted to take a step back but was frozen in her spot.

"Hello, Miss West, pleased to meet you. How are you enjoying Seară House?" She reached out a hand and Maddie shook it. Valora's eyes strayed to Maddie's birth mark and the woman halted, it was just a second but made Maddie feel uncomfortable.

"It's lovely, I can't believe you want to rent it to college students." Maddie tried to joke, but it came out flat. *Why is your picture in our dining room? A warning, vanity, or simply because you have nowhere else to put it?*

Valora's gaze rose and she finally let go of Maddie's hand.

"I love to see young people filling it with laughter. If I did not rent it out it would sit here collecting dust. I have no other family, and I live in Dulcara Mansion," she said, her voice was thick and lush, tinged with an accent Maddie couldn't place. As Valora spoke, her fingers gently touched a few of the petals on the roses Allison had brought.

Maddie was drawn to the woman's slender hand caressing the petals. They were such a pretty flower, pure white in a glass vase. Maddie didn't know how long they'd live but thought they might get a plant after they died, a plant in the foyer sounded so romantic.

"Sierra House is really wonderful, I'm so glad you like to rent it out," Jo said, laughing, breaking the spell that seemed to surround Valora and Maddie. Maddie turned her head away so neither of them would see the shame staining her cheeks, she really needed to work on the day dreaming.

"It's Seară, it means "evening" in Romanian," the professor corrected.

"I'm sorry," Jo quickly said.

"Do not worry. In my class you will be learning a bit of Romanian."

"We ordered pizza, do you want to join us?" Maddie asked, trying to be polite; she wanted their landlord and Jo's new teacher to like them.

"No, thank you. I always stop by to meet my new tenants and make sure everyone got here in one piece."

"Not all the girls are here, Allison is upstairs, I can go get her," Maddie volunteered.

"No need. I met Miss Hastings already and am acquainted with Miss Myles and Miss Jones from last year," Professor Dulcara said.

"I'm looking forward to your class," Jo told her.

"It will be an exciting year. It is too bad Miss West will not be joining us."

"I'm taking Anthropology with Professor Heeling instead," Maddie said. She didn't think it was her imagination that the older woman's mouth turned down in distaste.

"I am sure you will find his subject fascinating, if not a bit... imaginative. He actually does a section on social anthropology that touches on the natives of Puerto Rico."

"How did you know I'm Puerto Rican?" Maddie asked. *Great now here it comes, do I speak Spanish...Nope, not a bit.*

"I know a great many things, Miss West."

Maddie stood, stunned, she'd never felt so out of her element before.

"Now, Ms. Harper, I assume you will be applying for the first extra credit assignment of the year?" Professor Dulcara placed her full attention on Jo.

"I was thinking about it," Jo said.

"Do not think, simply do. Actions make for far better stories. I have reviewed your transcripts, and it would be a waste for you not to apply."

"I will put together my resume and application first thing this week," Jo said. The doorbell rang again.

"That's probably dinner." Maddie went to get her purse, when she came back, the professor had left, and Jo was talking to the pizza delivery guy.

"I already paid, Maddie, I told you not to worry about it," Jo said upon seeing Maddie's purse.

"I want to chip in."

"You can buy me gas later, here." Jo handed her the two large pizza boxes, gave the guy a cash tip, and shut the door.

"So, what did you think about your new teacher?" Maddie asked, as they took the food into the kitchen. The yummy smell of melted cheese and tomato sauce made her stomach growl.

"I think her class is going to be fun and interesting." Jo grabbed some paper plates from the cupboards and put two slices of pizza on each plate.

"No, I mean what about Professor Dulcara?" Maddie grabbed cups and filled them with water from the fridge. They really needed to go grocery shopping. They had some basics her parents bought but not much else.

"She seemed really great, a bit intense, but I bet she teaches an amazing class. I think I have a good chance of making it on that first extra credit team." They went into the living room and sat on the carpet. Jo grabbed the remote control.

"Hey, why did you introduce me as your best friend?" Maddie asked.

Jo put the slice of pizza she was holding down, slowly. "Well you are, aren't you?"

"Of course, but why not just tell her I'm your girlfriend?" Maddie was starting to lose her appetite.

"Maddie, it's pretty obvious I'm gay, okay? I don't want to announce it if I don't have to. What if she's super conservative and me being all up in her face about my sexuality hurts my grades or her opinion of me? She can assume all she wants but I wasn't going to spell it out for her."

Jo's words hurt Maddie. This wasn't like Jo at all, this was her father talking from miles away.

"You never had that issue before."

"Well, this is different. I'm not going to hide, but I don't feel the need to shout it from the rooftops right now either." Jo began eating again, ending the conversation.

Maddie stayed silent, processing Jo's words. She guessed they made sense, but they still hurt.

"Look, Maddie, you're bi, things will be easier for you. There's not nearly as much hate going your way these days."

Maddie didn't argue. Jo was wrong. Maddie knew how she looked to a lot of people, like she just couldn't decide, or wanted the best of both words. Some of the LGBTQ community didn't even really consider her to be like them. Maddie felt that sexuality was fluid and wished she wouldn't be punished for it.

"So, Professor Dulcara, she's kind of pretty," Maddie said, trying to lighten the mood, as Jo settled on a Buffy the Vampire Slayer rerun.

"What?" Jo paused, in the middle of chewing. "Sure, she's good looking for an older lady." Her attention focused back on the TV. "Not as hot as Buffy though."

Maddie looked away from the TV; she didn't agree. Professor Dulcara was a hundred times hotter than Buffy. As her eyes strayed from the room, she caught sight of something that wasn't quite right. Standing, she went to the doorway and looked at the blooms near the front door. Her eyes took a moment to make sense of what she was seeing; the snow colored flowers were now shriveled and black.

CHAPTER THREE

Transcript of Social Media Conversations

Allison Hastings
@princessallie
Went on a great date last night with a guy from my business class.
#crushingbigtime

Lucca West
Jo and I both got selected to be a part of Professor Dulcara's extra credit
assignment! Plus, I've been out with this great girl a couple of times.

Scarlet Jones
Yesterday at 5:00pm
Must interview a local psych patient for my final this year. Anyone want
to volunteer? Totally anonymous!

Comments:

Queenie Myles
I may be your only crazy friend, but not an actual psych patient- sorry!
Ask your fancy Dr. Mamma.

"So, you've seen Allison a few times since school started," Maddie commented, after sipping her iced tea. She was having lunch with Lucca at a café near campus. It was a quaint little place, with fake candles on the real wood tables and a pioneer décor.

It had a great outdoor patio that most people enjoyed sitting at. They'd stumbled upon it quite by accident, as it seemed no college kids ate there, just grizzled, old, white guys.

"She's really nice, and pretty," Lucca said, putting mustard on his veggie burger. They looked almost identical, except his eyes were blue, and he had no birth mark.

"Nice? I wouldn't say nice, but she is beautiful."

"Don't be catty, that's not you, that's Jo talking," Lucca said, frowning at her. Maddie thought he looked pale and tried not to worry.

"You're right, Allison has been nothing but polite to me. Did you tell Mom?" Maddie's eyes strayed to the road and sidewalk. She liked watching all the different kinds of people walking by. She liked to imagine their lives, where they were going to, coming from. Were they Christian? Liberal? An alien from outer space? *That would be funny, a liberal, Christian, lizard person.*

"In a way."

"Put it on social media, yeah?"

"Yeah." They both laughed for a few seconds and focused on their food. Maddie was having a roast beef sandwich, her favorite.

"I'm really excited about being chosen to help with the Dulcara family documents, I think it's going to be very interesting," Lucca said.

"Jo is ecstatic. I'm meeting her after class today, and she's getting the itinerary." Maddie was happy for Jo and Lucca and knew this was a big deal for both of them. She didn't get the appeal of spending hours digging through dusty documents, but hey, to each their own. She was much more into actually doing something, feeling like she could contribute to a cause that made things better for a lot of people, and if she couldn't do that, she wanted a good book.

"I got mine yesterday. It's going to be extra work, but it will look great on my resume." Lucca was practically beaming. Maddie felt inspired by her brother, he'd been sick most of their lives, and it was great to know he was enjoying college as much as she was.

"Is your schedule different than Jo's?" Maddie asked.

"She chose about ten of us, plus her three TAs. We won't all be working at the same time," Lucca explained.

She was about to finish her sandwich when there was an ear-piercing scream from across the street, where a row of houses stood, side by side. Every patron of the diner stopped and looked up, the waitress near them dropped a dish, the breaking sound of ceramic adding to the tension.

Maddie focused on a girl running from the front door of a two-storied house. It was white with a large porch in front, the paint was peeling in many places, but the place looked lived in and loved rather than old and neglected. Maddie had admired some of the details when they'd walked past earlier, like the pink flowers painted on the old porch and the design carved into the door.

Maddie's mind reeled. *It's a mass murder, a kid with their head spinning puking soup, a rerun of Cop Rock.*

The girl stumbled down the walkway, almost tripping over the bushes and knocking into the gate. She shoved against it hard until it gave and came barreling out into the street, almost being hit by a car.

"That's Lorraine, I have class with her," Maddie told Lucca, as she jumped up from her chair and ran out into the road. She grabbed the girl's arms and pulled her onto the sidewalk, just as another car drove by, honking their horn in annoyed tones.

The girl trembled against Maddie, she was a thin, mousy brunette with large eyes that took up half her face.

"Lorraine, right? It's Lorraine?" Maddie said. She wanted the girl to focus on her, but her eyes were glassy, so she gave her a squeeze and repeated her name again.

"Yes, I'm Lorraine... My...my family." Lorraine pointed, mouth thin, face pale.

"What's happened?" Maddie asked, aware a crowd was starting to form, and wished they wouldn't. Whatever happened probably didn't need an audience.

"Lorraine? What's going on?" a male voice asked. Maddie turned to her left to see a handsome, young man on the sidewalk. He held carnations in one hand.

"I don't know. She came from there, screaming," Maddie told him. She didn't know what had scared the poor girl, but it must be awful. She'd go look herself but not only a) did she not want to but b) she worried if she left Lorraine the girl would run back out into the road.

"I'm her fiancée. That's her parents' house," he told Maddie.

"Maybe you should go check," Maddie instructed. By now Lorraine was sobbing in earnest, heartfelt tremors wracking her entire frame.

"Is everything okay?" Lucca asked, stepping onto the sidewalk next to them. His hands were shoved into the pockets of his jacket. "Don't worry, I paid."

"I don't know but..." Maddie trailed off, as Lorraine's fiancé darted out of the house and fell to his knees, vomiting all over the front yard. He was pale and hollow eyed.

"Call the police, Lucca, please," Maddie said, cold enveloping over her. Whatever was in that house must be a nightmare.

Maddie tugged Lorraine's arm and brought her closer to the house, thinking maybe being with her fiancé would help, but the moment they got to the gate it was as if she woke up and started shrieking again.

"Lorraine, calm down, it's going to be okay." Maddie rubbed her arms, trying to maintain a firm calm tone as sirens began to blare in the distance.

"Cops are on their way," Lucca said, putting his phone in his back pocket.

When the police arrived, a female officer took over with Lorraine and instructed Maddie and Lucca to stand with the rest of the gathering crowd. Maddie gave her their information, assuming they'd want statements later.

As Maddie and Lucca made their way over to everyone else, she listened to bits of conversations.

"What's going on?'

"Can't you smell the blood?"

"What's going on? Murder? Rape?"

"She's just hysterical."

Maddie couldn't see inside the house at all. She couldn't take her eyes off Lorraine. She didn't know what happened, but it must be something awful. She'd never seen someone look so devastated before, not even when her parents were told Lucca didn't qualify for a heart transplant.

"Whatcha think happened?" Lucca asked her, as they held their coveted position, closest to the house. Police were all over, some rushing into the house while others began crowd control, and some roped off the yard and house.

Maddie liked the feel of being in the throng of people. There was so much to take in. What people were saying, doing, and wearing. It was invigorating and anxiety inducing. She only wished this was a protest and not a bunch of people gathered to find out about a crime of some sort. *I'll close my eyes and when I open them this will have been a bad dream, no one will be dead, and I'll get to start the day over. Remind me to pick somewhere else for lunch.*

"Please stay back, people!" an officer shouted, as they taped off the scene.

One of the officers who'd been first inside the house came out and threw up over the side of the porch rail. The steaming pile of retch frightened Maddie more than anything else. What could make a cop sick?

"It must be really bad," Lucca whispered to her, as people began to stop talking and just focus on the activity.

"Thanks, Captain Obvious," Maddie whispered back. The group of people outside doubled and then tripled in size, but everyone was strangely silent. It was eerie. This was a bustling college town at the end of summer, and not once in the weeks since she'd moved in had she seen it like this. There was a faint breeze and the sun beat down on Maddie's head. Police, paramedics, and firemen were going in and out of the front door, but everyone was quiet, just watching or working.

Someone put a blanket around the crying girl and began walking her and the man to a waiting police car. Lorraine tried to pull away and run back inside when Professor Dulcara showed up and grabbed her by the arms.

"Lorraine, no, you do not want to go back in there," the professor said.

"Oh, Valora, it's awful!" With her words, the world made sense again and Maddie heard the trickle of conversation through the crowd.

"I know." Professor Dulcara placed an arm around her. "You need to go with the police officers now, and with your fiancé."

"I should have been here, I should have been home!" Lorraine wailed.

"So you could die too? That does not make sense." The professor handed her off to her fiancé and the couple got into the back of the police car.

Professor Dulcara stepped further away, and Maddie strained to hear the rest of the conversation. There was a slightly pudgy, older man who Maddie assumed was the one in charge, striding over to the professor.

"Valora, I'm going to have to ask you to answer some questions at the station, too," he said, voice very deep, almost villain-like.

"Maddie, what..." Lucca had noticed his professor too.

"Hush!" Maddie hissed at her brother, edging closer to the tape to listen.

"That will not be a problem, Aaron. I was with the Ceres's just this morning, it is only natural I give you any information I can. I will stop by after my last class this evening."

Maddie was mesmerized by the expression on the professor's face, her eyes almost sparkled with intensity.

"This evening will be fine, Valora," the man said. He stood still and watched the professor leave. She didn't hurry, but strolled through the crowd, people parted for her, most greeted her in neutral tones.

"What was that all about?" Lucca asked her, just as the first gurney came out. There was a filled, black body bag on the gurney.

"Professor Dulcara was with those people this morning, now they are all dead," Maddie told her brother.

"I wonder what happened?" Lucca looked green around the edges, he'd never done well with blood.

"Whatever it was, it was bad," Maddie commented, as another set of paramedics brought out another body. People were making all sorts of exclamations around her as another, smaller, body was brought out.

Maddie and Lucca stayed until people began to get bored and start wandering off, probably to spread the gossip as quickly as they could. The breeze began to blow and with it came a stench of gore from inside the house, the rest of the stragglers moved away rather than smell death.

Lucca went off to his dorm, complaining of a headache, and Maddie went to find Jo. She'd counted five bodies coming out of that house. She hoped none of them were children. She hated it when kids died, it reminded her of too many uncomfortable and sterile afternoons at the children's hospital with her brother.

The main campus wasn't far so Maddie decided to process her

thoughts and walk. Jo's class was ending in a few minutes, Professor Dulcara had either left class to deal with the horror or went straight from all that awfulness to class. She wondered if the professor would mention it to her students.

"Maddie!"

Maddie broke away from her melancholy thoughts, as someone called her name. She stopped and looked around to see Queenie running in her direction. The little hippy had her blonde hair in braids and looked like an ad for COACH. *In another life, Queenie totally lived in a commune and talked to chickens or something.*

"Hey Queenie."

"Did you hear, an entire family was slaughtered just a mile from here?" she gushed.

"Lucca and I were having lunch across the street, it wasn't the whole family. At least one of their daughters survived."

"Wow, I would not have wanted to be anywhere around there. That sounds horrible." Queenie shuddered.

"It was pretty bad. Do you know what actually happened to them?"

"Some girls outside my Botany class said all their throats had been torn out." Queenie scratched her arm; Maddie watched as a few flakes of skin fell to the ground.

"Did you know any of the Ceres family? I only knew Lorraine in passing."

"One of their sons is a year older than me, but no, not well. The mom is a member of the historical society. Scarlet knew them better since she's actually from here," Queenie said. She looked behind her, as if to make sure she wasn't being watched. "They got on Valora Dulcara's bad side... that's what my uncle said."

"Professor Dulcara was there! I heard her say she was with the family just this morning," Maddie exclaimed.

"Not surprised. My uncle does work for the historical society. He told me that Professor Dulcara doesn't want to open Dulcara Mansion up for the annual Halloween Ball this year. It will cause a huge dip in their finances if she won't. They depend on the ticket money. She's being stingy with some records too."

"I wonder why she doesn't want to have it." It didn't make sense, wasn't cataloguing records for the historical society what Jo and Lucca would be doing?

"Because she is awful."

"You don't know that," Maddie gently reprimanded the other girl. Queenie had such a softness to her nature Maddie was surprised to hear such an angry tone in her voice.

"I know she makes me itch and makes my head all fuzzy. I swear I saw bats following her one night," Queenie said, eyes lingering over something in the distance. Maddie wasn't sure how to get out of the conversation when Queenie changed the subject, abruptly. "Hey! Do you want to go to a Planned Parenthood rally?"

"What?' Maddie asked. Queenie pointed to a message board a few feet behind Maddie. The girls walked over, and Queenie pushed her finger against a sign.

"Yes, I'd love to," Maddie said, after reading the paper. The local Planned Parenthood was holding a fundraiser, not a rally, over the weekend. "Jo will be busy." Why did she feel the need to add that sentence in?

"Good! I'll see if Scarlet and Allison want to join us. Gotta run! Don't get axe murdered on your way home!" Queenie yelled as she ran off.

"Weird girl," Maddie said to herself. She glanced at her phone and there was a text from Jo, wondering where she was. Maddie hurried, she was late. A fundraiser for Planned Parenthood would be fun. She'd volunteered at the one in her home town as a clinic escort and really enjoyed it.

As she came around the corner to where Jo's class was, she bumped into Jo. Jo grinned down at her.

"Going somewhere?"

"Sorry, Jo, there has been so much drama today!" Maddie hugged her girlfriend and felt warmth surge through her, as Jo kissed her forehead and played with the skin at the nape of her neck.

"I know, it's all over campus already, scary and sad." Jo took Maddie's hand, and Maddie realized they weren't alone. There was a boy standing next to Jo.

"Maddie, this is Byron, he's one of Professor Dulcara's TAs," Jo introduced them. The boy did not offer to shake her hand. Byron was pale, his face youthful and boyish. He was a little podgy, with dark hair and eyes.

"Nice to meet you," he said, voice soft and lyrical. Maddie took an instant disliking to him.

"He's going to be working with me this weekend at Dulcara Mansion," Jo said, grinning.

"Yes. Valora is especially looking forward to you coming to help Jolene." Byron touched Jo's arm briefly and Maddie watched in disgust, as Jo blushed. She couldn't be attracted to him, could she?

"Thanks for walking through the itinerary with me," Jo said. Byron gave a stiff head nod and went back toward Professor Dulcara's classroom.

"He's interesting. Is Byron his real name?" Maddie said, putting an arm around Jo's waist.

"He takes a little getting used to, but he's brilliant, and no, it's Brian, but Byron is more poetic. He writes poetry and has already been published. When he graduates this year, he's moving to France. It's true what Queenie and Scarlet said, being Professor Dulcara's TA gets you all kind of perks and benefits." Jo's voice had a fire in it Maddie had never heard before.

"So now you want to be a TA?" Maddie asked.

"Maybe, it would be a great honor. I gave up a lot of my father's contacts by coming here instead of Stanford." Jo was walking fast, Maddie had to take three steps to every one of Jo's.

"You didn't have to come here," Maddie said, feeling guilty. She already worried that Jo only decided to come to Humboldt State because Maddie hadn't gotten in anywhere else.

"Of course, I did! This is a great school, and you're here." Jo halted, put her hands on Maddie's shoulder, and kissed her. It was a solid kiss, warm and welcoming. Maddie breathed easier afterward.

"I love you, you know that."

"I love you, too." But Maddie felt weird saying it back, like maybe it had become habit instead of an actual feeling, had their time apart this summer changed things?

Jo was already walking again when a thought burst into Maddie's mind.

How had Professor Dulcara known someone was murdered when she spoke to Lorraine?

CHAPTER FOUR

Journal of Lucca West
September 25th

I feel so stupid even writing this down, but my therapist says it will help with the depression. I don't want to call it a diary, so I've chosen a normal three ring notebook and have decided journal is a better word. Diary makes me sound like a fifteen-year-old girl who has a crush on Justin Bieber. My doctors think the depression is a side effect of the medication for my heart.

I was supposed to start this months ago, but just couldn't get myself to write anything. What would I write about? College, my classes, my overprotective parents? I guess I could write about Allison, this cute girl I started dating. But it all seems so trivial and well...would I sound immature if I said: lame?

Something has been happening to me lately that I do want to write down, mostly so I can get over it. I don't put any stock in dreams, it's a bunch of woo woo that they can predict the future or any crap like that. However, ever since I started working on this project at Dulcara Mansion, I have been having the strangest and oddly erotic dreams. It's not just that they are strange or hot, but that I wake up feeling more tired than when I went to bed and I dwell on them all day. Hopefully this helps, I still say this whole journal writing thing is dumb as fuck, maybe I'll prove myself wrong.

Here's last night's:

I'm in my room, sitting on my bed, wearing only my boxers. I'm staring at the TV, there isn't anything on, only the reflection of myself. My roommate is snoring lightly from his bed, but I ignore him. The window is open and the cool almost fall breeze sends a shiver across my spine, but in a good way. I squish my toes into the thread bare carpet and enjoy the sensation. I feel my heart pounding in my chest, but I don't know why. There isn't anything to be anxious about or scared of. I briefly wonder if I should take the tiny, blue pills in my night stand for just this type of moment, but instead focus on my breathing.

I see a shadow move from the window and into the room, and my heart skips a few beats. "Hello?" I ask, feeling stupid—it's only a shadow. But I am so wrong. The shadow grows and turns into a beautiful woman. I wish I could describe her, but when I wake up, her image is shadowy and out of focus. All I know is she is beautiful, and I want her.

She kneels in front of me, wearing only a thin white night gown, I can see her nipples through it and am embarrassed as my cock twitches, growing thick, and heavy against my thigh.

"Who are you?" I ask.

"It depends, either a good dream, or a bad one," she says. I try to talk again, I have so many questions. What if the guy across the room wakes up? Who is she? How did she get in? What is she doing here? She places a finger against my mouth to quiet my questions and her hands begin to roam all over my body. They slip inside my boxers and—well I don't think I need to write down what's she doing.

Her mouth kisses a path up my chest to my neck. I have never felt so turned on before. I'm no virgin but her hands on my dick and mouth licking and sucking at my throat feel better than any sex I've ever had before. Not sure if that makes me pathetic or if dream sex is more like porn than reality.

I feel pressure on my neck; it kind of hurts and I move to push her mouth away, but before I can, I am distracted by her hands, and I cum. I cum hard and all over her soft fingers. She moans against my throat and licks the skin there, giving me goosebumps. Then she pulls away.

"You are sick, Lucca," she says, her voice sad and stern.

"I know," I whisper, a little sad that she has stopped touching me. She wipes her hands down the front of her gown, leaving wet streaks that almost make me hard again. Then she pushes me down into the bed and covers me with blankets, like a child.

"Sleep now," she says, moving toward the window.

"I am asleep," I tell her, closing my eyes.

"Of course, you are," she says, laughing.
I always wake up with her dark, poignant laughter ringing in my ears.

———

addie had just gotten home when there was a knock at the front door. She set her bag down in the foyer and gave an inpatient sigh. It had been a long day and she was looking forward to having the whole house to herself for a few hours before the rest of her roommates got home. She wanted to eat some soup, take a bath, and possibly get a nap in before starting on her homework.

Her feelings of annoyance disappeared the moment she opened the door. Valora Dulcara stood on the other side, looking radiant in a black pant suit.

"Miss West, isn't that right?" she asked.

"Yes, please come in, professor." Maddie held the door open and allowed the older woman to walk in. Maddie took in a breath through her nose, and a feeling of longing swept through her at the scent of Professor Dulcara's perfume—it was heady, floral, and quite seductive. Maddie shut the door and tried to shake off the sensation. She could not have a crush on Jo's teacher. She wasn't a child anymore.

"Call me Valora, you are not my student after all," Valora said. "I need to drop off some things for Jolene." She held out a manila folder.

"Oh, well Jo isn't here, but I'll make sure she gets it." Maddie took the folder; she didn't want Valora to leave so soon. She placed the folder on the entryway table, the dead flowers long since gone.

"Tea?" she blurted out, and instantly regretted it.

"I never drink tea," Valora said. "But if you have coffee, I would love some."

"Yes, follow me." Maddie went into the kitchen and got the coffee from the fridge, plugging in the little, black coffee maker.

"Are you enjoying college?" Valora asked. She was standing too close to Maddie. Butterflies fought in her stomach. Mixed emotions coursing through her.

"Yes, very much so. Though not as much as Jo and Lucca." Maddie put water into the coffee maker.

"They are working very hard at Dulcara Mansion. You should stop by sometime and see it." Valora leaned against the counter, her blouse shifting beneath her suit jacket, showing Maddie an extra bit of her cleavage. Maddie felt her mouth go dry and forced her eyes up to meet Valora's. Was it just her or was there a knowing gleam in the other woman's eyes? *You are going crazy, Madeline West, that's it, crazy. You're going to wake up in a sanitarium and be told this was all a dream caused by your meds.*

"I've been meaning to take the tour, I've just been busy with my studies." Maddie got out a filter and measured coffee grounds. Finally, she hit start on the maker and enjoyed the gurgling sound that came from the machine.

"Yes, Jolene told me about your activist activities. I am very impressed. Women need to stand up for the rights of other women. I was born in a country where the government does not respect its women. At least not without a show of force." Valora smiled after she was done talking, and Maddie noticed she had straight, white, beautiful teeth.

"Yes, that's important to me too. One of my main goals is to help keep abortion safe, legal, and affordable," Maddie said, as she placed two cups on the counter and got out milk and sugar. She jumped, as Valora's hand touched the nape of her neck.

The brief touch sent a tremor of attraction through Maddie that she wasn't used to and didn't understand. She turned to face Valora and found the other woman's face inches from hers.

"Sorry—you had a stray hair." Valora pulled back and handed Maddie a long, brown hair.

"Uh, thanks?" Maddie took the hair and wasn't sure what to do with it.

"Traditionally you burn it so no one can use it against you." Valora pulled a lighter from her pocket and offered it to Maddie.

"Do you carry a lighter for all stray hair emergencies?" Maddie joked, taking the lighter. She burned the piece of hair and wrinkled her nose at the acrid smell it caused; thankfully, the scent of coffee quickly overpowered it. *Maybe Valora was a witch, card carrying, and broom riding. That would explain the dreams I had before coming here. She put a spell on me, from a distance.*

"No, today I lit candles in class for some ambience." Valora poured the coffee for Maddie and herself. Maddie noticed that she took it black, while Maddie had to add copious amounts of cream and sugar to make it palatable. She really was more of a tea person, it just seemed to come in more flavors and variety. To Maddie, all coffee tasted the same.

The two of them stood in silence for a few moments, drinking.

"Did you know I once lived here briefly?" Valora asked.

"No, makes sense though since your portrait is in the dining room."

"During renovations to the mansion. I stayed here for a few months. I have fond memories of this house. It's always felt like home to me. You must tell me if I ever overstay my welcome." Then she chuckled and half to herself said, "I'd forgotten that painting is in there."

"I don't think you could do that," Maddie said. If anything, Maddie wanted Valora to come by more often and she felt guilty as hell for even thinking it. Valora was so elegant, there was just something mysterious and wondrous about her. Maddie didn't know if she wanted to fuck her or simply be in her platonic company. Either way she needed to stop thinking about it, she was in love with Jo, after all. It would hurt Jo if she knew Maddie was having these kinds of thoughts about someone else. It was her eyes, they were so familiar. Maddie needed to get them out of her thoughts.

"Did you put up that mirror?" Valora asked, the tone in her voice unpleasant. Near the breakfast nook, there was a pale yellow wall that had been bare when they moved in. Now a pretty, if not ornate, mirror graced it. It reflected most of the kitchen, but not the corner where the coffee maker was.

"No, one of the other girls probably did. Allison maybe," Maddie said, shrugging, not sure why Valora looked upset.

"You can decorate your rooms any way you like, but as it states in the rental agreement, I would appreciate it if you didn't decorate the main living spaces." Valora was glaring at the mirror, as if it offended her personally.

"I'll take it down...I'm sorry." Maddie didn't want Valora upset and didn't want Allison in trouble. She went over to the wall and took the mirror down. As she moved it, she noticed it must be dirty or something because Valora's reflection in the glass seemed fuzzy and out of focus. She placed it on the bench seat; she'd clean it and find out who it belonged to later. *Wouldn't it be fun if was a mirror that you could talk to other people through?*

"Thank you." Valora's face went back to being relaxed.

"No problem, sorry again."

"I'm reading a book I think you might enjoy. It's about Mary Shelley and her mother, quite a scandalous tale of single motherhood and feminist ideals for their time. Would you like to borrow it?" Valora asked.

"Yes, I think I know what you're talking about, it's on my to-be-read list. A list which seems to get longer every year," Maddie said, excited. Jo read, but aside from *Nightmare Abbey,* not usually the kind of stuff Maddie was interested in. She had considered trying to find a book club on campus with some of her fellow Women Studies classmates.

"I will bring it by once I have finished it then." As Valora took a deep sip of her coffee Maddie's cell phone buzzed from the pocket of her jeans. She checked it: Mom.

"I have to take this, sorry," Maddie said and left the room to answer the phone. Walking into the dining room, she hit the green button on the screen. "Hello?"

"Hey sweetie, do you have a minute? It's about Lucca." Her mom's voice was thin sounding on the other end.

"Yeah, one minute, Mom." Maddie frowned. She didn't want to ask Valora to leave, but her mom sounded upset. She poked her head around the door to ask if Valora didn't mind waiting while she finished the conversation with Mom and found the room empty. Valora's half-drunk coffee was on the counter, but no professor. Maddie went out into the foyer, the file was still on the table and the front door was shut, but Valora was gone.

"Strange," Maddie said to herself. She checked the living room and the downstairs bathroom just to be sure, but she turned up empty.

"Okay, Mom, sorry about that, what's up?" Maddie made herself comfortable on a couch in the living room.

"I'm worried about your brother. When we facetimed last night, he looked really pale and tired."

"I just saw him a few days ago, he seemed fine. I mean maybe he's staying out too late having a good time. Remind him to eat more protein," Maddie said. She understood her mother's concern but knew Lucca wouldn't appreciate any unnecessary meddling.

"Will you check on him tomorrow? Your father and I would feel better."

"Yeah, Mom, but Lucca won't like it if he thinks any of us are hovering," Maddie warned, rolling her eyes and glad her mother couldn't see her.

Getting up, she wandered back into the kitchen and grabbed a rag to clean the mirror.

"Thanks, sweetie. Have a good rest of your night. Love you." Her mom hung up. Putting her phone away, Maddie went to get the mirror. Picking it up, she checked out her own reflection and that of the room behind her, everything was clear and perfect, in fact, the mirror was in pristine condition. So, what had caused the earlier issue? Maddie wondered if she simply needed to have her eyes checked and put the mirror back down.

CHAPTER FIVE

Psychology Term Paper
Interview a psychiatric patient part one—transcribed from recording.

October 1st
   Mr. R.M. Rainier by Scarlet Jones.
   Mr. Rainier has been a resident of Sempervirens Psychiatric Hospital for over ten years. He is one of their longest staying residents. His care is paid for by one of the many Dulcara Foundation yearly donations to Humboldt County's hospitals and clinics. Mr. Rainier is a forty-five-year-old white male. He used to be a real estate agent and property manager.
   Mr. Rainier is on several medications and when medicated is considered completely harmless. He and the staff at Sempervirens have agreed and consented to this interview.
   SJ: First off, Mr. Rainier, thank you so much for speaking to me.
   R: It's not a problem my dear, I'm glad to be of assistance to local college students.
   SJ: Let's start off simply, then. Do you know why you are here, at Sempervirens?
   R: Yes, my wife caught me drinking the blood of our family dog.
   SJ: Why were you doing that?
   R: At the time, I believed that it would prolong my life.

SJ: But you don't believe that anymore?

R: I know, scientifically, that it is impossible for the blood of one creature to prolong the life of another. Sustain it in nutrients maybe, but I thought I was getting a version of immortality.

SJ: If you no longer believe that, then why are you still kept at Sempervirens?

R: I hate to take my medication. They do make my mind fuzzy and stop my good dreams.

SJ: What happens if you stop taking your medication?

R: I want lives.

SJ: Lives?

R: Any life I can get: bird, spider, kitty.

SJ: So essentially, you stay here so that the staff can make sure you take your medication?

R: Yes, and they are so good about reminding me.

SJ: Do you ever feel like hurting people?

R: No, people are too complicated. I do wish they would let me have a pet here. Could you ask them for me?

SJ: I'll see what I can do.

End of first interview.

"*N*ow, this next section we will be focusing on Thanatology and ancient death rites," Professor Heeling said. He was standing in front of the class. A handsome, older man with sandy blond hair and steely eyes behind wire rimmed glasses. He was wearing a cream-colored button up shirt and tan trousers. Maddie could see the family resemblance between him and Queenie the first time she saw him. Like someone who used to be a pot smoking surfer but didn't want anyone to know.

Maddie didn't know what Thanatology was and hoped he was going to explain. She rather enjoyed anthropology but realized early on that she didn't know nearly as much as she thought she had on the subject. She'd had no idea there were different kinds; social, biological, archaeological and linguistic. She waited for him to explain, she didn't want to be the one to ask the stupid question—maybe it was in her text book somewhere?

The class was packed today; Mr. Heeling's class was almost as popular as Professor Dulcara's. Usually they had a few empty seats; kids nursing hangovers or just decided they couldn't deal with the early morning class, but not today. Today every seat had someone in it.

"Aside from covering the basics of Thanatology, we will go over in detail death rites from ancient Egypt, Greece and..." Professor Heeling didn't sound or look too pleased at his next sentence, "Professor Dulcara will be stopping by to give a special presentation on Moldavian and Wallachian rituals."

Maddie perked up at this, thumbing through the index in her text, she found Thanatology and flipped to the pages listed. The definition read: *Thanatology is the scientific study of death. It investigates the mechanisms and forensic aspects of death, such as bodily changes that accompany death and the post-mortem period, as well as wider psychological and social aspects related to death.*

Wow, that sounds interesting. Death could be such an interesting subject! Maddie smiled at herself. She knew a lot more about death than the average person, it's what happened when you were forever afraid your brother was going to die.

"At the end of the semester you will have a paper due on any aspect of Thanatology you would like from any of the cultures we will be discussing." The professor kept talking, as Maddie scribbled the assignment down.

"3000 words, minimum three peer reviewed references. No, Wikipedia does not count. You can find all the details on the class website."

There were a few laughs over the Wikipedia reference. Maddie felt the assignment more than reasonable. Glancing at the clock behind Professor Heeling, she was happy it was almost time for class to be over. She had a few hours before her next class, and Jo was at home. Maddie wanted to talk to her as they'd missed each other over the last few days, and Maddie wanted to hear all about her assignment at Dulcara Mansion.

"Alright, that's all for today, everyone get out." Professor Heeling grinned as he said it. Maddie was one of the last students to make it to the door, one of the problems with sitting all the way in the back.

"Miss West, can I speak with you a moment?" Professor Heeling asked before Maddie could get out the door.

"Sure thing, is it about my test?" Maddie was worried she hadn't done as well as she expected to on the first exam of the year.

"No, while I think you could have done better, you seemed to grasp the concepts behind the different forms of anthropology," he said.

"Then how can I help you?" Maddie asked, curious.

"Queenie says that your girlfriend and brother are both helping Valora with her project at Dulcara Mansion." He didn't wait for confirmation. "I don't like to get involved in my students' private lives, but you should keep an eye on your loved ones." Taking off his glasses, he blew onto them and began rubbing them with his sleeve.

Maddie was becoming uncomfortable with every word he spoke. "Ummm, thanks?" Was there any other way to respond?

"I warn students every year against accepting any favors from Valora Dulcara as they always come with strings attached. Sometimes complicated ones that don't show up right away." Professor Heeling had a look in his eyes Maddie didn't like. This didn't sound like a man who didn't meddle in the affairs of his students, it sounded like someone who reveled in them.

"I don't think Lucca or Jo have accepted any favors, but thanks for the warning. I'll keep an eye on them," Maddie said, trying to placate her teacher.

"They won't know they have until afterward. Anyway, you may go, Miss West." He walked away abruptly and went to his desk, obviously ending the conversation.

Maddie left quickly, not wanting to risk him saying anything more. It couldn't be okay for him to talk to her like that, could it? Should she say something to her student advisor, or just ignore it all together? Maybe she should tell Valora that Professor Heeling was spreading rumors. *If Valora was a witch then he might be a troll, it'd fit. Ugh, take a breath, Maddie, you know what mom says about your mind filling with nonsense.*

The thoughts occupied her until she got home. As she opened the door, she decided she wouldn't say anything to anyone and ignore that the conversation happened altogether. Maddie went upstairs and put her things away, and slipping out of her shoes, she sat down on her bed for a few moments and got out her phone. She sent a rapid text to Jo to see if she was home yet.

The response came only seconds after Maddie hit send.

Yes—come here ASAP.

Maddie left her room and went down to the second floor. She gave a quick knock on Jo's door and went in. The room was dark, and Jo was laying on her bed, music playing softly from her computer.

"Jo? Are you okay?" Maddie sat down next to her and placed a hand on Jo's back. The girl shuddered and turned over, her face was pale and her eyes wide.

"I guess so...just tired," Jo said, meekly.

"What's wrong, did something happen?" Maddie slid into bed next to her, wrapping her arms around Jo. Jo snuggled into her embrace.

"It's just this extra credit at Dulcara Mansion, it's more complicated and time consuming than I thought it would be," Jo said, kissing Maddie's shoulder.

"Well you're almost done, right?"

"Right...weird stuff just keeps happening. I can't explain it all."

"Like, the house is haunted or something?" Maddie could understand why Jo was upset, scientific Jo didn't believe in anything she couldn't see or touch. If the mansion was haunted, Jo would be in a small crisis of scientific faith.

"No, ghosts aren't real, don't be stupid," Jo snorted.

"Sorry," Maddie said, a little hurt by Jo's words.

"It's not like that. I just find myself really uncomfortable, Professor Dulcara has three TAs right now, and they all watch us like hawks. We have to come and go at very specific times and she gets angry if we try to leave early. She's quite demanding about what she wants from us. Out of the ten students she assigned there are only five of us left. Some quit because the work was too time consuming, but she told others to go because she didn't think they were a good fit after all." The words bubbled out of Jo's mouth.

"What does Lucca think?" Maddie asked. Jo was worrying her. She didn't like how stressed out she sounded.

"He doesn't seem to mind, but he's looking really sickly lately."

"I know, I spoke to him about it. I think he's stretching himself too thin or forgetting to take his medication." This was something Maddie could comment on.

"I don't know how to explain how being at the mansion makes me feel, it's like once I get there I really want to leave, but when I'm away all I can think about is going back," Jo said.

"And you said Lucca doesn't seem to have any issues with it?"

"No, I even asked him, but he laughed and told me I was crazy."

"Then I think it's simply that Lucca isn't the only one who's over done it this semester so far. Blow off your classes tomorrow and just sleep in. I know you don't go to the mansion on Wednesday so take a day off. You haven't been to the ocean or hiking in the forest once since we moved here, and they were part of the appeal." Maddie felt like her advice was solid. Jo just needed a very small vacation. Maddie knew that on top of this extra credit assignment her course load was ridiculous.

Jo was silent for a few moments and then sat up. Maddie sat with her. "Yeah, that sounds like a good idea. Would you come with me?"

"Sure, forest or ocean?" Maddie asked, praying it was ocean.

"Why don't we see if we can camp a night in the forest? I bet we could camp in the Redwoods," Jo said, excitement was filling her face with color.

Maddie groaned internally, she hated to camp, and it would be cold.

"Can we ask the girls if they want to come?"

"Sure, the more the merrier. I'll get started making plans and getting supplies, while you go see who wants to come. We can pile into the Jo-mobile and leave in the morning!" Jo jumped out of bed and rushed over to her computer.

Maddie went downstairs, a little disappointed Jo didn't just want to do a day trip to the beach or go for a solo hike. Of course, she would want Maddie to tag along on a camping trip in the first week of October. *It will be cold, awful, and Jo will make fun of me because I don't like the outdoors.*

She heard voices in the kitchen and followed them, a little surprised to find Allison and her brother kissing near the sink.

"Ugh, get a room," she teased. The couple broke away, both flushed. Lucca looked guilty, and Allison looked smug. Maddie noticed there were bags under Lucca's eyes and his skin had a sallow tint to it.

"My house too, I have a room if you really want me to take him up to it," Allison said, jokingly.

"I'm kidding. Question: Jo wants to have a small getaway and spend tomorrow night camping in the Redwoods. Interested?" Maddie asked.

"Sounds fun, I don't have class Wednesday and can skip out Thursday.

I'd like a break," Lucca said. "I'm pretty sure I packed my camping gear too."

"Are you crazy? It will be cold and dirty, I do not camp," Allison said, she motioned at her expensive labeled clothes. "What would I even wear?"

"Well, it is an excuse to go shopping," Maddie said. She didn't always like Allison, but wouldn't mind extra company, especially extra company that hated to camp.

"Plus, we can share a tent, I'll keep you nice and warm, babe," Lucca said, tickling her gently. Allison blushed and giggled, her whole face softened when she looked at Lucca.

"I guess, but you have to come shopping with me," Allison bargained.

"Deal." Lucca grabbed her hand and kissed each knuckle.

"I'll text you when Jo has all the information. We can all go in the Jo-mobile," Maddie said, relieved.

"Let's go, princess," Lucca said, dragging Allison out of the room, her laughter filling the front hall and trickling back toward Maddie.

"Your brother is such a happy guy," Scarlet said, coming into the room. "Just passed him and Allison leaving. I swear he always has a smile on his face."

"Yeah, even when he's sick. Lucca has always been like that," Maddie said, pride filling her words.

"Did I overhear something about a camping trip?" Scarlet asked, opening the fridge and pulling out a can of orange soda.

"Jo needs a break so we're skipping town to camp tomorrow night. You wanna come?"

"I wish I could, even camping in the cold fall is pretty around here," Scarlet said, disappointment in her features and voice.

"Class?" Maddie hadn't figured Scarlet for the type to care about missing a few days of class.

"Oh no, I have an appointment to interview that patient again, I can't miss it."

"How's that going anyway?"

"It's interesting. Sometimes Mr. R can be so normal and then he'll say something weird. I just know I'm going to get an A on this assignment," Scarlet said. She took a long drink out of the can. "I'll mention it to

Queenie though, how's that? I bet she'll want to come. She tells the best ghost stories."

"Her uncle is odd." Maddie hadn't meant to mention it. Scarlet stopped drinking and just stared at her for a moment. Slowly she put the can down on the counter and crossed the space between them so she was only a foot away from Maddie.

"He tell you to watch out for Lucca and Jo?" Her voice was low, almost a whisper. Maddie nodded, wide eyed.

"He does that all the time. I don't know if it's his version of hazing or what," Scarlet confided. "But Queenie believes him. Something happened between him and Professor Dulcara when she first started teaching here, not sure what...I don't think even Queenie knows."

"How can he be allowed to say that kind of stuff to students? Doesn't anyone complain?" Maddie couldn't believe what she was hearing.

"He shouldn't, but he has tenure, so does Dulcara. It wouldn't matter even if someone did complain. Most students don't."

"Do you think there's something up with Val...I mean Professor Dulcara?" Maddie asked, almost afraid to hear the answer.

"I don't know. I think there must be some reason Professor Heeling doesn't like or trust her. I grew up here and some of the things she and her TAs get away with are pretty remarkable. Though it could just be her standing in the community. The Dulcara family gives a lot of money...all over the place," Scarlet said, shrugging. She went back to the counter and grabbed her drink.

"Don't say anything to Queenie about it, she gets all crazy conspiracy theorist if you do. I'll let her know about the camping trip," Scarlet said.

"Thanks." Maddie felt uneasy about their conversation, she should never have brought up Professor Heeling's comments, and she vowed not to do so again.

CHAPTER SIX

Personal Journal of Jolene Harper
Entry #210

The work I am doing at Dulcara Mansion is interesting and tedious at the same time. Professor Dulcara has tons of documents on her family and the numerous properties they own around the world, all in physical form. We are gathering the data and entering it all electronically for her as well as putting aside certain pieces to be displayed for the historical society here in Arcata.

Many of these records were kept in an abandoned church on Dulcara property that had recently been torn down. Many of the pages are damaged from the elements.

So far, I've mainly seen deeds to property here, in England, and in Romania, most of which the professor assures me she already has updated. The Dulcara family owns a vast amount of ruins and old cemeteries.

Today, however, I was able to help Vaughn go over some birth records. It is interesting to note that while Scarlet's family, the Jones', can trace their roots back to around the time of the civil war as can many of the prominent families, the family that died...the Ceres, I believe? They are new to the area.

Vaughn is a weird sort of guy. He has a unique sense of humor and puts me on edge. They all put me on edge, except Byron—though he can be simpering. Mircalla is cold, and Vaughn is quite off putting. They don't talk to me or each other much. They seem to watch me more than they work. I've mentioned this to Lucca, but he just laughs it off in his normal jovial way.

Sometimes documents I've found and catalogued go missing. Professor Dulcara states they are part of her personal collection and not available to the public. I can't find any rhyme or reason to it.

Something is wrong in this place. There were about ten volunteers to start with, but over the last few weeks, it has dwindled down to just Lucca and me. Some quit because of the stress, which I blame solely on the environment as the work load isn't difficult. Professor Dulcara let others go who she said, "didn't seem up to the task." Which I find hidden meaning in, as again...the task isn't that complicated. One girl left and the rumor is she dropped out of school. Lucca says that happens all the time to freshmen who can't handle college life. I'll have to look that up and see if there are statistics.

I don't like to indulge in fantasy and sometimes must remind Maddie that magic and the supernatural are just stories, but if I were going to believe in it, it would be here in this mansion, on these grounds.

I hate to put it in writing, but hopefully I'll look back on this later and laugh.

A list of things I've found peculiar:

I swear in the right light Professor Dulcara's eyes are red.

Mircalla seems to float everywhere she goes, it's ridiculous, but it is as if her feet do not touch the ground.

Every mirror in the house is covered.

Vaughn and Byron shared a burger the other night that practically mooed. I know people like their meat raw, but at the restaurant, they ordered it rare. I've written down the exact language here. "Have the chef simply touch each side to the grill for no more than 20 seconds."

Enough of this, it's late and all nonsense I will be able to explain away later.

---

*M*addie loved the little coffee shop at the far end of campus. It was quiet and mostly used by introverted hipsters who kept to themselves and rarely looked up from their Chromebooks or phones.

The inside was dark, a weak light illuminated the simple menu that consisted of about five different types of beverages and a few pastries. The tables were all made from a deep cherry wood with matching chairs, and lush, green plants filled the empty spaces. She imagined little imps or tiny fairies lived at the base of the plants, laughing at all the foolish humans. Maybe the owners were fae themselves.

Elves, or Brownies maybe, if they're Unseelie this place could take a turn for the worse, fast. Again, what's with the fairytale creatures, Maddie? What has gotten into your brain? I should probably start writing this stuff down, maybe I'm meant to be an author.

She didn't know how it managed to stay in business; why a large coffee chain hadn't bought them out or been offered a contract by the school, but she was glad she'd stumbled upon it. She didn't even mind paying almost four dollars for the small vanilla latte she always ordered. The quiet ambience suited her needs.

Sitting down, she placed her bag on the table and pulled out her anthropology book.

"Are you enjoying that class?"

Maddie glanced up and almost dropped her recycled cup. Valora Dulcara stood looking down at her. She was immaculate in a silver blouse and charcoal linen pants, her hair in a French twist, rubies glittering at her ears, matching her lipstick.

"Mostly," Maddie said, wishing she wasn't in a purple maxi dress and sweater. Why couldn't she have worn something prettier or more sophisticated? She probably looked about twelve with her hair in pigtails connected with a ribbon.

"May I join you?' Valora asked.

"Of course!" Maddie put her bag on the floor to make room and the other woman slid into the chair next to her in a fluid motion.

"I didn't know you enjoyed coming here. It's one of my favorite places on campus," Valora said, fingers wrapping around her cup.

"It's quiet, sometimes that's nice."

"Yes, sometimes it is, though other times a bit of excitement can be... pleasing." Her lips tilted at the corners, eyes sparkling, and Maddie swallowed, throat dry.

"Of course, life's all about balance." Maddie was glad she sounded so sure of herself.

"Did you enjoy the novel I sent you?"

"Oh yes, it was brilliant."

"I have another you may like, you should come by my office later this week and pick it up." Valora took a deep drink and made a satisfied sound that caused Maddie's thoughts to go to decadent places.

"Yes, I'll do that."

"Now, your anthropology class, you said you only mostly enjoy it?"

"The professor is a little odd," Maddie admitted, feeling guilty about talking about Professor Heeling.

"Ah, Professor Heeling, yes he can be...different?" She gave a throaty laugh. "I will be coming in to discuss some of my culture as a cross over program later in the semester."

"He mentioned that."

A young man walked by, smiled, and greeted Valora. She made about a minute's worth of small talk before focusing her attention back to Maddie.

"Do you come here often?" Maddie asked, a little jealous someone else had spoken so intimately with Valora. *Her eyes were in my dreams again last night. What does it mean? Should I talk to someone about it? Is it all in my imagination?*

"Yes, I enjoy being out and about with my students."

"Oh." She shouldn't feel sad about that answer, but she did.

"Sitting with you, however, is a bit more than that," Valora said slowly. Hidden by their cups, her hand reached out and she caressed one of Maddie's knuckles, sending shivers down her spine. Valora pulled her hand away and wrapped it around her cup.

"You will enjoy learning about my culture. It truly is a shame you weren't in my class this year," Valora continued like nothing happened.

"I am hoping to score a seat next year," Maddie said, though she had to fight to get the words out past her heart, as it was in her throat, beating furiously.

"I believe I can guarantee you'll be there."

"Thank you." What else was she supposed to say? Instead, she made herself busy by sipping her drink and checking her phone. She didn't have any messages, just a few Facebook updates.

"You haven't seen the Mansion yet, have you?" Valora asked.

"No, I've been meaning to."

"You'll love it. I'm sure you'll find at least one room, exhilarating."

Maddie felt Valora's hand on her knee. The other woman didn't blink or show any sign she'd moved, but her hand danced lightly over the silky fabric of her dress and gave her a light squeeze before moving away. Maddie let out the breath she was holding, sure her cheeks were bright pink. Was Valora really coming on to her?

"I'll come by as soon as I can," Maddie said. What was she agreeing to?

"Good. Anyway, I must go. Enjoy your coffee and your quiet." Valora stood up and left. Maddie had a hell of a time looking away from her. She took over the whole room with her presence.

Getting her heart rate and breathing back under control, guilt radiated through her. What the fuck was she doing? Jo would be terribly hurt if she knew that Maddie was honestly considering whether Valora Dulcara had a romantic interest in her.

Maddie knew she should study, but she couldn't concentrate. Valora was a puzzle. It was wrong to be thinking romantic and sexual thoughts about her while still in a relationship with Jo. It was as if she couldn't help herself. The more time she spent with Valora, the more time she wanted... no, needed, to spend with her. She'd never felt this way about anyone. She didn't know what to do; break up with Jo and hope she was reading Valora's signals right?

What if Maddie was just entertaining a fantasy and Valora was simply being kind and friendly? Valora was a teacher, after all. In books and movies, students had affairs with teachers all the time, but did that truly happen in real life? *Well if it is all a fantasy, it's an R rated one.*

Deciding to put those thoughts away for another time, if she decided to explore them at all, she began to study. Wasn't that the reason she'd come here to begin with? To drink a not so great cup of coffee and be left alone so she could get some work done? Resolved to at least try to do homework she dove into the chapter.

After an hour or so, she closed her book and rubbed her eyes. It was time to go home and she didn't think she could read one more word on anthropology without a break for food and possibly TV or conversation that wasn't about dead people.

Gathering her things, she stood up and took her empty cup. Noticing Valora had left her cup, she picked it up, surprised the other woman had left trash lying around. Oh well, it wouldn't strain a muscle to throw away two cups instead of one.

Then she saw something odd on it, something that shouldn't be there.

Scrawled on one side of Valora's cup, in red ink were the words: I want you to believe...to believe in things that you cannot.

CHAPTER SEVEN

Transcription of Social Media Conversations

Madeline West
Yesterday at 7:15pm
Can't believe I agreed to go camping with Jo. I hope it will be a nice time. We need a break from school. Jo- I am worried about you!

Comments:

Jolene Harper
Thanks, you know I appreciate it. Besides next weekend I won't see you at all so we will have to use this time as special. We are going to have fun.
Madeline West
What do you mean you won't see me at all next weekend?
Jolene Harper
Crap. I forgot to tell you. Coming to see you now. I don't want to discuss this online.

Queenie Myles
@offwiththeirheads

Going camping w/ friends from school. Have the best story to scare them with! My uncle passed it along.

*M*addie sat in the back seat of Jo's car, pissed, cramped, and uncomfortable. It was 11 a.m. and already her day was off to a shitty start. Last night Jo had dropped the bomb that she was spending the entire weekend at the Dulcara Mansion with Valora and the TAs to finish up the project. Jo felt that if she put in an entire weekend that the project would finish up sooner rather than later and then she would be done.

Maddie didn't know if she was jealous that Jo got to spend so much time with Valora or angry that Jo would be gone all weekend and hadn't even discussed it with her first. It meant their evening had ended in a small fight and she'd still been upset when she got up this morning.

Though, if she admitted it to herself, she didn't have the right to be angry, not with the path her thoughts and emotions were taking of late.

Lucca was sitting up front with Jo because he got car sick easily, a side effect of one of his heart medications. They were talking quietly while NPR played in the background; sometimes it seemed like Lucca and Jo had more in common than Maddie and Jo.

"This is going to be awful, isn't it?" Allison asked, a whine in her voice. She was stuck between Maddie and Queenie, because she was the smallest.

"It won't be awful, a bit cold or uncomfortable, but last time I camped with Jo I did laugh, a lot," Maddie said.

"Have you ever peed outdoors?" Queenie asked, and Jo and Lucca started laughing from the front seat.

"No!" Allison looked appalled, she leaned up and shook Lucca's shoulder. "Please tell me you are taking me somewhere with a proper bathroom!"

"Sorry, babe, we've got a shovel and toilet paper, but you'll have to do your business behind a tree like the rest of us," Lucca said, teasing.

"You're kidding me—you better be," Allison practically growled.

"The campsite probably has a bathroom, but you might feel cleaner peeing near a bush," Jo said.

"Yeah, that's more likely," Maddie agreed. Last time she agreed to camp with Jo, the camp toilet had been smelly and disgusting. She'd felt more sanitary taking a dump behind a big oak tree, if not a little more exposed.

Allison groaned and put her head in her hands. Maddie worried it would be a long drive.

"Don't be such a girl. It's bad enough I'll have to listen to Maddie whine about dirt and bugs, I don't wanna hear it from you," Jo said, her tone suggested teasing, but Maddie knew the words were partly sincere.

"Hey, don't be like that, Jo," Lucca said defensively, giving Maddie a conspiratorial wink.

It took an hour to get from Arcata to Albee Creek, where they were camping. They bumped down a gravel road until they reached their campsite. It was shaded by giant redwoods and other trees, the ground covered in rich brown loam and bark. The first thing Maddie noticed was that it smelled good and everything was green, but the sunlight barely penetrated the forest. She was glad she'd packed sweat pants and a hoodie, because it was at least ten degrees colder here than in Arcata.

"Wow, what'd you do, pick the camp furthest away from anyone?" Allison asked, getting out and stretching her legs.

"I got what was cheap and available. This trip was last minute. Apparently, they have a few marathons around this time of year," Jo explained. Opening the hatchback of her car, she started unloading equipment.

"It's pretty and secluded, like Camp Crystal Lake," Queenie said, giggling.

"Not helpful," Allison said. She walked over to Lucca and hugged him, giving the forest the evil eye.

Within a few hours, they had set up three tents and gotten enough wood to last them through the night. Allison and Maddie checked out the nearest toilet, and Lucca gloated about being right, it would smell nicer to pee in the woods. Queenie quickly found a tree she deemed "perfect" to squat behind and Jo showed them how to dig a hole to take a shit in. Maddie vowed to hold in any shits she had to take until they were home tomorrow.

By 2 p.m., they were all hungry, so Jo broke out sodas and sandwiches and they sat at the picnic table and ate together. It was chilly but beautiful and Maddie felt about as relaxed as she was going to get. She wondered what this forest might have looked like a hundred years ago and how it would change in another hundred years when some other girl sat here because her, possibly robotic, boyfriend wanted to go camping.

"Well I admit, it is pretty out here," Allison said, taking a bite of her sandwich.

"Kind of romantic too, I say we ditch everyone and go for a walk," Lucca told her, smiling.

"Be careful," Maddie warned. She would hate for Lucca to get sick out here, it was a bit away from the nearest hospital. She had his meds and a first aid kit, but she was still apprehensive.

"Don't worry so much, Maddie," Lucca said, giving her the stare, the one that meant back off. He stood up and went to the tent he and Allison were sharing. After a few minutes, he came back with a large blanket and both their jackets.

"Not far okay, I don't like to hike." Allison put her coat on; it was a neon purple and puffy.

"Just far enough for some privacy," Lucca agreed. Hand in hand, they started off down a path into the forest.

"Stay on the path!" Jo yelled after them. The three of them sat in silence for a while, not uncomfortable should-we-be-talking silence, just nice and peaceful. Maddie could hear birds, and she was pretty sure the sounds of other campers down the road. She looked at the trees hoping to catch a glimpse of the bird that was singing but couldn't find it. She thought it might be a goldfinch, but it was almost too late in the year for that.

"Might be a rowdy bunch down that way," she said, pointing. She could hear music and tinny sounding laughter, it drowned out the pretty bird song.

"Possibly, but they won't bother us," Jo pointed out.

"Oh, I'm not concerned, a bit relieved actually." A breeze blew through camp, and Maddie shivered. She was in black leggings and a long green sweater with brown ankle boots. Maybe she should have put on layers.

"Cold?" Jo asked.

"A little, but it's fine. I have other clothes in my bag." She didn't want Jo to fuss over her or lecture her.

"You guys are dull, dull, dull!" Queenie suddenly exclaimed, jumping up from her seat. She'd finished her food and was digging around in her bag for something.

"Sorry, did you need entertainment?" Jo asked, laughing.

"No, but if I did, you would fail." She pulled out a camera. "I'm going to take some pictures, and I'll be back in a few hours." Then, like Lucca and Allison, she wandered off.

"So whatcha wanna do?" Jo asked, a teasing gleam in her eyes.

"Here?" Maddie's eyes widened, knowing exactly what Jo wanted.

"Why not? The tent is private, everyone is gone, and we have a few hours to kill. Besides, we've never done it in the woods before."

"Not true, we did it at the party Mary Anne Mollison threw end of junior year."

"Doesn't count. That was just some trees behind her house, not a proper forest," Jo said, standing. She held out her hand to Maddie. Maddie hesitated for a second, as they hadn't had sex in over a week, and she wasn't sure it was just because they were both busy. Making up her mind, Maddie put her hand in Jo's and let her lead the way to their tent.

It didn't take long for Jo's mouth and hands to dash all the doubts from Maddie's mind. With the smell of trees in her nose and the soft rustling sound the tent made in her ears, Maddie could lose herself to sensation and enjoy the moment. She returned Jo's kisses and touches with passion, enjoying the feel of Jo's skin and the taste of Jo's mouth.

When they were both spent, they lay curled against each other, naked and warm. Jo played with a lock of Maddie's hair.

"That was nice," Jo whispered against the bare skin of Maddie's shoulder.

"I thought so too." And she did, in fact it was the nicest it had been in a while.

"Maybe we should fuck in the forest more often." Both of them laughed.

"Maybe, we could just buy air fresheners that smells of pine and put some plants in our rooms instead."

Jo growled and began to tickle Maddie. After a few moments, they both settled down again, the laughter dying. Maddie's eyes closed for a second.

When they opened, she was alone in the tent. She must have fallen asleep. She scrambled to get her clothes on and unzip the door. She could hear voices coming from outside and smelled the acrid aroma of smoke, which made her think about hot dogs and marshmallows. Her stomach growled. She hoped no one could hear it.

"There's Sleeping Beauty!" Jo called when she saw her.

"What time is it?" Maddie asked, yawning. *Sleeping Beauty? For reals? I'd rather be Snow White.*

"Dinner time!" Queenie yelled.

"Five," Lucca answered.

"Yeah, it'll be dark soon, so we figured we should start cooking," Jo explained.

"Why didn't you wake me sooner? I would have helped."

Maddie sat down on a log surrounding the fire. Jo had her grill on the coals and several hobo dinners were cooking. Hobo dinners were ground beef, veggies, salt, pepper, and some gravy mix wrapped in tin foil and then cooked over a camp fire. When Jo first made them for her, she'd asked why they were called that. She doubted real hobos ever ate that well. Jo hadn't ever answered her.

"Well, go get the beers out of the ice chest," Jo instructed. "Camping is so much more fun when someone will buy you booze." She grinned at Queenie who gave her a thumbs up.

"I'll help," Lucca said. He and Maddie went back to the car.

"Allison and I had a great walk, and she's such an interesting person," Lucca said as they opened the hatchback.

"I'm glad you are having such a nice time." And she was, Lucca looked happy, if not a little gray around the gills. "Are you feeling okay, though?"

"Yeah, I mean not one hundred percent, but not shitty. I'll take a pill with dinner and be right as rain."

"No booze."

"No booze." Lucca demonstrated by grabbing a water bottle while Maddie got the six pack out.

"Want us to grab the marshmallows too?" Maddie called back to Jo who nodded emphatically. Lucca grabbed the bag of giant, white, sugary puffs, and they made their way back over to the fire.

"I have never eaten anything so... horrible-looking in my life," Allison said, as Jo fished the tin foil wrapped dinners from the grill.

"Says the woman who admitted to eating snails," Lucca snorted.

"Eeew you ate snails?" Queenie sounded appalled; she grabbed a plastic fork and carefully opened her special, veggie meal. Taking a deep sniff, she grinned and dug in.

"They taste like garlic butter gummy bears. Good stuff," Allison said, opening her own dinner.

For a few moments the only sound was of eating and drinking, which seemed to echo through their little camp site. From each person chewing to a can of beer being popped open and slurped up, it was an interesting symphony. Maddie noticed, dismally, that her brother only seemed to be picking at his food.

CHAPTER EIGHT

A page from a book—front and back:

BLOOD BORN

Chapter 3

I wake in pain and fury, confusion echoing in me. Nothing but darkess surrounding me, air barely filling my lungs. My hands reach out, feeling, trying to make sense of where I am. I touch wood, hard and prickly. It is to my side, beneath me and above me. I am in a wooden box. Am I dead? Did they bury me alive?

I feel strong, stronger than I ever have before. I use that strength to tear my way out of the box, up through the earth. Dirt gets in my mouth, gets in my eyes. It tastes of minerals and blood. I crawl from my hole, an unclean thing. I know I am not alive, not as I once was.

I can see, oh how I can see. I am in the forest, there is nothing around but trees. I can see each leaf as if I hold it in my hand. I can smell food cooking from a village miles away, a deer trembles yards from my right. There is to be rain tomorrow, and the stars are fiery glimmers in an unreal sky.

I am naked, and there is blood on my skin. I do not smell good.

"You are awake." A voice from my left. I turn and it leaves me dizzy, so fast the world around me is a blur.

I try to cover myself, modesty from an old life ingrained. I know there is no need for it now.

There is nothing, just more trees and darkness, but the darkness moves. I can see red glimmering eyes, but nothing else, nothing but shadow.

"Your soul cried out as it died. Few cry like yours did." The voice speaks again; it is not male or female. I can barely stand to listen to it. I cringe away from the awful sounds.

"I have woken you up, you are not as you were before."

"Are you the devil?" I ask. I killed myself, I killed the girls, and now I will be punished for my sins.

It laughs, a hard sound between a screeching bird and metal against metal. "No, I am not the devil."

"What am I?"

"That is for you to figure out, I can only give you three pieces of wisdom."

I am kneeling on the ground, still confused, but not cold, perhaps I will never be cold again?

———

BETHANY STRATTON

*"Y*ou are something special now, what you choose to do with it is up to you. However, to keep your specialness, you must return home every six years and sleep in the earth, alone and unprotected for one whole night."*

"Why six years?" Yes, I must ask questions, no matter how muddled I feel, how out of sorts. I know I will not get the chance again.

"Because you slept for six months," the shadow answers. Six months, so long? I have been in the ground all that time? Doing what, changing, becoming... What am I? Fear pools in my belly. Where are the girls? Where are my sons? My husband.

"You must stay away from the sun and feed often as you become used to your

new form." The shadow moves and it sounds like insects crawling, swarming just feet from me.

"I must be a monster." I cross myself and it burns, my arms wrap around my naked form. This is not what I wanted to happen, it must be a nightmare.

"If you wish to be, then yes." It hisses the last word and the red eyes flash.

"Lastly, your actions stemmed from love, I cannot touch love." It sounds disgusted. "You must be rewarded for the strength of your love."

"If my husband is dead, I can never love again, if my children are beyond my reach, love will never be attainable." As I say it, the ground on either side of me stirs. I can feel something, there are other things, like me, beneath the dirt.

"That makes this task more amusing for me. You will not have true love again, until you find the one who already has your mark." Then the shadow is gone and I am lost. What was it? What did it mean?

In horror, I watch as a pale hand with bleeding, broken fingernails breaks through the dirt near me. I know that hand. I scramble to it, clasping it in my grasp. It is cold and clammy. No, no, no. It cannot be.

"So, who's got a good scary story for tonight?" Jo asked as everyone seemed to be done eating.

"Me!" Queenie exclaimed.

"Well, it's almost dark now. Once it gets properly dark, we'll roast marshmallows and you can tell us," Allison said. She crinkled up her tin foil, having finished her food, though Maddie figured she hadn't eaten it all. Allison seemed to be very strict about what and how much she ate.

"There's a bag in the car, put all the trash in there, we want to keep this place looking nice," Jo told her.

"What about the trash can?" Allison asked, pointing to an old metal can near the picnic table.

"We'll toss all our trash into it before we leave, but we don't want to attract animals tonight," Jo explained.

Eventually everyone finished their food and cleaned up. Maddie gathered up all the little tin foil balls and took them back to Jo's car. Maddie was still hungry and thought about digging into some chips she saw in the back of the car. Their salty goodness would top off her small, kind of sad dinner perfectly. As she reached a hand toward the yellow bag, she decided against it and gave herself permission to eat a few extra blackened marshmallows instead.

Wrapped in blankets and with long sticks, they reconvened around the fire as night fell. Jo had a lantern she placed on the picnic table to help fight off some of the gloom, but the main source of light came from the flickering flames of the campfire.

"Eerie," Allison said, cuddled up next to Lucca.

"Awesome, I mean it is October." Lucca put his arms around her. The firelight made everything seem dimmer and more sinister. Maddie knew it was just an illusion, but she didn't care for it. She could barely see her tent in the dark and gripped the flashlight under her blanket tightly.

The flames were beautiful, orange, white, and blue, they licked at the wood, and she could feel the heat from where she sat. Every so often, a puff of smoke would float her way, dousing her in the wood heady perfume, and Jo would nudge her, whispering, "Smoke follows beauty."

Queenie passed around the bag of sweet treats and Maddie, grateful to have something else to do with her hands, eagerly stuck her marshmallow topped stick into the fire.

"I guess this is the time in the evening where we scare the shit out of one another." Jo laughed, pulling a toasted marshmallow off her stick and shoving it into her mouth.

"Finally. I have a great story!" Queenie said, she put her own stick down and brought her knees to her chest.

"Nothing with ghosts, alright?" Allison requested, she squished in tighter against Lucca.

"The best stories have ghosts, and I'll protect you," Lucca whispered in her ear.

"Not that we need a scary story, a whole family was murdered a mile from where we live, real life is scary enough," Allison said.

"This one doesn't have a ghost, it's about a monster," Queenie consoled her, looking a little annoyed.

"Fine, go ahead." Allison waved a hand at her.

"Once upon a time..."

"Ugh, seriously?" Jo wrinkled her nose at the obvious starting line.

"Hey, I'm a forestry major not a creative writing major, give me a break."

"Let her tell it her way." Maddie came to Queenie's defense. *I hope it's*

*so scary Jo regrets being mean. Maybe Queenie will tell us these woods are haunted
or a serial killer preys on young women during fall.*

Queenie gave Maddie a thankful grin and started again. "Once upon a
time, there was a castle, and in the castle lived a wonderful family. They
had everything: beauty, money, and fame."

"Sounds like my kind of people," Allison snorted.

"The castle was surrounded by several tiny villages, each that looked
to the residents of the castle to protect them and govern them. One day a
horrible raid happened, and hundreds of villagers were slaughtered by a
raving war lord and his followers." Queenie sat forward, eyes intense.

"The lady of the manor sent out her best warriors to try and deal with
the warlord, but it didn't help. They too were all killed. One night, the
war lord and his followers snuck into the castle and attacked. They killed
the lady's husband and her two sons before she and her daughters fled
into the catacombs beneath their home."

Maddie put her head on Jo's shoulder, entranced in the tale; this
wasn't quite the type of spooky story she'd been expecting. She hoped the
woman and her daughters didn't die.

"When the warlord finally caught up to her, he told her if she gave one
of her daughters to him as his bride, he would leave their home and spare
the rest of the villages and people. One daughter volunteered, the other
cowered behind her mother. Knowing that she had little option, and that
the man was more than likely to be a horrible husband and not keep his
word, she killed both her daughters with a knife she'd kept in her pocket."

"Are you serious? What kind of story is this?" Lucca asked.

"A good one, shut up," Maddie told him, horrified at the thought of
some mother murdering her kids.

Queenie paused to take a deep swig of her beer. "The warlord and his
people were so appalled, they killed her quickly and left her body to rot in
the catacombs. They were excited to take over her home and possess the
family's riches and land. The remaining villagers were afraid and in
mourning, their new ruler was a harsh master, cruel, demanding, and
disgusting. He raped their daughters, beat their sons, took their crops,
and raised their taxes. The people prayed for salvation."

"Six months later, the people of the village woke up from a long night,
worried about what awful things the new day would bring. However, the
day brought nothing, no men rode from the castle, no smoke rose from

the chimneys and then the servants who worked in the castle were found, alive, wandering in a daze in one of the meadows. Finally, a group of brave men went to the castle and broke in. They found nothing, no people, no blood, no signs of life. It was empty, cold, and abandoned." Queenie paused, possibly for dramatic effect.

"That is creepy," Maddie said, "Then what happened?" Her eyes darted to the darkness behind Queenie and then back to the fire, she didn't want to speculate about what she couldn't see out in the dark.

"The villagers went back to their homes, rumors spread throughout the area, and others tried to come and claim the castle and the riches, tried to rule the people, but it never worked. People would come and each morning there would be no sign any living soul had ever crossed the castle's threshold. One night, a child was dared to run up to the castle and peak in a window, when he came back the brown hair on his head had turned stark white. He raved about seeing a lady floating around the castle, eyes glowing red. None of the villagers would approach the castle after dark again. Instead, they started leaving gifts during the day, live animals, clothing, bread, eggs...whatever they could spare, and it would always be gone the following day.

"For a century, the castle and surrounding villages were left in peace and prospered under their invisible guardian, even while other areas around them were torn apart by war. The castle was quiet, and then over 100 years later, war came to the castle gates, and men burned the castle to the ground. It had been decided it was a symbol of evil and must be destroyed, that a monster lived within. A few days later, hundreds of villagers came to the smoldering ruins to mourn and found dozens of heads impaled on stakes posted around the remains of their beloved castle. It was every man who had helped light the fires. Soon after, the surrounding villages were abandoned. No one goes near the ruins of that old castle anymore. It is said if you venture there after dark, you too will see the monstrous lady with the glowing red eyes."

Everyone sat in silence for a while, just staring at each other.

"That was great," Maddie said, forcing a laugh.

"Yeah, where did you hear that?" Jo asked.

"My uncle. He says it's based on a true story."

"I doubt it, but it's decent fiction. I've never heard it before." Lucca stood up, stretching. "Now I think it's time for bed." He reached out and took Allison's hand.

"Agreed. I'm creeped out and cold, let's go." Allison smiled up at him.

Jo covered the fire with dirt and grabbed the lantern while Queenie and Maddie cleaned up the rest of the food and trash, then one by one, they all made their way to their tents. Maddie ducked inside her and Jo's. With giggles and awkwardness, they managed to change into what they brought to sleep in. Mainly sweat pants and t-shirts with big fluffy socks, not quite attractive, but warm.

"What did you think of Queenie's story?" Maddie asked, as she spread out one of the sleeping bags, straightening it and putting their pillows at the top, no easy feat while on your knees.

"I think it sounds familiar," Jo said, grabbing the heap of blankets from the corner, and stepping on a tiny spider that was trying to make a home in the warm tent.

"Really? I didn't think so at all. Do you really think it was based on a true story?" Maddie laid down and pulled the blankets on top of her, rolling to her side she propped up on an elbow to face Jo.

"Maybe. I swear I've heard or read something like that before." Jo got into bed beside her and turned off the lantern, dousing the tent in almost total blackness, a shaft of moonlight was penetrating through the trees, illuminating a bit of where the tents were set up. Maddie squeezed her eyes shut, the moonlight made the shadows look even more terrifying, she really didn't care for camping.

"You'll be gone all weekend, huh?" Maddie asked, snuggling with Jo, relaxing as Jo's bigger frame curled around hers.

"Yeah, but it should make it so I'm basically done at Dulcara Mansion. I may have to go back once or twice after that but then it will be done," Jo said, relief tainted her words.

"Are you going to try and see about going on her Yule trip?"

"I don't think so. I don't have any real interest in Romania, besides it's only to..." Jo trailed off. "That's it!" she exclaimed, causing Maddie to jump and shush her.

"What's it?"

"She's taking students to the ruins of a castle she said burned down over a few hundred years ago. That's where I'd heard part of that tale before."

"I doubt it's the same castle. Wasn't that region torn apart by war? I bet there are a lot of castles that were destroyed. It's not even a true story, something Queenie's weird uncle made up. Come on, let's go to sleep." Maddie wanted to change the subject. She didn't like anxious Jo and would be glad when she was done with this project.

"Yeah, you're probably right. G'night." Jo kissed Maddie's head.

Maddie waited until she heard Jo's breathing deepen and knew her girlfriend was asleep. She thought about the trip to Romania and how she might like to go with Valora, away to a foreign country, learning about such an exotic woman's heritage might be fun. She felt her cheeks burn as she thought about how her touch had felt the other day in the kitchen, then remorse swamped her. Jo was sleeping right next to her!

Maddie tried to sleep but couldn't, erotic images of the older woman filled her mind. After tossing and turning for over an hour, she was just about to try and find her book and a flashlight when there was a sound outside. She froze. It sounded like footsteps, and then there was a rustling.

She held her breath, should she wake up Jo? Whatever it was, it was getting closer. She saw a partial shadow outside the tent. Then she saw the faint brightness of a flashlight beam.

"Maddie?" a voice called through the tent door. Maddie let out the breath she was holding.

"Allison?" Maddie sat up, scrambled over to the zipper and unzipped the door. "What's up?"

"Is your brother with you?" Allison asked. She was in a fuzzy, blue robe and matching slippers, her red hair in a high pony tail and a very worried expression on her pretty face. She was gripping a large black flashlight like a weapon.

"No, what's wrong?" Maddie grabbed her coat, boots, and got out of the tent without waking Jo, though it would have taken a marching band to wake Jo; the girl slept like the dead.

"We fell asleep, I woke up to pee, and he was gone," Allison told her.

"Gone?" Maddie put the jacket on and stepped into her boots. "Maybe he had to pee too?"

"I waited for about twenty minutes, but he didn't come back, it doesn't take that long to pee, especially for guys. Now I'm worried," Allison said.

Maddie felt her heart start to pound, and she shivered inside her coat. What if Lucca had gotten up to use the bathroom and his heart had given out? He could be dying out in the woods! She had to find him! Her mind reeled with all the possible awful scenarios that could have happened. She pictured having to tell her parents that Lucca died less than thirty feet from her while she'd been day dreaming.

If Lucca dies, wouldn't life be easier? OH MY GOD, what did I just think? Does that make me a horrible person?

"Check the car, and I'll wake Jo," Maddie instructed. Waking Jo was a harder task than she wanted but within a few minutes, Jo was awake and dressed. They woke Queenie, and the three of them met Allison by the car

"He's not here," Allison said, panic in her voice.

"We'll find him. I'm sure he's sleeping up against a tree with his dick out." Jo tried to make light of the situation. Maddie was grateful, but her own worry was a cold lump in her stomach and an ache in her throat.

Jo got into the back of her car and pulled out a few things. She gave them each a flare and a whistle. "We'll each take a path, if you see anything light the flare and blow. Not only will the others be able to find you, but it will scare off anything else."

"That doesn't make me feel safe," Queenie said, rubbing her eyes, tired.

"I am not walking in those woods alone." Allison shook her head.

"Alone wandering around in the dark sounds like a bad idea," Queenie agreed.

"Fine, you and Allison go together, toward the main road. Maddie, will you be okay by yourself?" Jo asked.

Maddie didn't think she would be; she didn't want to wander the dark by herself. She reminded herself they were looking for her brother, who might be hurt or worse and this was a campground, other camps were not too far away, right? The dark was simply the absence of light and nothing to be afraid of. None of these thoughts helped the fear coursing through her, but the annoyed look in Jo's eyes did. She simply nodded yes.

Maddie began to walk in the direction Allison and Lucca had gone earlier that day and soon she couldn't hear or see her friends. Her flashlight bobbed, as she stepped and while the dark pushed in against the sides of the path it did a decent job of making sure she didn't trip and fall on her face.

"Lucca!" she called softly. She checked behind every tree just off the path, each time praying she found him. Maybe he was constipated, or Jo was right, he'd fallen asleep taking a piss. That would be so like her brother.

As she got further down the path, she became more nervous. Lucca wouldn't have gone this far from camp. Her eyes strained to see past the flashlight's glow. She wanted to find him, but she wanted to go back too. Maybe they should get in the car and go for help. A park ranger might have better luck. They may have to wait for daylight.

The thought of her brother out in the forest all night made her nauseous. Then she saw something, it looked like a person up ahead, just outside the beam of light. She quickened her pace, feeling like Snow White in the forest, trees looming around her, casting evil shadows, playing tricks on her mind.

"Lucca?" she called again, then stopped dead in her tracks. It didn't look like just one person, but two, two people embracing near the edge of the path, shaded by the trees. Maddie didn't know if she wanted to go further—this may not be her brother at all. She didn't want to disturb a couple making out or a serial killer either.

She heard a groan and a sigh that she was positive sounded like her brother and pointed the flash light at the couple. Yes! It was Lucca, she would recognize his yellow coat anywhere, but the other person was hidden by him, it almost looked like a woman, but she was to in the shadows to be clear.

"Hey!" Maddie shouted. She lit her flare, put the whistle to her mouth, and blew. Lucca didn't move, but the shadow startled. Maddie swore she saw red eyes flash at her before whoever or whatever it was ran off into the woods. Maddie's heart thumped wildly in her chest as she made her way to her brother. Her hands were shaking with cold and fear as she kept her sight on Lucca. She didn't know what she just saw and wasn't sure she wanted to.

Jesus Christ, maybe there are monsters in these woods. Or I was right earlier, insanity is kicking in. Maybe I need to be tested for schizophrenia.

"Lucca, are you okay?" she asked when she got to his side. He didn't respond. His eyes were open, and he was breathing but he didn't move when she grabbed his arm. He was in his pajama pants and a thin, white cotton t-shirt. His feet were bare, and she worried about hypothermia. She had no idea at what temperature frostbite would kick in.

"Lucca?" She shook him and he still didn't seem to be awake, at least not really, he wouldn't say anything.

Maddie heard her name being called, Jo! "I'm over here!" Putting an arm around her brother, she waited for Jo to find her.

"Is he okay?" Jo was panting like she'd been running.

"I think so, I think he is sleep walking," Maddie explained.

"Has he ever done that before?"

"Not that I know of. Let's get him back to camp. It's cold out here." Maddie spent a second trying to decide if she should tell Jo about the weird person like shadow she'd seen and decided against it. It may have just been her tired and over active imagination...combined with the fear, cold, and Queenie's story. That made a whole hell of a lot more sense than a shadow with red eyes.

"Okay, we should wake him up first, right?" Jo asked.

It took a few tries but eventually they managed to wake Lucca up. He blinked and then a filthy string of curses came out of his mouth as he realized he was standing in his pajamas in the middle of woods.

"What the fuck? Where the hell am I? It's god damn freezing!"

"It's okay, Lucca, you were sleep walking. You don't remember anything?" Maddie asked.

His eyes glazed over for a moment and then he mumbled, "Nothing but a weird dream." Shaking his head, as if to clear it, he put his arms around himself.

"Here," Jo said, as she wrapped him in a blanket.

"Come on, let's get you back to camp and warm you up," Maddie said.

Jo found her flare and made sure it was out, she picked it up, and together they led Lucca back to camp.

Allison and Queenie were already at camp when they got back. They'd started a fire and were huddled around it with blankets. Allison jumped up when she saw them.

"Lucca!" She threw her arms around him. "I was so worried."

"I found him sleep walking," Maddie explained.

Allison checked him all over and when she found his bare feet, she quickly remedied it by going into their tent and not only bringing out his socks but another blanket.

"You should probably go back to bed," Jo told them.

"I won't get any more sleep tonight, my adrenaline is too high," Queenie said. "But I'm glad you're safe, Lucca."

"Yours might be, but I'm exhausted. Come on, baby," Allison tugged Lucca's hand. "And this time I'm sleeping so you'll have to step on me to get out of the flap!"

Maddie watched them disappear into the tent and sighed in relief. Her brother was safe and not dying alone in the woods somewhere. But what had she seen? Had there really been some shadowy figure with Lucca or had her tired and scared imagination taken over her brain? Maybe she should talk about it with Jo. She opened her mouth to start saying something and snapped it shut as Jo's words registered.

"See? Nothing frightening or weird. Sleep walking is a natural human response to stress, so why don't we go back to bed?" Jo snuggled up next to Maddie and kissed her cheek.

"No, I'm with Queenie, I couldn't sleep again if I tried."

"Suit yourself. I'm going back to bed." Jo kissed her again and stood up, stretching and yawning.

"Come over here and share my blanket. We'll keep each other company until morning," Queenie said. She was curled against a log, close to the fire, under a huge blanket. She'd gotten the beer and marshmallows back out.

Maddie stood up. Sounded like the perfect end to a shitty evening. Maybe she could lose the anxiety in her chest amidst booze and sugar.

CHAPTER NINE

Personal Journal of Jolene Harper
Entry # 213

I don't even know what to write, or even if I should be writing this down. I fear if I don't though I will think I've gone crazy. Today started off normally enough. I had breakfast with Maddie ~~omg poor Maddie she would be heartbroken~~ *and then left for the Dulcara Mansion. I am spending the whole weekend here to try and finish up my part in this project. I wish I'd never agreed to do this.*

The house is amazing and beautiful, if not a little strange. The Dulcara family enjoys their dark tapestries depicting murder, mayhem, and darkness. They also don't care for mirrors and religious art work of any kind, but I guess most old families have strange habits. The historical documents I've been going through have mainly been boring, I wrote about them a few entries back. Just a list of who married who and deeds to property, meetings with slightly famous historical people.

However, the farther back I go, the weirder the information becomes, like the Dulcara family doesn't even seem to exist before the 17th century, and they have a very odd habit of naming every female heir Valora. I have found no records of male children either or any death or burial records aside from the deed to a cemetery in Romania that must be 1000 years old (exaggeration).

I've mentioned some of this before in other entries and written about how only Lucca and I are left, and her TAs. Spending more time with them, I have found that while slightly unconventional and weird, Valora's TAs are brilliant people. I still feel like they are watching me a little too closely.

There's Mircalla who is a junior, Vaughn who is in a PHD program and then Byron who is a senior. Being able to converse with such bright people is a treat. I love Maddie, but smart isn't a word I'd use to describe her.

I've mentioned Byron before because he's who I am paired up with most often. Mircalla is a fashion major who has already sold a line to a prestigious label, and Vaughn is obtaining his PHD in History and has already had several colleges reach out about hiring him once he graduates. It is true what Queenie and Scarlet says, Professor Dulcara has amazing connections that she uses on her favorite students.

Last night, the three of them brought booze to the mansion to celebrate—we didn't get a lot of work done. I was in good spirits. The camping trip with Maddie had helped relieve a lot of tension. After a few drinks, they started telling me that Professor Dulcara might be interested in me as another TA and would I like that? I didn't know what to say so I simply shrugged and said I wouldn't get my hopes up until she officially asked me.

Though by this point I knew my answer would be no. She's unnerving. Though until last night I had been fond of Byron, we'd been casual flirting enough for me to feel awkward and guilty. Awkward because it's been a while since I've been turned on by a boy, in fact until recently I would have said it was impossible. Guilty because if Maddie could read my mind, she'd find way too many things in it that would hurt her.

I'm off subject. Shortly after the booze, things took a weird turn, like an alcohol induced dream, or maybe a nightmare. Maddie can never read this, she'd be so upset! I am upset writing it down, but the more time passes the more I seem to be forgetting what exactly happened. I remember Mircalla helping me to my room, her soft feminine laughter filling my ears. I recall Byron's soft fingers undressing me, caressing my skin as Vaughn kissed me all over. It felt good, like I was floating far away in my mind.

This wasn't like when I kissed the girl over summer break; that felt wrong but nice at the same time, my main thought was not to hurt Maddie. This was decadent and sensual, and Maddie didn't enter my mind once.

I seem to remember trying to push them away a few times, telling them no, that I really shouldn't because I have a girlfriend and I don't like boys...I mean at all. I have never been interested in them, ever. They ignored me and after a while, I didn't care. I blame the booze, I've never been that drunk before, but I've never felt that peaceful or that turned on either. Ugh! I am a horrible person.

We all got on my bed, Mircalla watching us, Vaughn touching my breasts and Byron with his face in-between my legs. I have never wanted to come so badly in my whole life, but they wouldn't let me, they also wouldn't let me touch them. Mircalla came closer, and I thought she would kiss me, but no. Her mouth attached to my neck and I almost surged off the bed, the feel of her teeth was electrifying.

"You will like this," Mircalla whispered in my ear. Byron was naked now and he slid up my body. I could feel his hard on pressing against me and knew I was about to have sex with a man for the first time in my life, but instead of repulsion I only felt want. It sickens me now.

Then my door flew open and Professor Dulcara stood on the other side. She looked furious.

"Stop!" she yelled, and they all scrambled away from me. They looked afraid of her. I just laid on the bed, still craving the orgasm that was so near.

"But you said..." Byron muttered, hands reaching out to her.

"I said nothing of you acting without my permission. Leave. I am ashamed of you." She glared at each of them. Byron and Vaughn got dressed, with haste.

"Are we to have nothing then?" Mircalla asked, angrily.

"There is a gift in the dining room," Professor Dulcara said. She came into the room and the three of them seemed to flee from her presence. The professor covered me with a blanket. I was starting to feel normal again and was embarrassed and nauseous. I leaned over the bed and threw up. When I was done, she helped me clean up and get into my pajamas.

Was it all my imagination or did I hear sobbing coming from down the hall, like a woman terrified?

"I am so sorry, Jolene. Do not fear, you won't remember and that will never happen again. You are safe in my home." She kissed my forehead and the next thing I knew it was morning.

No one has said anything about last night, in fact they all act like nothing happened. I don't know what to do. Could it have been a dream, some drunken thing my mind created? Or did I seriously almost have a threesome with these people? Maybe they roofied me? But that seems farfetched, all three of them hatched a plan to drug me? Who would believe that? I don't even believe it.

I have thought about reporting the incident, but as what? We were all drunk, so it wasn't sexual assault, was it? I willingly participated. It makes my head hurt and I just want the memories to fade as fast as they can. I can't wait to finish this project and never come back to this place again.

"*J*o's gone for the whole weekend huh?" Scarlet asked, plopping down on the couch next to Maddie.

"Yeah, I will be glad when she's done with this stupid project," Maddie said. She crossed her legs and wriggled around, getting comfortable. She was flipping through channels on the TV, but there wasn't anything on.

"I tried to warn you," Queenie said in a sing song voice. She was splayed out on the rug, staring at the ceiling.

"What? There's nothing to warn me about." Maddie was glad for their company, though she still wasn't quite sure they were all actually friends. *Yes, you are, you enjoy their company, and they seem to like you. I wonder if everyone gives themselves pep talks like this.*

"Professor Dulcara is bad news bears. My uncle says there is something wrong with her," Queenie explained.

Maddie looked at Scarlet. The girl was going to be a psychologist, and surely, she didn't believe all of Queenie's weird nonsense about Valora being evil or weird.

"I hate to say it, but I agree. This is your first year here, so you haven't had time to see what we have. Professor Dulcara could get away with murder and no one would bat an eye. She donates tons of money to everywhere and the mansion brings in tourists like crazy." Scarlet looked a little sheepish as she talked.

The word murder brought back the site of the Ceres house to Maddie's mind. "I haven't seen much in the news about those people who died. I wonder if they will ever catch who killed them?"

"I only know the surviving daughter has moved in with relatives in Ohio. There have been rumors they might have a suspect but honestly? I don't think anyone has a clue," Scarlet said.

"Has anything like this ever happened before?" Maddie asked, pausing her channel flipping on a documentary about cats as Queenie made an excited noise and sat up, focused on the TV.

"My uncle said something similar happened on a ship about a hundred years back. Everyone dead, throats ripped out," Queenie said, off handedly.

"That's a hundred years ago, so it's not like it's the same person."

Maddie sighed and leaned back, watching a particularly large tabby cat jump a small fence.

"About ten years back, a doctor and his family from the psychiatric hospital all disappeared. It was quite the scandal. I don't remember much, just my parents being really freaked out," Scarlet told them. Maddie didn't respond. Disappearances also weren't the same thing as a family murdered.

Why did a family go missing though? Maybe witness protection, or they decided to move to a small island and live off the grid? Or maybe they were all dead, in unmarked graves somewhere. Maddie thought that'd make a really interesting story.

"Have you been to the mansion yet?" Queenie asked.

"No."

"Really? All the elementary schools do a field trip there so I've been half a dozen times. You should take the tour. It's freaky and interesting," Scarlet said.

"What's freaky about it?" Maddie asked.

"Aside from the old cemetery out back? A ton of stuff. You'll have to go and see. Halloween is coming up, best time of year. Maybe we'll all go. I need a break from my psych ward interviews, since the guy I am talking with goes from zero to crazy in less than thirty seconds." The humor in Scarlet's voice sounded forced.

"I don't want to go. People go in that house and don't come back. I think Professor Valora killed that family because they knew something about her history she didn't want out." Queenie's statement filled the room like a tangible thing. No one said anything for a few minutes.

Maddie felt anger in her chest and the need to defend Valora, the woman had been nothing but nice and accommodating since she moved to Arcata. They were all living in her house and the rent was super cheap. "That's a pretty powerful thing to say, got any proof to back it up?"

"Just a feeling," Queenie said. She was still staring at the TV.

"Maddie," Scarlet's tone held a warning.

"What? She's the one saying ridiculous things!"

"Don't jump on Queenie. It's true, over the years a few students have gone missing."

"Kids who dropped out of college," Maddie argued.

"Probably, but..." Scarlet lowered her voice. "To someone like Queenie the pieces all fit together, okay? You don't have to humor her, but don't be condescending or mean, all right?"

Maddie took a deep breath and looked at Queenie who had never lost the slight grin on her face as she watched kittens play. "Yeah, okay, sorry."

"Don't talk about me like I'm not here," Queenie said suddenly and spun around to stare at them.

"Sorry, Queenie." Scarlet slid off the couch down to the floor and gave her best friend a side hug.

"I didn't mean to upset you, I guess I just don't see things the way you do," Maddie tried to explain.

"I know, one day you will though." A dark look came over Queenie's face. Maddie was about to ask her what was wrong when her phone rang.

"Hello?" Maddie answered. She didn't recognize the number.

"Yes, Ms. West?"

"Yes."

"I show here you are the emergency contact number for a Lucca West?"

Maddie froze, heart racing. "I'm his sister, is everything okay?"

"You need to come down to Mad River Community Hospital."

"I'll be right there." Maddie hung up.

"What's wrong?" Scarlet asked.

"Lucca's in the hospital!" Maddie stood up, feeling frantic, she didn't have a car, she could call a cab, or take a bus, maybe Lyft or Uber? She looked down at her phone but couldn't make her fingers work.

"Okay, calm down. Do you need a ride?" Scarlet was standing up as she spoke. Maddie could only nod as tears flooded her eyes.

"Not a problem, that place is like my second home. My mom's a resident." Scarlet put a hand on Maddie's arm. "Go get your purse and shoes, it will be okay."

Maddie darted up the stairs as fast as she could go. She slammed into her room and crammed her feet into boots, feeling relief she hadn't changed into her pajamas early. Slinging her purse over her shoulder, she was back downstairs within minutes, an anxious, sick feeling in the pit of her stomach.

"Queenie, will you text Allison and tell her?" Maddie asked. She was still sitting on the floor, but her smile was gone. She looked worried and pale as she nodded.

"Come on, you can call your folks from the road." Scarlet had her keys in her hand, and they went out the front door. Scarlet drove a dark red four door Honda; the back was slathered in #imwithher and ACLU stickers.

Maddie buckled in. She was cold and starting to shake. If Lucca was in the hospital, that could only mean something bad happened. With stiff fingers, she dialed her parents, and her mom picked up on the first ring.

"Maddie? We just got a call from the hospital, we're on our way." Her mom's voice held tears and frustration.

"I am too. Don't worry, Mom, I'll call you as soon as I have information," Maddie said, trying to remain calm for her mother's sake.

"They wouldn't say anything over the phone except he was in serious but stable condition."

"I'll be there in a few minutes. Drive safe. I love you!" Maddie could feel her throat burn and clench, as she tried to hold back tears.

"Love you too." Her mom hung up.

"I'm sure he's fine," Scarlet said, gripping the wheel, as she pressed her little car to go faster.

Maddie didn't know what to think, but it wasn't until much later she realized she never even thought to call Jo.

CHAPTER TEN

Psychology Term Paper
Interview a psychiatric patient part two- transcribed from recording.
October 28th

Mr. R.M. Rainier by Scarlet Jones.

RM: I wondered if you were going to come back.

SJ: Of course, we aren't finished with our conversation.

RM: Aside from the doctors, not a lot of people want to speak with me.

SJ: Well I do, you are a great topic for my paper.

RM: I am glad I could help, though there's another patient you might want to interview.

SJ: Another patient? I don't think so, you're pretty interesting.

RM: I can be, but she would make a much better subject. She's been here for years!

SJ: Tell me about her.

RM: I can't, not really, it's a secret.

SJ: Well then, we should move on. Let's talk a little about your history, is that all right?

RM: Sure, what do you want to know?

SJ: Have you always lived here in Arcata? Where are you from, what did you do before coming to the hospital?

RM: I was born in Arcata, but my family has long worked for the Dulcaras. You can find many links between the Rainiers and the Dulcaras if you trace the family history.

SJ: Wow, I had no idea, so your family is from Romania too?

RM: No, no (chuckle) we are from England, nothing but plain, white stock in the Rainier line, I'm afraid.

SJ: I was told you were a real estate agent before...well, before you got sick.

RM: Yes, and a property manager for several places that the Dulcara Foundation owns.

SJ: So that's why it pays for all your medical care.

RM: (Laughs again) That and other things. I hold their secrets, like my father and mother before me.

SJ: Secrets?

RM: About the lives, but I mustn't tell you.

SJ: Your parents knew that if you drank the blood of animals you'd live forever?

RM: YES! Yes, but they never partook, they just held the secret, close to their bosoms. That's why they are dead, dead, dead, cold in the ground and I will live forever.

SJ: But the staff here doesn't allow you to have lives.

RM: (More laughter, louder than before) That's what you think, that's what they think, but I find a way. I always find a way.

(Door opens and an attendant comes into the room)

A: I think that's all for today, Ms. Jones. Come on, Mr. Rainier, let's get you back to your room.

SJ: Yeah, I think that's a good idea.

RM: But we're not done! I have more to tell you!

SJ: I promise to come back and listen to more.

RM: (In a whisper) You promise?

SJ: I promise.

––––––––

"*A* party? Are you sure that's a good idea? Lucca just got out of the hospital," Maddie said. She was sitting on her bed looking at Allison and Scarlet in disbelief. The afternoon sunlight filtered through her room, giving the colors more warmth and texture.

"It's a perfect idea! Lucca wants things to get back to normal and this is a great way to show him that it can," Allison said, excitement in her voice, worry in her eyes.

Lucca had spent the last two weeks in the hospital. When Maddie got to the hospital, the doctor told her Lucca had been found sleep walking outside, barefoot, and collapsed. Testing showed his heart seemed to be weaker than previous exams showed.

It wasn't just his heart that was the issue, he also had a condition called Pulmonary Hypertension: high blood pressure in his lungs which causes shortness of breath, fatigue and is the #1 reason they wouldn't qualify him for a heart transplant.

They changed his medicine and kept him in the hospital until they were sure he was better. Though the doctor warned her and her parents that at this point Lucca could live many more years or die suddenly.

Her parents went back home only a few days ago. Maddie and Lucca had to practically beg them to go. Their mom almost pulled Lucca from school, but the doctor said that Lucca needed normality, and to go about his life as usual.

"I think it's a great idea, Maddie. We can hold a small get together here at the house, have some drinks, games, pizza, and all just relax," Scarlet agreed.

"It's not just Lucca who needs it, Jo has been acting erratic and nervous ever since she finished that project at Dulcara Mansion." Allison sat next to Maddie.

"I know." Maddie nodded her head; it was true. Jo had not been Jo in over a week. She'd thought Jo would be happy that she was done with the project. Lucca certainly seemed to be. However, Jo was starting to skip Professor Dulcara's class all together and Maddie was worried she'd flunk it. What would Jo do if she flunked the class? Having that on her transcript would make it much harder to get into a graduate program in a few years.

"Jo's just bitten off more than she can chew for a freshman. We'll get her to lighten back up, she just needs some old-fashioned booty shakin'!" Scarlet laughed.

"You guys have already started planning this, haven't you?" Maddie asked, suddenly suspicious.

Scarlet looked sheepish, Allison puffed out her chest in pride.

"Yes, for Halloween night, we knew we could convince you and you'd convince Jo," Allison said.

"A Halloween party? Tomorrow? Where am I going to find a costume this last minute?" Maddie thought about what was in her closet, maybe she could put something together. Possibly a Stevie Nicks type person or a pirate maybe?

Great, knowing Allison, she's gotten me a princess costume, or worse a salsa dancer. She still hasn't figured out the difference between Mexican and Puerto Rican.

"I've got that all under control, me and my bestie, Amex, went shopping," Allison told her.

"I've taken care of the music and guest list, Queenie's got the food and decorations, you don't have to do anything but look fabulous and bring Jo," Scarlet said.

Maddie was silent for a few moments, it might be nice to go to a party and relax, maybe have a few beers, and laugh with her friends, the past month had been stressful.

"Fine, I'll go talk to Jo," Maddie stood up.

"I knew you'd see it our way!" Allison slung an arm around one of her shoulders and gave her a light squeeze. "I'll send your costumes up that night. Don't ruin them, they are rented."

"Nothing too slutty, okay?" Maddie said, already slightly regretting her decision to say yes.

"Of course not. Maddie, you couldn't pull off slutty even if you wanted to." Allison left the room.

"We'll tell Lucca he has to sit and can't drink. Don't worry we all like your brother. We'll make sure nothing happens to him." Scarlet tried to comfort Maddie and it worked, a little. Lucca wouldn't be happy at the rules, but better than trying to tell him he couldn't come at all. Maddie made a mental note to not mention anything about the party the next time her mom called.

After they both left, Maddie squared her shoulders and made her way down to Jo's room. She knocked, tentatively. Waiting, she bounced from foot to foot and stared too hard at the wood that made up Jo's door. She wondered what kind it was and how old the tree was that died to make it. She frowned at the wood and knocked again. Was Jo asleep?

"Come in?" Jo's voice sounded off, but that was how she usually sounded...now.

Maddie went in and had to shield her eyes since every light was on in Jo's room, the ceiling and a desktop lamp and what had to be a brand-new floor lamp near her bed. The three different shades of yellow clashed, making the light not only jarring but almost frantic.

"Damn, Jo, afraid of the dark?" Maddie asked. Jo didn't seem to appreciate the humor. She was sitting cross legged in the middle of her bed, it was stripped bare, her blue striped sheets pooling on the floor.

"Did you hire a maid?" Maddie came in further, closing the door behind her. Jo was a messy person, smart, but unorganized. However, her bedroom was currently immaculate, which scared Maddie. Wasn't personality changes a major sign something was wrong?

"No, I just cleaned it, I was tired of the clutter."

"You took down your Kate Bush posters, even the signed one I gave you." Maddie felt hurt. Jo loved Kate Bush, and when they first moved in, she'd helped Jo carefully put up posters of the singer. They'd even used the special adhesive so it wouldn't ruin them.

"I'm going to put them back up, I just wanted to clean first," Jo said. That's when Maddie noticed that Jo had nailed a few large, silver crosses to the wall, one over the door, one near the window and one above her bed.

"Jo, what's going on? You don't believe in the 'all powerful sky daddy.'" Maddie used her fingers for quotations, as she used a saying stolen from Jo herself.

"I know...They just make me feel safer."

Maddie crawled up on the bed and put her arms around Jo. Jo was stiff for a moment and then relaxed. Maddie nuzzled her neck smelling the cologne that Jo preferred to wear and feeling how fast Jo's heart was beating.

"What's wrong, Jo? You never leave your room, except for classes, you don't even want to talk to me."

"I'm sorry, I just feel...like something bad is going to happen. You don't know, you can't know what working at the Dulcara Mansion was like," Jo told her.

"Try to tell me, and I'll try to understand." Maddie didn't like Jo acting like this, afraid and weak. She was used to take charge Jo, fearless Jo and she wanted her back. The last few weeks were like her best friend had gone missing. While Maddie was having small doubts about their romantic relationship, the one thing she never questioned was the friendship they'd spent the last few years cultivating. Jo was her best friend and if something was wrong, she wanted to help fix it.

"It was like a nightmare. The place just doesn't feel right. The work I was doing made me feel like I was being watched, as if each piece of paper was a bit to a horrible puzzle I just couldn't understand," Jo said. Maddie opened her mouth to talk and decided against it.

"Professor Valora is doing something awful in that house and her TAs are no better. It's like there are monsters just beneath their skin, but you can't tell, you can't tell until one day you aren't paying attention and bam! Their hands are on you and you can see it in their eyes." Jo continued to ramble. None of it made sense to Maddie, she only knew that Jo was traumatized over something.

"You don't have to go back there, Jo," she said, rubbing the other girl's shoulders. She couldn't believe Valora was some sort of monster. Maddie hadn't told Jo, but she'd spent one on one time with the professor over the last month and really enjoyed herself. Valora was well read, educated and had the time and money to make a difference in the world. She'd already read two novels Valora recommended and had an impromptu coffee date. Maddie was hoping to get a spot in her next class, she really liked listening to Valora talk.

Maddie could believe that maybe one of the TAs were freaky or awful. She'd met all three and they all gave her a vibe she couldn't put her finger on. Perhaps one of them made a pass at Jo? Or did something to make her uncomfortable?

Whatever it was, it had obviously spooked her girlfriend.

"Did something happen? Did one of the TAs...do something?" Maddie asked. Jo blanched but shook her head no.

"They are all evil. You'd never see it, but I saw it. They know I saw it... they don't want me to tell anyone else," Jo said, squeezing her eyes shut.

Maddie was even more convinced now that Scarlet was right, Jo had taken on too much work and too many classes. This was just stress leaking out of her mouth in the form of craziness. It couldn't be anything else, right? Maddie tightened her arms around Jo, hoping it made her feel better.

"I don't want to go to her class anymore either," Jo whispered.

"You'll flunk if you don't. Plus, if Professor Valora is some sort of scary monster you don't want her to know she got to you, right?" Maddie prayed her half ass attempt at psychology would work. Lucca thought the world of Valora. Still, if she really was horrible, wouldn't her brother have noticed something too? Instead, he'd appreciated the extra credit, even though he hadn't been able to finish the project.

"I guess you're right." Jo gave her a genuine smile the first Maddie had seen in days. Maddie gave Jo one last squeeze and dropped her arms. The bed was too soft underneath her and the mattress felt scratchy against her bare feet. Maddie wanted to tell her about the party and leave, now that Jo seemed calmer. Maddie noticed a slightly gross and pungent smell in the room. It was just a hint, like if she turned a certain way it was there and then gone. She glanced around and tried to find its source. It really wasn't like Jo to leave food spoiling in her bedroom. Something with garlic in it? Maddie tried to remember if they'd brought home left over pasta from their last date night.

"What's that smell?" she asked.

"What smell? I don't smell anything," Jo said, but Maddie knew she was lying.

"Huh, okay." Maddie changed the subject. "I need to talk to you about something."

"Shoot," Jo said.

"The girls are going to be throwing a Halloween party here tomorrow night, nothing major, just a few people, some drinks, food, and costumes. Lucca is even coming. I think it will be good for us to have some fun, don't you?"

"That does sound nice. I have some homework to finish but then we can spend the whole weekend together. I've been neglecting you, I'm sorry." Jo angled her body so she could kiss Maddie.

Maddie tried to enjoy the kiss, but something was lacking in it and made her more anxious. She didn't want to lose Jo. Hopefully this party and free weekend together could fix what was wrong with them. Maddie felt there was this giant divide between them of late and she was desperate to either fill it in or build a bridge across it. She loved Jo, right?

"Allison got us costumes," Maddie said after Jo's lips left hers.

"Hopefully something sexy for you." There was a twinkle in Jo's eyes, one that usually meant Maddie was about to end up naked in Jo's bed, but today she wasn't in the mood for it. Maddie was worried she'd have to fake enjoyment and involvement. Valora's image swam in her mind and she pushed thoughts of the other woman away, feeling mortified and dreadful.

"I don't really do sexy," Maddie said, grinning, happy that at least Jo seemed to be trying to get in better spirits.

"You could." Jo grabbed her shoulders and kissed her, mouth hot and full of need. Her hands gripped Maddie's shirt and Maddie could feel desperation leaking off her girlfriend.

"I want you," Jo whispered, kissing Maddie's jawline and licking the skin beneath her ear. Maddie shivered. It did feel nice, and she held her breath as Jo pushed her back on the bed, fingers touching the skin beneath her shirt and crawling up to cup her breasts. Maddie pushed her hands away and tried to sit back up.

"Not now, Jo." Even to her it sounded lame. Jo kissed her again, a smile on her lips, even though her eyes were still shadowed and strained. She put her mouth near Maddie's ear, tugging the lobe with her teeth. Maddie sucked in a breath. It didn't feel bad, it felt kind of nice. She made herself relax under Jo.

"Please, Maddie, don't make me beg," Jo said, laughter in her voice tickling against Maddie's ear.

Maddie nodded her consent, though her body was still not quite willing. She loved Jo. Jo was her girlfriend. What kind of person did it make her if she didn't want to fuck her own girlfriend?

She found out, several minutes later; it made her the kind of girlfriend who thought about another woman when she came.

CHAPTER ELEVEN

Journal of Lucca West
October 30th

I still don't know if this journal is helping me. When I read back on old entries, I just think I'm crazy.

I'm still having dreams of the woman, but now I also dream of this fluttering noise outside my window and I wake up more tired than when I went to bed. The only time I sleep well is when Allison is next to me, and she can't sleep with me every night.

I almost don't want to sleep at night, the weird sounds and dreams are becoming almost nightmarish. If I could smoke pot or drink, I would, maybe it would keep the dreams away.

I don't like to dwell on the negative, my life is short enough without being a glass-half-empty kind of person. I wish I could talk to Maddie or my parents, but it would only worry them more. It was hard enough to get Mom and Dad to let me come to school and live in a dorm away from Maddie. After my last attack, I'm lucky they haven't swooped in and locked me in my room at home.

When they found me this last time, the doctors were puzzled at my lack of blood and I had to have a transfusion. I feel better now but I can tell the ordeal put a strain on me, one that has accelerated my heart condition. I don't fear death, but I am sad for those I would leave behind. I have so many good friends and so many people who love me, so much to be thankful for.

Ugh, I sound like an emo teen girl.

We're having a Halloween party at Maddie and Jo's. I'm excited, I need to do something besides watch movies in my room, see my unattractive male doctor, and go to class. I couldn't finish the project at the Dulcara Mansion which was a bummer.

Professor Dulcara is the reason kids become teachers, she's the reason you learn to love school. Listening and watching her teach is amazing. She never stops trying to get you to improve yourself and is always so passionate about her subject. Maddie says Jo hates her and wants to stop going to class. She's crazy. The professor has never been anything but nice to me. I'm not surprised though, Jo is a hard personality to get along with. I don't even always like her. I think she tries to control Maddie too, like her father, is my guess.

What do you get when two huge personalities mesh? Conflict. Jo and Professor Dulcara are very strong, dominant women.

I guess that's all for now.

$\mathcal{M}$ addie looked again at the costume Allison had put on her bed. It still hadn't changed.

"I can't wear this," she said. Jo, who was already in the process of getting dressed, stopped, one leg in and one leg out of her pants.

"You can, I think it looks cute."

"You would. Anyway, your costume is perfectly fine." In fact, Maddie loved it, the green and brown of the Robin Hood costume was complimentary to Jo's coloring, plus it was pants, a tunic, vest, little jaunty hat, and a fake bow. Fairly simply and rather fun. Maddie wouldn't have minded being Robin Hood. Why did people always assume she was should be the one in the dress?

"Maid Marian is a fine costume, it might be a little tight, but I'm sure it'll be fine." Jo finished dressing and shoved the cap on her head, placed her hands on her hips and gave her best 'Welcome to Sherwood' stance.

"This isn't just Maid Marian; it's slutty, corseted Maid Marian." Maddie sat down next to the costume, it wasn't even a flattering color. A short, pale pink shirt dress with a soft leather yellow waist cincher and matching veil type head piece.

"Yeah, not really a flattering cut on you, but your breasts will look great," Jo kidded.

"It's really short," Maddie complained, as she got out of everything but a pair of black boy short underwear. A little hurt Jo was agreeing with her, wasn't Jo supposed to compliment and tell her she was beautiful no matter what?

"Wear something under it if you're that uncomfortable." Jo leaned into the mirror and took a black eye liner pencil, in one deft move she drew a swarthy looking mustache above her lip and winked at Maddie.

"I'm glad you're feeling better at least," Maddie said, giving in and getting dressed. She had a pair of white pajama shorts she'd wear under the dress. She didn't want to flash anyone should she sit wrong or fall over. Why in her imagination she'd be falling over was in question, but her mind often went places unexplainable.

"I am. Meet you down stairs!" Jo kissed her check and sauntered out the door.

By the time Maddie made it downstairs, Halloween music was playing and everyone who had been invited was there, though that wasn't saying much. It was only them and Lucca, after all.

"Wow, that's some outfit," Lucca said when Maddie came into the room. He was lounging on the couch in a tight, black t-shirt, matching pants, with his hair slicked back greaser style, obviously Danny Zuko.

"I chose it. Not half bad, huh?" Allison said, she walked into the room holding two cups and handed one to Lucca.

"So sweet Sandy, not bad Sandy?" Maddie asked, annoyed. How come she had to wander around all night uncomfortable, but Allison was in a sweater and a poodle skirt?

"I didn't think yours would be quite so...short...sorry," Allison said, a sheepish grin on her face. Probably underestimated how much more fat the outfit had to cover on Maddie versus herself. Maddie pushed away the uncharitable thoughts. Showing off your body wasn't a big deal, she had no issue when other women did it, more power to them. She just wasn't comfortable in a skirt that came above her knees.

"I thought with your heritage a salsa dancer would be good, but Lucca reminded me you guys aren't from Mexico," Allison added.

Just like I don't enjoy spicy foods or celebrate Day of the Dead. Though it would be cool to dress like one of those skeleton candies.

"There's food in the dining room!" Scarlet called out from the hallway.

"You coming?" Maddie asked her brother, he was still paler than she would have liked, but seemed so much better since his trip to the hospital.

"Nah, Allie and I are going to stay right here." Lucca placed an arm around Allison and squeezed. The look on her face made Maddie happy, the girl was obviously head over heels for Lucca.

Maddie wondered if she still looked that way when she was with Jo. Once upon a time she must have had that soft stupid glow, but she didn't feel like it was there anymore, did that happen in all relationships, eventually? Was it something you desperately clung to and did anything to keep or did it fade away as deep love and comfort took its place? Maybe it disappeared altogether, and it was a sign things were over.

"What did you guys make?" Maddie asked, her nose picking up delicious aromas as she went into the dining room.

"Queenie's the cook, not me. I make about three meals and they all require a casserole dish and chicken, 'cause my grandma taught them to me." Scarlet laughed. She was in a white flapper's dress, a band around her forehead, nestling into her black curly hair with a feather sticking out. She looked wonderful.

"I can make eggs," Jo said. She was leaning against the wall, beer in one hand.

"Scrambled with too much hot sauce," Maddie said, her stomach growled, and she began to load up a plate. She wanted food, especially if there was also booze.

"Scarlet, let's play games now!" Queenie complained, bringing in a tray of food from the kitchen. She was dressed as a large, yellow flower, all in green with a ring of yellow petals around her face.

"I've told you before, its food and mingling, drinking and games and then passing out on the floor."

Everyone laughed at Scarlet's comment.

Maddie was impressed by the spread. There were little meatballs that tasted sweet and spicy, leaves (she was told it was endive, whatever that was) stuffed with onions and goat cheese, and deviled eggs with bacon. The tray Queenie was currently bringing out was filled with all kinds of vegetables and dips. There were even purple carrots, what makes a carrot purple? Does it taste different from a normal carrot? Maddie was tempted to try one, but she hated carrots.

"Thanks for going to the fundraiser with me, by the way." Queenie came and stood by Maddie. "Did you have fun?"

Maddie had just taken a huge bite and quickly chewed and swallowed before answering. Why did people have to ask you questions while you were eating?

"Yes, I did. I found out they raised a few thousand dollars. I wish I could have afforded more."

"As long as you do what you can, isn't that what matters?" Queenie asked.

"Yes, I spoke to the head of this chapter's PP, and they are sending the money to clinics in states less hospitable than ours. I'm probably going to be a clinic escort," Maddie said, she was really excited about the prospect.

"A clinic escort, really? Be careful, you put that on a resume as your community service it might limit jobs in the future," Jo said from across the room. She was making her disapproving face.

"Isn't Maddie a Women's Studies major?" Scarlet asked.

"Yes, so the kind of jobs I am going to want will probably like it," Maddie said, defensively. *Jo should know that, she knows I want to fight for abortion rights and women's equality.*

"Maybe you could come to a Green Party meeting with me later this month." Queenie was petting one of her petals and had a faraway look in her eyes.

"Uh...maybe?" Maddie didn't want to commit to anything. She liked that Queenie and Scarlet were activists, but thought the Green Party was pretty ridiculous.

"Your brother looks pretty good tonight. We've all been worried about him," Scarlet said, changing the subject.

"Yes, I hope he can relax and have a good time tonight. He wants so much to be a normal college student."

"Well, he certainly looks like one, he really is adorable," Queenie said. "Adorable?"

"I know he's your brother, Maddie, but yeah Lucca is too cute. I considered making a play myself, but I could tell he was already way too into Allie." Scarlet grinned.

"Seriously?" Jo asked.

"You've already had too many drinks, Scarlet," Queenie said, laughing at her BFF.

"And why not?"

Scarlet looked like she was going to say something more, but the doorbell rang.

"Who could that be?" Scarlet wondered. Maddie was curious too. Had someone else been invited? Did they have a surprise guest? Please, God, do not let it be her parents.

Maddie froze coming into the hallway as she saw Professor Dulcara being greeted by Allison.

"What the fuck?" Jo hissed from behind her. Maddie felt Jo grab her waist, fingers digging into her skin through the fabric of the dress. Out of the corner of her eye, Maddie could see Jo was frightened.

"It's okay," Maddie said. It was more than okay, honestly. Valora looked stunning. She was in a black cape, black tights, and a matching tunic with a silver belt slung low on her hips, holding a very realistic sword. Her hair was in a braid and a silver and black hat was on her head.

"Professor Valora just stopped by with some things for Jo and Lucca," Allison was saying, as she ushered the professor inside and closed the door.

"Yes, sorry to crash your gathering, but Mr. West told me you both would be here tonight, and I had some parting gifts for you," Valora said, her smile wide. She caught Maddie's gaze and Maddie looked at the ground. Fawning over your girlfriend's teacher was super tacky.

But I really want to fawn over her. I want my hands and lips on her skin. I also want to stop feeling this drawn to another woman when I am still with Jo. What is wrong with me? No, no...go away images of us in a hot tub in the Alps.

"Come in! Lucca's in the living room," Allison said, leading the way.

"Make her go away," Jo muttered.

"That would be rude, come on Jo, you can do this," Maddie said. They were alone in the hallway.

"I can't, she's awful."

"It's fine. You have like two more months of her class," Maddie gently reminded her.

"You look so pale, Mr. West. You really need more red meat in your diet," Valora was saying as Maddie and Jo entered the room.

"I've been telling him that!" Allison exclaimed.

"She's not a doctor," Queenie said from her seat on the floor, she looked almost as unhappy as Jo did.

"You are quite right, ah, Ms. Harper! I am very happy with the work you've done for me. I've brought you both a little something as a token of my appreciation." She handed Lucca and Jo each a little brown package.

"Thanks, professor!" Lucca said, beaming. "I really enjoyed working with you."

"Thank you," mumbled Jo, still partially behind Maddie.

"Do you want a drink?" Scarlet asked, being a good host.

"No, thank you, I am actually on my way to a costume party of my own," Valora told them.

"Really? Who are you?" Maddie asked.

"The devil," Queenie whispered as she walked past Maddie and left the room.

"What did she say?" Valora asked, a slight glare on her face.

"Nothing, it's just...Queenie, being Queenie." Scarlet forced a laugh and rushed after her friend.

"Hmm, well I thought it was obvious. I am the Sherriff of Nottingham."

"Oh, my God! How funny. Jo and Maddie are Robin Hood and Maid Marian," Allison said, laughing.

"Yeah, quite a coincidence," Lucca agreed.

"Well then, perhaps I shall steal Ms. West away for the night." Valora's words brought laughter to the room. They sounded light, but the look in her eyes as she stared at Maddie was anything but.

They lapsed into silence as Lucca began ripping open his gift. Jo stood there, still as a statue, staring at her feet. Maddie nudged her.

"What?" Jo asked, voice low.

"You're being rude, c'mon...what'd she give you?" Maddie asked, her cheeks burning under Valora's gaze. Jo was being awful. She hoped it didn't affect her grade, or worse...Valora's opinion of Maddie.

"Sorry. My mind wandered." The smile on Jo's face was tight and insincere.

"I understand, I too would be...preoccupied." Valora said, her eyes never leaving Maddie's face.

"Professor, thank you! I have no idea what it is, but I know it must be special," Lucca said, his laughter infectious and bringing joy to everyone. He held a small, murky brown bottle with a label Maddie had never seen before.

"It's *divin*, Moldovan brandy. It should help bring color to your cheeks again, Mr. West," Valora explained. "One of my family's holdings makes it."

"How does it differ from normal brandy?" Allison asked, grabbing the bottle and inspecting it.

"Like many beverages from the time and area, it is made with plums."

"Thank you," Jo said, finally opening her own package. She held the gift like it was a snake.

"You are most welcome, now I need to be going. See you both in class." She turned her attention to Maddie. "Ms. West, I hope you will consider applying for my Yuletide trip, I think you would enjoy my home country."

"Oh…I hadn't considered, yes, I'll think about it," Maddie stammered.

After Valora left, Jo gripped Maddie's arm and yanked her into the hallway. Maddie stood, irritated, rubbing her arm. There would be a bruise there in the morning. What had gotten into Jo?

"You are not going to Romania with Professor Dulcara," Jo stated it like the decision was already made.

"It sounds like fun, I don't know…maybe."

"No, I mean you are not doing it. Haven't I made it clear there is something wrong with her? Really wrong, Maddie, if you only knew…" Jo tore off her hat, threw it to the ground, and ran a hand through her hair.

"If I only knew what? You haven't told me anything!" Maddie yelled and quickly clamped her mouth shut. She never yelled, and she certainly didn't want their housemates to know they were fighting over an imaginary trip or a possibly monstrous teacher.

"I can't really…remember…it hurts my head. I wrote it down, but when I went to look for it, it was gone." Jo's hand moved from her straight, dark hair to her forehead. Her eyes were pained and wide, Maddie felt her anger leaving her, and instead she put an arm around Jo.

"Maybe you should go to bed, Jo." She didn't know what else to say. Something had obviously happened, but who knew what it was? Maddie worried something was wrong with Jo, something she couldn't help her with. Was the girl stressed, overworked, and exhausted? Or did she need to see a therapist?

"Yeah, that might be a good idea. Here, take this and get rid of it." Jo thrust the bottle into Maddie's hands.

As she watched Jo go upstairs, she held the bottle to her chest, feeling lost, confused, angry, and just a little happy Valora wanted her to go on the Yuletide trip.

CHAPTER TWELVE

Transcription of Social Media Conversations

Madeline West
Yesterday at 10:00pm
OMG JUST APPLIED FOR PROFESSOR DULCARA'S YULETIDE
TRIP!!! WISH ME LUCK!!

Comments:

Queenie Myles
Why would you do that?
Scarlet Jones
Better yet, why are you typing IN ALL CAPS?
Jolene Harper
Why can't I dislike this status?

Lucca West
Yesterday at 2:55pm

Sorry I haven't been on much. I've been sick, go figure. Not sleeping well. I'm having bad dreams. Allie is taking good care of me.

Comments:

Jolene Harper
I wish I could have bad dreams. At least that means I'm sleeping. BTW talk to your sister about her crazy idea to go to Romania

Allison Hastings
@princessallie
Super worried about boyfriend. He's not acting like himself ☹

ou should check on Lucca. He's been acting so weird!
Maddie stared at the text message and frowned. If Allison was texting her about Lucca, there must be something very strange going on. She and Allison weren't super close by any means. She didn't even realize Allison had her phone number, this was quite possibly the first text she'd ever received.

Weird how? Maddie sent back quickly. She hoped she didn't have to deal with it right now, as selfish as that sounded. Glancing up from her phone, her eyes had trouble taking in all the Dulcara Mansion at once. It was a huge mismatched rambling house, at least three stories tall.

Well...TMI but even though he looks like death he's trying to get on me in the worst way.

Maddie rolled her eyes, was that all? *Sounds just like a horny boy,* she responded.

I know, but it's not like your brother. I have a hickey for God's sake!

Okay, okay. I'll call him in a bit. Maddie hit send, put her phone on silent, and stuck it in her purse.

Pulling out the guide book she'd bought from a skinny guy near the bus stop, she looked to see if it said how big the house was. The guide book, though it was more a pamphlet than anything else, was crinkled and a little worse for wear, as was Maddie. When she'd set off that morning to finally get a look at the infamous living quarters of Professor

Dulcara, she didn't realize that unless you were part of a group it was hard to get to the house.

The bus dropped off in front of a large iron gate, which stood open Monday through Wednesday from sunrise to sunset—according to a sign attached to the front. Then there was a mile walk up a winding, paved road, with no sidewalks, but plenty of shade from giant, scary trees. If she'd come with a designated tour group, the pamphlet said, there was a shuttle from the bus stop to the house.

The guy at the bus stop, who'd smelled a little like garlic, also sold hats and other touristy type things. He said that the mansion didn't have a gift shop. Maddie asked if she would even be able to get inside, thinking maybe she needed to schedule it.

"Sure, walk up the path and go right inside. Someone will greet you. The house is open to the public, it's just normally big groups like school classes, tend to be what I see most often." After that, he turned his attention to hocking his wares to a couple walking by.

So, a little out of breath, Maddie now stood in front of the mansion. It was this dark, almost living thing, the windows all small and covered, the yard was overgrown, the plants seemed to have taken over. How was this a public place when it didn't look that well cared for?

Jungle cats could live in here. That would be awesome, though that would mean they're hunting me right now...so let's skip that.

Maddie couldn't imagine Valora living in such a place, as she walked up the stairs, she noticed cobwebs in the corners near the rafters and heard a flapping shuffling noise her imagination was sure were evil bats about to fly into her hair.

Quickening her pace, she pushed against the large door, surprised at how heavy it was, and went inside. It took her eyes a few moments to adjust to the dark, but when they did, her mouth made a tiny O shape.

The inside was beautiful, like she'd stepped into a renaissance painting. There was artwork and tapestries everywhere, antique furniture in golds and mauves, statues and shelves filled with giant, leather tomes.

The ceilings were high, and old-fashioned wall lamps illuminated the space, giving off a specific scent, musty and spicy at the same time, while their yellowish light left the room feeling like a different time period.

Velvet red ropes lined a path through all the beauty and every so often there was a plaque next to an item. Maddie couldn't read any of them from the front door, but she assumed they gave history about the object they were attached to.

Several doors led away from the main room, some stood open and others were shut and on the other side of the rope.

Maddie walked further in. "Hello!" she called out. There had to be someone to greet guests, right? Or was this an abandoned, haunted mansion and the front door would lock behind her, keeping her in with all manner of devious spirits?

"Welcome to Dulcara Mansion."

Maddie spun around, hand to her chest. Professor Dulcara was leaning against a bookshelf. Her black hair was in a tight bun, accentuating her pale and sharp features. She wore a dark purple A-line skirt and a black camisole, which barely covered her generous bosom.

Maddie licked her lips, her mouth suddenly dry. This was a magnificent creature standing before her. How could Jo be afraid of her?

"Oh, I'm sorry, are you not...open?"

"Of course we are. I'm just on staff this morning," Valora said, she had a strained tired look around her eyes that Maddie had never seen before.

"I just wanted to see, I mean...I've lived here almost three months and thought..." Maddie didn't know why she was having a hard time putting together sentences.

"Of course, you wanted to see the mansion. I bet you were a bit shocked by the outside, yes?" Valora moved closer to Maddie, her grin friendly.

"Well, maybe."

"I do not like to change things very much. I fix up the house, nothing is broken or dangerous, but I have tried to keep everything as original as possible. It's not history once you add siding or plastic," Valora explained.

"And the cobwebs? The bats?"

"Just creatures of the night. I have no fear of them and do not mind sharing my space. They are not welcome inside the house, however."

"That's an interesting way of looking at it," Maddie said, in awe. This woman was sophisticated, and Maddie felt ashamed at every fantasy she'd had about her, what could a woman like Valora see in her? She was a baby.

"The paths are pretty well defined, any door on the other side of the rope is off limits and most likely locked. They are private," Valora was saying. Maddie focused on her words, they were probably important.

"Don't touch anything, bathrooms are on the second floor and the tour ends when you reach the cemetery. Any questions?"

"Yes, do I get an app on my phone, head phones, or anything?" Maddie asked, looking around for equipment and puzzled when she saw none. Valora looked confused at her words, then her eyes sparkled in amusement and glowed just a moment with a light Maddie was sure she'd imagined.

"Ms. West, there is no technology here. I am your guide today."

Maddie couldn't believe her luck, a tour of Dulcara Mansion by the one person who would know the history better than anyone else? Her heart sped up as she also realized that she and Valora would be alone in this large, dark house for at least an hour. Her palms grew sweaty and she wiped them on her dark blue, cotton skater dress. She'd chosen this one because it was cute, comfy, and had tiny lace skulls sewn in at the bottom.

They started in what Valora called the living room but wasn't like any living room she'd ever seen. There was no TV or big comfy sofa.

"Before we get started, I wanted to tell you I received your application for the Yuletide trip to Romania," Valora said.

Maddie's throat went dry; she'd only turned that in a day before. Was this Valora's way of letting her down nicely? Maddie knew she didn't have near the credentials that were probably required. She'd heard people talking about Professor Valora's yearly trip to Romania, how she only chose a handful of students, mostly upper classman, and most who had at least taken her class previously.

"When you suggested it, I thought, hey, there's no harm in giving it a shot." She hoped she didn't come off sounding immature or disinterested.

"No there is not, and I think for you this will be a great experience," Valora told her. She reached out a hand and placed it on Maddie's shoulder. The pressure was light, and Maddie could feel each of her fingers through the thin fabric of her dress, it was a comforting and electrifying touch. Maddie wondered what it would be like to have those long thin fingers on her bare skin instead.

Blushing furiously at her fantastical thoughts, Maddie pretended to be interested in a piece of pottery dated back to the 18th century and moved away.

"Yes, filling out the application was good experience."

"You misunderstand me again, is it on purpose? I am curious why you always assume the farthest outcome from what the facts are telling you?"

Did she do that? In retrospect, it was obvious that Valora was to be her guide, she'd seen no evidence of anything to suggest otherwise. Maddie studied the colors in the pot until her eyes burned, and she turned Valora's sentence around in her mind for a few seconds.

"So...I am coming with you to Romania?" She hated how timid she sounded, but she was afraid she hadn't understood.

"Yes. I wanted to tell you in person. I would have come by the house, but as luck would have it you stepped into my house today."

Why did that sound too much like "said the spider to the fly?"

"Wow, thanks!" Maddie's smile hurt it was so wide and full of delight. She turned to Valora who was studying her with a severe and serious expression.

"You are welcome."

"No, really, this is amazing! I can't wait, it will be better than Christmas!" She'd never been out of the country, and now she got to go with this perfect woman and learn about history in a way she'd never imagined. Her smile faltered as another thought drifted into her mind. How was she going to tell Jo?

"There is something else I want to discuss with you, if that pot is done taking up your time." The joke caught Maddie off guard, and she began to laugh. Valora joined her and the humor in her face made her skin shine and even more beautiful than before.

The two women laughed together for a few minutes, Valora dabbed at her eyes.

"You are amusing, Ms. West, and good company."

"Please, it's Maddie."

"Short for Madeline, yes?"

"Yes."

"Then, if you don't mind, I shall call you Madeline."

"Alright." A humming warmth in her chest was all Maddie needed to know that this was something special. No one called her Madeline, it had been Maddie since she was born.

"I was wondering if you would like a TA position next year. One of my currents will be graduating."

This statement shocked Maddie far more than the realization she was going to Romania.

"Are you serious?" Maddie asked before she could stop to consider her words.

"I am almost always serious. You have everything I want in a TA," Valora said.

"I figured you'd be asking Lucca, or Jo." Maddie heard noise from behind them and saw a girl in a deep green dress with a name tag come in the front door followed by a group of three or four. She looked at them, nodded her head to Valora and instead of taking the path they were on she opened a door to the west that said "Parlor" across the top. Maddie could hear her speaking softly to the people until the door shut with a loud click.

"No, they are not...appropriate for this position," Valora said.

"Can I think about it?" Maddie asked, upset, their bubble of privacy and intimacy felt like it burst with the arrival of more people in the house. *Jo and Lucca weren't appropriate? Then why had Jo told her she thought Valora might ask her, what had changed?*

"Of course. Now, the tour?"

Maddie nodded her consent. Her head felt like it had way too much information buzzing about. These first few months at college were so much better than she expected. She didn't know if she was having a typical college experience, but she was having something much deeper.

"This house was built in 1870, ten years after the town was officially named Arcata, but the Dulcaras lived on this land since 1850. In the cemetery you will see graves older than that, but the first written record we have in the archives is from 1850," Valora said proudly as they stopped at a large, oil painting of the house. Next to it was a huge portrait of Valora in period costume.

"Pretty picture of you, I've never had mine painted."

"Thank you, but that is actually my great, great, great aunt. She helped fund Trinity Hospital in 1911, which eventually closed and was moved and is now known as Mad River Community hospital."

"Your family donates a lot of money to healthcare here, right?" Maddie asked, fascinated.

"Yes, Mad River and Sempervirens Psychiatric Hospital."

"My friend is interviewing a patient there that used to work for you."

They wandered by several other paintings of the house and various family members, slowly they turned into photographs. Maddie was amazed at the familial resemblance between Valora and her kin.

"I think I know who you're talking about. He's been a family friend for years."

"He tells some crazy stories."

"I should probably pay him a visit." Valora's mouth tightened into a slight grimace, then relaxed. Maddie worried she'd said something stupid by bringing up Scarlet's paper. Jo always accused her of saying the wrong things at the way wrong times.

They passed through a doorway that had lettering above it saying, "Study."

"I thought you'd have more books," Maddie commented. There were a few book shelves with leather bound volumes, but mostly the room was filled with furniture and more art.

One plaque, next to a painting that looked like just a bunch of colors on a canvas, read, "Marcel Janco—Romania and Israeli artist—Marine Landscape." Maddie cocked her head to one side. She didn't care for art, especially art you had to translate, but she guessed she saw something that might be a crab.

"I do, in my library upstairs, but it is private. I know you enjoyed the last novel I recommended, perhaps we could make a habit of getting together and discussing literature?"

"That sounds wonderful. I wish I could get Jo to read more."

Another painting, this time of a girl in a white dress and head band. "Nicolae Grigorescu—Peasant Woman from Muscel." Maddie liked this one much better.

"Ms. Harper does not seem the type of woman who would enjoy the books we like to read, especially those about powerful women."

"I don't know, Jo's all for equal rights," Maddie defended Jo.

"Not like you are, not as I am. You and I are alike in this way. We see intolerance and wish to remove it." Valora led her through another room, filled with musical instruments, a soft symphony playing from hidden speakers.

"I know, right? How difficult is the concept that everyone should have equal rights? Jo is going to be a lawyer, she will be able to fight injustice."

"Do you really think so? I believe you shall fight more injustice than she."

Maddie opened her mouth to deny it, to call Valora out on what she was saying about Jo, but a look on the other woman's face made her pause. She stopped walking and pretended to be interested in an antique piano forte. Jo never mentioned what kind of law she wanted to practice, she didn't want to attend Stanford, riding on her father's coat tails, that much was true. But her dad was a high-profile litigator. Maddie and she just never discussed it. Maddie assumed she wanted to defend victims or go pro bono for immigrants, but was that Maddie being idealistic? Was she putting her own beliefs onto Jo?

"I don't know. I guess Jo can do whatever she wants," Maddie finally answered.

Silence followed as Valora led her out of the Music Room, through a hall and up some stairs. Maddie excused herself to use the restroom, her mind reeling from her inner thoughts. She'd always assumed she and Jo would be together forever, but that wasn't realistic. Her thoughts strayed to the woman waiting outside the bathroom for her. Why did she have to say anything at all? What would she get out of a conversation like that?

A little angry, Maddie splashed cold water on her face and told her reflection, "You're here for a tour and only a tour. Keep the topics light and to history."

"Are you ready to continue?" Valora asked, concern in her voice as Maddie appeared back in the hallway.

"Yes, please."

"This is one of my favorite rooms, it used to be just another guest room, but I have so many I decided to put up one of my favorite tapestries for all to enjoy."

The room was very bright and had electric light. Three of the four walls were covered with a tapestry that seemed to be telling a story, the first was of a beautiful woman, face obscured, standing in front of two cowering women, a knife in her hands. The second was of a castle, the dead littered outside, the third was the woman again, this time her eyes were red, and she was covered in blood.

"This is gorgeous, and familiar." Maddie moved closer, she dared not touch it, but she wanted to see the details up close.

"It's a very old tale from my homeland. I doubt you would know it."

Maddie stared at the woman cowering in the first section and it stirred a memory. "Is that their mother holding the knife?"

"Yes, in the tale she is being threatened by a warlord who wishes to rape her daughters. Instead she kills them and then herself." Valora came to stand next to her.

"I have heard this. Queenie told us on our camping trip. Professor Heeling told her. Though in her tale the warlord murders the mother."

"He did, did he? Like he would know what really happened? It's a common mistake in the translation." Valora's words held a bite, an edge to them.

"It was scary but beautiful." Maddie turned to face Valora, who was much closer to her than a few minutes prior, Maddie could smell her perfume, feel the warmth from her body. *That tapestry makes my nose twitch, but in a good way. In fact, standing here with her is like pages from a book, unreal and amazing.*

"Have you always had these?" Valora asked, fingers alighting on Maddie's birth marks.

"Yes, I was born with them," Maddie answered, suppressing the urge to shiver under Valora's touch. Why did she affect her so much? It was like her brain became foggy with everything but thoughts of Valora.

"Beautiful. I've been waiting for you. I thought I didn't need this in my life. I have since discovered how wrong I was."

Maddie didn't understand. Valora had been waiting for her? It didn't make any sense.

"We are so alike, Madeline. You have a darkness in you that mirrors my own, and I want it," Valora whispered, seconds before her mouth descended.

Valora's hands wrapped around Maddie's waist, her lips pressing, warm, moist, and passionate. Maddie was lost, a sea of passion and heat flooded her system. She'd never wanted anyone or anything as much as she wanted this woman.

Valora was a skilled lover, she knew where to touch Maddie, how to make her wet, to make her tremble and finally come with a shattering force, in only a few minutes. Valora took Maddie on the floor in front of the red eyed woman, licking and biting her, riding her with an energy that could never be matched. Valora placed her lips on Maddie's neck, there was an intense pain and then a quickening inside her as arousal became the beginning and ending of everything, all she wanted was to be touched and loved by this woman.

Maddie laid beneath her, arching, begging for more. She touched and kissed in response, enjoying the taste and feel of Valora's skin. When she was spent, sweating and half naked, carpet burns on her back, she gently used her own skills, to Valora's surprise. Maddie's love making had a tenderness to it Valora's lacked. The difference didn't seem to matter as Valora's breath sped up and climax claimed her.

Afterward they lay quivering in each other's arms on the floor, Valora stroking her hair.

"I knew it would be like that, Madeline," Valora whispered, kissing her deeply and softly. "It will always be like that. I will come to you, whenever you want me." Valora used her fingertip to trace Maddie's swollen lips.

"I...I don't know what to say, but I have to go." Maddie was confused, she'd never felt so wonderful or so awful in her whole life. She stood up, shivering, and rushed to put her clothes back on. Valora stayed on the floor watching her, naked, her breasts perfect, begging Maddie to come back to the floor and touch them again.

Maddie pushed aside her carnal thoughts, grabbed her shoes, and ran, she ran past all the artwork and woodsy smelling books, past a tour guide showing off a set of historical dishes, past the Dulcara Mansion history and the interesting pottery. She threw open the front door and burst into the open air and sunshine, tears starting to stream down her face, even as what she really wanted was to go back inside.

She couldn't go back inside, this was real life, out there, walking barefoot to the bus stop. What had just happened was like a dream, an erotic, amazing dream. Out here, she was just a girl who'd cheated and now wanted to throw up.

Checking her phone, she saw she had over a dozen missed called from her mom, Jo, and Allison. Heart speeding up with fear, she quickly dialed her mother.

"Maddie, where have you been?" Her mother sounded desperate and tearful.

"What's happened?" Maddie asked, but she knew. She knew it by the sound in her mother's voice and she knew it by the coldness leaking down her spine.

"Lucca is dead."

CHAPTER THIRTEEN

Obituary in the Arcata Daily and Clear Lake Register

Lucca Arthur West died unexpectedly in his dorm room on 11/7/2017 in Arcata, California at the age of 19.

Lucca is survived by his parents, Rebecca and Marcus; twin sister, Madeline; grandparents, Thomas, Nadine and Loraine.

Lucca was born on 11/13/1998 in Clear Lake, California. He was a student at Humboldt State, studying business management.

Lucca was born with a heart condition that had him in and out of the hospital. He was an advocate for heart health awareness and healthcare reform.

A memorial service is scheduled for 11/10/2017 at The Dulcara Mansion. All are welcome to attend and celebrate Lucca's life. In lieu of flowers, please send donations to The American Heart Association. The family would like to thank Valora Dulcara and the Dulcara Foundation for covering the costs of Lucca's last stay in the hospital.

*M*adeline stood in the gardens at Dulcara Mansion, in shock. She couldn't feel anything. A part of her was missing. She never thought there would come a day when she wouldn't feel Lucca anymore. He had always been there, like something in her peripheral vision.

The afternoon was chilly, or at least that was what the app on her phone said. Maddie wasn't sure she could even feel the cold. She wore a dark maroon skirt, boots, and a striped sweater, but her clothes didn't matter. Her mother chose this outfit based on the weather. Maddie couldn't have cared less if she wore a pretty put together ensemble or a burlap sack.

Reaching a hand up, she touched a straggly end of her hair. Had she even bothered to brush it or her teeth today? Did it matter? Who cared if she looked like a bum or had breath that would knock over an elephant?

The days between Lucca's death and the memorial service felt long and drawn out, and yet fuzzy, she couldn't quite remember what she'd done, said or even ate. Her eyes wandered over to the other side of the garden where her parents stood, wrapped around each other, pale and hollow eyed. They greeted everyone with the same tight smile and head nod. A line of people waited to shake hands and give their condolences. Maddie had stood by their sides for over an hour, before she couldn't take it anymore and retreated to this corner of the garden.

Maddie watched as another person hugged her mother and recalled the litany of repeating statements of remorse coming out of a dozen different mouths. She thought maybe she should go back over, help or relieve them, but she didn't want to. Selfish? Sure, but she knew Lucca would understand.

Oh, Lucca... A sob threatened its way up from her chest, a deep wretched thing that she squashed down with sheer force of will.

She knew this day would come, eventually. Lucca was never going to live a long and full life, but it still felt so wrong. How do you prepare for something so devastating? You don't.

Wrapping her arms around herself, she took a few steps back into the shadow of a large tree near the edge of the garden. As the shadow hid her, she kept backing up. She felt ivy brush against her clothes and then the give and coldness of the chain link fence that surrounded this part of the property. The fence and foliage supported her, and she closed her eyes.

"You'll be covered in bugs soon." A hand gripped her shoulder and pulled her away, just a few inches from the rough and earthy smelling plant life. Queenie and Scarlet stood in front of her.

They were both in black pant suits. Scarlet looked smart, but Queenie looked like she was playing dress up in her mother's work clothes. Queenie had a camera around her neck. Maddie's parents asked her to take pictures of the memorial. Maddie didn't understand why, why would they want forever reminders of today? Wasn't the urn they were taking home enough?

"You should eat something," Scarlet said.

"And not lean against ivy, there are bugs…and snakes," Queenie said.

"I don't care." And she didn't, so what if she got bitten by a spider or a snake? That wasn't as concerning as the urn full of her brother's ashes that sat on the table near her parents. It was shiny and gold, like it should have flowers in it instead of her dead brother.

"We know, that's why we're here." Scarlet's voice was trying for light hearted, it failed.

"I don't know half these people," Maddie said. She'd noticed that most of the guests were strangers. She saw her grandparents, a few friends from the town she grew up in, but mainly faces she didn't recognize.

"Classmates. I think the American Heart Association should thank your family for the amount of money that's been donated in Lucca's name the past few days," Scarlet said, giving a tiny chuckle.

"Allison's dad donated at least a grand," Queenie told them.

"Allison…Oh, where is Allison?" Maddie didn't know why she felt badly that she hadn't checked on her brother's girlfriend. Maddie was the one that lost a brother, Allison lost a boy she'd known less than three months. She did feel bad, she knew Allison was grieving too, she'd seen her own sadness mirrored in the other girl's face every time they'd been in a room together.

Why hadn't she called him when Allison asked? Apparently, he tried to bite her during foreplay, and she got pissed off and sent him home. He died soon after that. Allison blamed herself, but Maddie didn't, it was simply coincidence. Failure to have sex did not kill someone, but she wished Allison didn't feel such responsibility. Any other time or event and Maddie would tell her that, but she just didn't feel like being compassionate or empathetic.

"She's around here somewhere. We thought we might convince you to take a break, go somewhere not everyone is crying or talking about Lucca," Scarlet said.

"Where is Jo?" Queenie asked.

The ice around Maddie's heart cracked a bit, but the crack wasn't a good one, it was filled with anger, not mourning. Resentment tried to melt the shield she'd put up around herself. Bitterness that Jo wasn't there, and that Jo had made today about herself and not Maddie and Maddie's family. This gathering should have been all about Lucca, and it wasn't because of the scene Jo caused earlier.

"She's not here."

"What do you mean she's not here?" Scarlet asked, incredulously.

"She wouldn't come because the memorial is being held here, in the Dulcara gardens." Maddie could feel her throat burning and swallowed frantically, she didn't want to cry, especially not over this. Her eyes ached with the pressure behind them and she struggled to regain control.

"I guess I get that," Queenie said.

"What?" Scarlet and Maddie said at the same time.

"She is uncomfortable here, around Professor Dulcara and that the professor paid for everything," Queenie answered.

"So? If she loves Maddie that shouldn't matter," Scarlet argued.

"Enough. I don't want to talk about Jo." Maddie took a few steps away from her friends. "She could have been here, she chose not to come. End of story." Maddie had never felt so alone, Jo wasn't with her and Valora had barely been in contact either. A part of Maddie hoped she'd show for the memorial service, but so far, she hadn't.

Maddie's eyes darted to the mansion as she thought about Valora. Where was she? What was she doing? Didn't she know that Maddie was in intense amounts of pain? Did she even care?

She wanted to leave her friends, to go in through the doors and find Valora, ask Valora to help her forget her pain. She needed to know what happened between them was real. On the other side of those thoughts she was racked with guilt. Guilt because of Jo and because shouldn't she just be thinking about Lucca? How could she even be contemplating a romantic entanglement with Valora when her brother was dead?

"Let's walk." Scarlet linked her arm with Maddie's and pulled her deeper into the garden. They took a smaller path, shaded and covered in vines.

The three of them walked in silence for a while and it was nice, a cool breeze pushed against Maddie's skin and she watched the sky, a mixture of blue, orange, and red, as the sun started to set. The tiny puffs of white clouds against all that color was like a painting, a perfect moment on a horrible day.

"What the hell is he doing here?"

Maddie came out of her thoughts and gave a sharp look to Scarlet.

"I don't know." Queenie shrugged.

Maddie glanced to where her friends were focused, leaning against a large rock off to the side was Professor Heeling, he seemed agitated and as if he were waiting for them.

"Queenie?" Scarlet asked, accusation in her voice.

"I told him not to come, I told him to wait," Queenie said, absentmindedly. She gave her uncle a soft smile and shook her head.

"What's going on?" Maddie asked. She paused mid step as the one person she didn't expect to see stepped out from behind him; Jo.

"We need to talk," Jo said as they came closer.

"I don't want to talk to you right now," Maddie said, her frozen shield was being blasted away by a passionate bout of pissed off.

"Please Maddie, please listen to us," Jo begged.

"I really don't think now's the right time for this," Scarlet said.

"It never will be. She needs to know," Professor Heeling reasoned.

"What's going on?" Maddie asked, confused and considering turning around and ditching them all. It may be morbid, but she knew the cemetery was near here, she could easily lose them among the large mausoleums and creepy statues.

"Maddie, we think, well, we think Professor Dulcara is responsible for Lucca's death."

Jo's statement made Maddie instantly queasy.

"What?" she hissed.

"I told you the woman was a monster, I've...remembered some of the things that happened to me. She and her TAs, they're evil... they aren't normal..." Jo spoke quickly, trying to get it all out at once.

"That's crazy, there are no such things as monsters."

"I beg to differ, Miss West. I've done extensive research. I've long thought Valora Dulcara was unnatural and she turns others into similarly unnatural creatures," Professor Heeling said.

"Like what? A vampire or a werewolf? Do you know how ridiculous you sound? I ought to report you to the school board," Maddie exclaimed.

Feelings of betrayal and amazement coursed through her blood. These were crazy people, she needed to get away from them.

This is a joke, breathe Maddie. Alright, super bad timing, but any minute now Lucca will jump out from behind them and tell me he faked his death as one big prank. I'll be pissed and relieved and hit him with my shoe. Because this cannot be real life, right?

"Come on, Jo, let's go home, we'll cozy up in my room and read *Nightmare Abbey* together, It's our favorite book and it will make us feel better," Maddie pleaded. She thought that if she tried to change the subject this would all go away. Instead, she saw Jo flinch.

"I thought you said you hated reading," Queenie said, unaware of the tension.

"She does, but not *Nightmare Abbey*."

"I'm sorry, Maddie, no more secrets, not with everything that's happened," Jo said.

"I really don't think think now is the time for this." Scarlet tried again to make them stop.

"Secrets?" Maddie repeated, what was Jo talking about?

"I hate that book, I only pretended to like it because I wanted to meet you, I'm sorry." Jo rushed her words, like you do a bandage on a wound, as if saying it fast will make it hurt less.

"You're kidding. Please tell me you're not serious? Are we living in the Twilight Zone? None of today makes any sense." Maddie took a few steps back. This simply couldn't be happening.

Putting her hand in her pocket, she squeezed the paper that rested there, tightly. It was a piece of reality in what was fast becoming a surreal moment. She needed something to keep her grounded as those she called friends turned on her. Especially now that she'd found out the original building block of her relationship with Jo was a lie.

She'd received the official invitation for the Yuletide trip yesterday and a request to be a TA next year. She hadn't responded to either of them. However, it was the personal note scrawled on the bottom from Valora that captured the most of her attention.

CHAPTER FOURTEEN

Madeline,

I hope you will accept both these offers. I do not wish to go to Romania without your company. I truly believe we are two parts of the same whole. I have been searching my entire existence for someone like you. The next few years are so critical in your life and I would be honored to be there while you grow, change, and learn.

V

"We don't have time for your drama, we need to discuss the monster." Heeling's angry voice cut through Maddie's dark thoughts.

"Valora isn't some kind of horrible creature," Maddie stated.

"It's true, Maddie, please listen. Her TAs, they are all in her thrall and then when's she's done with them they receive rewards, the perfect life, position, money... Scarlet's seen it time and time again, right? My uncle has taught here for years. We all know it's true," Queenie said. The determined look on her face made Maddie take another step back, she squeezed the letter harder and then, worried she'd rip it, let go and brought her hand out, crossing her arms over her chest.

"Are you serious? Is this a joke? Scarlet?" She faced her other friend and was shocked to see resignation on her features.

"I don't think now is a good time, but I agree with them."

"It's not a joke, Miss West."

"What the fuck! You're all crazy. My brother just DIED!" Maddie yelled, slightly frightened. She should leave, go find her parents and mourn with them.

"You haven't read the rest of my psych paper report, Maddie, the guy, he talks about how Valora offered to give him lives in return for him keeping her family's secrets, that the Dulcara's drink the blood of the living to maintain their youth, wealth, and position," Scarlet quickly explained.

"He's a nutter, in a psych ward. I can't believe you would think anything he said was the truth." Maddie looked for an escape route, she could only hope this was a sick practical joke. They couldn't all be telling her this fantastical nonsense, could they? They couldn't all be serious. What they were was fucked up.

"Normally I wouldn't, but when matched with Professor Heeling's research, Jo's memories, and what she discovered during the project...it all makes sense," Scarlet said.

"You don't know what my uncle has been through. He's seen vampires, up close and personal, he's even killed a few of them," Queenie exclaimed.

"You all believe he murdered people?" Maddie asked, stunned.

"I didn't murder people. I killed vampires that would have fed off the blood of innocents," Heeling said.

"He showed us pictures, told all of us what happened. We can tell you, show you..." Jo began.

Maddie cut off Jo, "That just makes you all his accomplices, if what you saw was real and not just his snuff porn."

"Maddie, that's unfair," Scarlet argued, out of all of them she seemed the most uncomfortable.

"I need to find Allie," Maddie mumbled. They weren't friends, but at least she was sane.

"Allie agrees with us," Jo said, and her words were like horrible nails in the coffin.

"Fuck you," Maddie growled.

"She found your brother's journal. He has detailed accounts of a woman coming to him in his dreams. She told us how he tried to attack her, drink her blood right before his...last moments," Jo said, trying and failing at being tactful.

"You're lying, or she is. She never said anything about Lucca attacking her, he tried to bite her, you know, before sex." But in the back of her mind, she remembered Allison asking her for help that day, telling her Lucca was acting strange. It had to be because his body knew something was wrong, there was a logical explanation for it.

"You remember the story I told you, when we went camping? Valora is related to the monster in it," Queenie explained.

"She is the monster in it," Heeling countered.

"It's a favorite story of hers. I've seen the tapestry in her house," Maddie admitted. Fear was tingling around the back of her spine. The mention of the camping trip made her recall the woman she'd seen with her brother, the one with the red eyes. She'd tried to convince herself she was seeing things. It had been late, she had been worried, scared, and tired. Maybe her mind played tricks on her.

Or maybe they are telling the truth.

No, she was sleep deprived and in mourning, this craziness was another stage of grief.

"Valora Dulcara is a vampire, Miss West, and I believe she has turned your brother into one as well." Professor Heeling made the statement and it startled Maddie from her thoughts.

"No. First off, there's no such thing as vampires and two, why would she turn Lucca?" Maddie said, a small smile forming around her lips, vampires...this was...how many times could she roll the word ridiculous around in her mind before it stopped sounding like a real word?

She used the word existence instead of life in her letter. Even as she thought it, she felt as if it betrayed Valora. How could she doubt someone who had done so much for her family? Valora never did anything to warrant the kind of abuse these people were hurling.

It took her a few seconds to realize they were all staring at her, but it was the wary look in Jo and Professor Heeling's eyes that struck her the most.

"You've taken quite a liking to Valora and her culture, haven't you?" Heeling asked suspiciously.

"Yes, she has, and she's spending a lot of time with her recently," Jo answered.

"And what business is that of yours?" Maddie asked, angrily. Now Jo was interested in her comings and goings? Where had that concern been a week ago?

"I think she is trying to seduce you, to compel you against your good nature," Heeling said.

"She has seemed to take an interest in you, Maddie, and you aren't even her student." Jo was hesitant.

Maddie stayed silent. Valora did seduce her, she'd fallen into that trap, but she wasn't sure she regretted it. Compel her, though? That sounded absurd.

"May I see your neck, Miss West?" Professor Heeling asked.

"No."

"Why not, Maddie?" Queenie questioned, softly.

"Because it's a perverted thing for a teacher to ask a student. I'm this close," she said as she held up fingers, "to telling the school about this."

"Just show us," Scarlet pleaded.

Maddie stared at her friends, appalled. What was it they expected to find on her neck? She'd already checked, Valora hadn't left a hickey of any kind.

"See for yourself." She turned her head left then right, sweeping her messy hair away from her neck.

"Nothing," Heeling said.

"Look, I've had enough of this." Maddie was furious at them; tears of anger and frustration were burning her eyes from being held back. This felt like a nightmare, one where she's trying to teach everyone about simple addition, but they were arguing trigonometry.

"Please listen. We have a lot to show you," Jo begged, stepping forward, hands out, trying to take Maddie's.

It was easy to evade the contact, the thought of Jo touching her right now was repulsive.

"We need to find Lucca. Find him and put a stake through his heart." Heeling was adamant.

"What? No one said anything about desecrating a corpse," Scarlet said, horror on her face.

Bile rose in the back of Maddie's throat. Put a stake through her brother's heart? What sort of barbaric mumbo jumbo was this sicko into? Why were her friends listening to him?

"It's the only way. Then we must cut off his head, or he will rise as a vampire and feed off the living, already it's been more days than I would like." Heeling sounded apologetic.

"That's twisted, Uncle. Are you sure it's the only way?" Queenie asked.

"Yeah, it doesn't sound so great," Jo agreed.

"He was cremated, you idiots!" Maddie screamed at them. They all stared at her like she was the unhinged one, not them.

"A ruse, I'm sure," Heeling snorted.

"I bet Valora took his body and buried it. Your parents are holding an urn full of vacuum dust," Queenie said.

"You guys cool it, this is hard enough as it is," Scarlet warned. "Maybe we should do this another day. I can walk Maddie back to the memorial service."

"No, we do this now," Jo said.

Maddie's breathing quickened with each word, goosebumps rising on her flesh as they spoke about this as if it were all normal and fact.

"Keep pushing me, Jo, and we are done."

"You don't mean that," Jo said.

"Don't make a rash decision, Lucca just died," Scarlet warned. The concern in her face almost made Maddie feel better.

"You're all insane. Did you smoke the same crack or something?" She couldn't keep the words or the venom in them to herself.

"Here's a copy of everything we've gathered. Maddie, please, just read it." Queenie handed her a thumb drive shaped like a blue whale.

Maddie closed her fist around it, the small device smooth and warm in her hand.

"I'm leaving," she whispered.

"Don't go near Valora, promise me," Jo demanded.

"No." Maddie shook her head. She wasn't promising these cracked up fuckers anything.

"Let me walk with you," Scarlet said.

"No!" Maddie exclaimed, she turned and fled down the path toward the back entrance to the Dulcara Mansion.

She heard them call out to her but refused to stop.

She didn't want to see anyone else, not her so called friends, her girlfriend, her parents, any well-meaning guests, or family members. She wanted to see Valora. Why hadn't she been at the wake? Where was she when Jo and company were making horrible allegations and talking about Lucca's corpse like he hadn't been cremated? What was going on, had the whole world gone insane with Lucca's death?

She knew she should go back and help her parents, but the emotions raging through her weren't sad and peaceful ones. She didn't want to traumatize her parents more by showing back up in a fury of sorrow and not be able to tell them why.

She pulled out her phone; *Mom, I went home. I can't be here anymore. I'm sorry. I suck as a daughter.* She fired the text off.

It's okay, sweetie, we understand. Meet for dinner at the hotel tonight. We love you. It took less than a minute for her to get a reply.

Bounding up the back steps of Dulcara Mansion, she didn't know what she was doing, she just knew she needed to be some place Jo and the rest wouldn't come looking for her.

She burst in through the back door and sagged against the cool wall of the hallway, the rough texture pressing into her skin. The hallway was dark, and she didn't know where in the house she was. The tour she'd taken with Valora hadn't covered this section, she was glad the door had even been open. Thick beige carpet covered the floor, looking soft and new.

The air around her felt still and slightly warm, if not a bit stale. Through the small rays of sunlight that made their way past the hazy glass of the door she could see dust floating. She wanted to sink down into the carpet like a cat and just stay there, sleepy and cozy.

Something was pressing against her palm and it kind of hurt. Glancing down she remembered it was the thumb drive, the metal part dug into her skin and the eyes of the whale looked at her, mockingly. She shoved it into her pocket. She didn't even know if she'd look at the crazy it contained, though she was curious about Lucca's journal. She hadn't even known Lucca kept a journal!

"Madeline?" a rich accent-laced voice called from the other end of the hallway.

"Valora!" Maddie sobbed, relieved.

"What is the matter?" Valora rushed toward her, incredibly fast, inhuman even. Maddie swatted the thoughts out of her mind, at least she cared about her! Maddie couldn't let the others uncharitable statements about her color anything.

"I've had a horrible day," Maddie finally said.

Valora looked tired. She wore a black silk robe, and her hair was down, flowing around her shoulders.

"Oh, Valora, I'm sorry...I didn't think, I just..." Maddie couldn't form a coherent sentence.

"It is fine, come with me. I imagine today is trying." Valora took her hand, skin cool against Maddie's. She led her into another room and Maddie was surprised to see a bright, modern, white and blue kitchen.

"Sit," Valora commanded and pointed to a barstool at a white marbled island. The stool was made of black metal with a deep blue cushion. Maddie sat on it and her feet thanked her. She was so exhausted.

"Why weren't you there?" Maddie asked. She didn't mean to, but she had to know. Valora's dark eyes found hers across the room, concern and sadness seemed to flicker within their depth.

"I do not care for funerals of any kind, plus on non-school days I rarely rise before dusk." Valora went to the chrome refrigerator and opened the door. Pulling out a water bottle, she opened it and then placed it in front of Maddie. "Drink."

Maddie obeyed and took a deep sip, the cold water making her feel even better than sitting down. When was the last time she had anything to eat or drink?

"I wished you had been though," Maddie admitted, feeling weird. Was that saying too much?

She didn't rise before dusk. Isn't that a vampire thing?

Maddie ground her teeth trying to make the doubting thoughts disappear. Sure, vampires came out at night, but Maddie had seen Valora during the day too, end of story.

"I know and being at your side today was all I thought about. It would have raised questions however." Valora placed a hand on Maddie's arm. "Questions I do not think you are ready to answer."

Shame and embarrassment colored Maddie's cheeks. Valora was right, Maddie was still technically with Jo. How would it have looked to be hanging onto Valora's arm while they all grieved over her brother?

"Something besides your brother's death is bothering you, I think." Valora sat down opposite her.

"Where's your staff?" Maddie deflected the question, badly. She wasn't sure she wanted to tell Valora about the out of this world conversation she'd just had.

"The museum is not open when there are private functions. Now, tell me what else is bothering you."

Valora was obviously the kind of woman used to getting her way. Maddie had to admit it was a quality she found attractive.

"Professor Heeling really hates you, and he's insane, did you know that?"

Valora's expression shut down, her mouth and eyes narrowed. "What did he say?"

"He's convinced my friends you're a monster." Maddie tried to laugh about it, but it didn't feel funny and the expression on Valora's face wasn't amusement.

"I really do need to do something about him," Valora said offhandedly.

Maddie ignored the odd statement and went on.

"He says that story, the one from your tapestry is a true tale, and you're some sort of immortal being. It's absurd." Maddie wanted to take the words back as soon as she said them. They didn't seem as silly now, sitting here alone with Valora, whose expression was not quite what Maddie expected.

"I am not a monster, Madeline," Valora finally said after a few moments of uncomfortable silence.

"They think you turned Lucca into one and now they need to find him and...I guess re-kill him," Maddie said, hoping Valora would laugh over the ridiculousness of the entire conversation.

"They will not find Lucca. Do not worry."

"What?" That was not what she wanted to hear.

"I will not allow them to harm your brother."

"Harm him? He's already dead!" *That's it, this is a dream, the whole damn day*. Maddie stood up from the bar stool and pinched herself, hard.

"Don't hurt yourself, dear girl," Valora said.

"I don't understand what's happening." Maddie moved away from Valora until her hip bounced off another counter. It hurt, and Maddie closed her eyes tightly. She felt the throb in her arm and hip, took five deep breaths and then counted to ten. When she opened them, she'd wake up.

Opening her eyes, she gasped as Valora stood right in front of her, eyes ablaze with red light, just like the woman in the woods.

Maddie screamed but Valora had her cornered and there was nowhere for her to go.

"I will not harm you, Madeline. I am the only person you can trust right now," Valora said. Reaching up she traced Maddie's cheek with a tip of her finger. Fear embraced Maddie like a freezing cold lake.

"Do you recall our time together?"

"Of course." She could never forget it.

"The tapestry is based on my life, it is a true story."

"Impossible."

"It seems that way on many days. My family was slaughtered, and I awoke hungry for vengeance. I protected the villagers for centuries until the modern world caught up with us and people who did not understand ruined my home," Valora explained as she played with a lock of Madeline's hair.

Maddie pulled back, she didn't want Valora to touch her.

"You're a vampire?" She squeaked out the question and this time Valora's luscious mouth turned up into a smile.

"It's as good a word as any, if not entirely accurate."

"You murdered Lucca?" Just another betrayal. If Valora killed her brother then she would help her friends, no matter the cost. Anger gathered just below her veins, she caught a glimpse of a knife set on the counter.

"Not exactly. I knew he would soon die the first moment we met. We will see if immortality has embraced him."

"You killed him? Why would you do that? There's no 'not exactly' about death," Maddie said. She wondered if she could get away from Valora fast enough to arm herself.

Valora met Maddie's gaze. "It would not be fast enough."

Fear turned the anger in her veins to ice and Maddie stilled, keeping eye contact.

"Please listen to me," Valora said. Maddie gave one small nod. "I did it for you, dear girl. So you could have him with you, forever. As a vampire he would be healthy and young, but it hasn't worked as I wished."

"I am tired of saying this, but I don't understand." Tears began to leak from her eyes, she'd spent too long trying to hold them back. This was all unbelievable!

"I know, sweet Madeline. Becoming as I am isn't a science. When your brother died, I hid his body. If he will rise again is still a mystery. I hope so, I saved him for you." Valora kissed her then, gently, a cool whisper on her skin.

Maddie knew she should pull away, but she didn't. Her mind was too busy with new thoughts and feelings.

"I'll get Lucca back?" It was incredible. Happiness surged through her, she didn't care how he came back, only that he did. A little flutter of happiness was taking over the empty ache. She might be able to see and talk to Lucca again?

"Why me? Why do this for me?" Maddie asked, tilting her head back, the red light had left Valora's eyes.

"You are even more than you know. I can always sense it. I have spent my life raising up the special, taking care of those in need, and living my life to the fullest." Valora pulled away and held out a hand. "Come with me, Madeline, I have stories to tell you and I want you in my bed."

"Did you drink my blood?"

"Yes, and I want to do it again. I promise just like before you will enjoy it. I would never hurt you."

Maddie hesitated. It was like when she was four and her dad wanted her to jump in the pool. He'd been there, ready to catch her, but she'd been afraid. As much as she wanted in the water and trusted her father, she feared drowning in the cool blue liquid. She'd eventually jumped and had a blast with her dad. Lucca spent that same day sitting with their mom playing Legos, envious of her.

She knew she should take more time, consider her actions and their consequences, but the only happiness she'd had in days was given to her by Valora.

Maddie put her hand in Valora's.

CHAPTER FIFTEEN

Dream Journal of Queenie Myles

04/02/2016
    ~~A bird is flying over my head and it poops on me. The poop is green and smells like roses.~~

06/11/2016
    ~~(I really need to be more consistent, mom would be so disappointed if she saw this.)~~
    ~~I'm wandering the halls of a house, it is filled with pot smoke. I can hear mom's laughter, but I can't find her.~~

06/22/2016
    ~~I am in front of my eighth-grade middle school class. I am dressed in my favorite sweater it is yellow. Every time I open my mouth to talk I sound like a dog barking.~~

09/03/2016
    ~~(Maybe I should give up on the dream journal, dad says my talents are not suited for writing, that I should start a photo diary instead)~~
    ~~Uncle Austin is sitting at the table eating tofurkey with us; that sneer on his~~

~~face he always makes during holiday meals. He goes to take a bite, but his hands are~~ ~~covered with mittens. I start to laugh and sparks snort out my nose. The whole~~ ~~room lights on fire.~~

11/13/2016

I decided to give up the dream journal. Dad's idea is much better. I did want to have a place to write a few things down. I don't want to forget, this has all been like Alice falling down the rabbit hole.

Today is Maddie's birthday, well, it's Lucca's too, but he's dead now. Though he's a vampire, so does that mean he still has a birthday?

What I wanted to write about was how relieved I am now that everyone knows Uncle Austin's secret. I've kept it to myself for a long time, even from Mom and Dad. Which would make them angry and they'd think he was crazy, so they can't ever read this. Mom and he already have a strained relationship.

So anyway, here it is, in writing.

My uncle got married right out of high school when he was 18. Mom says the stick in his ass wasn't full grown yet. I never met his wife, she was gone long before I was self-aware.

They moved to Sacramento so he could go to UC Davis. She wanted to be a painter or a sculptor...Not sure about that.

He began studying Anthropology and she stayed at home.

The story goes that he threw himself into his studies and ignored his wife. Mom says cheating happens in truly monogamous relationships where partners don't talk about their sexual needs. Maybe that's what happened, maybe not.

She began having an affair with a man who owned a well to do art gallery. He was quite famous, and his art gallery very well known within the right circles.

She left my uncle, very suddenly, and Uncle Austin was furious. He was 20 at the time and he confronted her and the new guy. Apparently, this confrontation led him to Valora Dulcara's mother, also Valora. I know, confusing? Though probably the same woman since she's a vampire... Sorry, babbling.

Uncle Austin tried to drown himself, not on booze or pot (which my mom said would have been way healthier) but in school work and research. By the time he was twenty-eight, he had a P.H.D in Anthropology and History. He'd never gotten over his wife leaving him and thought to rub it in her face how accomplished he was. He was shocked when he tracked her down and found her living in Oregon, looking no older than she had at twenty, not one line or wrinkle. He stalked her for over a month (yes, I know creepy, but no one ever said my uncle had good people skills) and saw many things he deemed "unnatural."

Taking the name Dulcara he began to do research which led him to Arcata and then back through England and Romania.

(I've seen so many documents my head began to swim. I've seen blurry pictures of vampires feeding and flying and smelled way too many musty tomes full of arcane knowledge. I spent every summer with Uncle Austin from ages thirteen to eighteen while my parents did, well anything from acting like pioneer settlers with Mormons to spending months in silence in over grown communes.)

He tells me he made an educated guess that Valora and her family were vampires. He applied for a teaching position at Humboldt State to keep an eye on things and that's when he saw the creepy pattern with the TAs. At that time, Valora had only been a teacher for about ten years. My uncle says she proclaimed to be ten years older than him. Which is crazy cause that would mean she was 40 twenty years ago! No way does she look 60.

Anyway, to continue with my tale. Five years ago, armed with instruments that are supposed to kill vampires, he went back to Oregon and confronted his ex-wife and her new husband. He managed to kill both of them, though from the photo's it was amateur and sloppy work. He took pictures of their fangs and held their faces up to a hand mirror. They cast a reflection, but not the way a human does. The pictures are weird, their reflections look more like shadows cut across their features.

He tells me he panicked about what to do with the bodies, but after a few hours, they turned to dust. I've seen pictures of that too. He says he sucked them up with the vacuum and cleaned himself up and walked away. They're both still listed as missing persons.

When he shared that with Jo, Allison, and Scarlet, that's when I knew we'd convinced them of the danger. Uncle Austin told us he's never been strong enough to take on such an ancient vampire like Valora. With all of us working together we stand a chance.

Now we must find Lucca and put him to rest. I hope I'm brave enough.

"Are you sure there isn't anything you'd like to do for your birthday?" Jo asked, leaning against the porch rail, the sun setting behind her. Maddie wished she was good with a camera, it would be a great photo. Jo, short hair disheveled, wearing a tight white t-shirt and slate gray slacks, tiny beams of half-light illuminating her silhouette, but Maddie sucked at taking pictures. Every photo she ever took caught someone right as they looked their most frumpy and goofy. Lucca hid every time she pulled out a camera, or at least he had. She wouldn't laugh at him dodging her cell phone ever again.

Queenie could probably take it and make it look amazing.

Rubbing her eyes, she took a deep breath as the pain swamped her, fresh and new, it probably would never leave.

The only consolation was that Valora said she could see Lucca soon, though Valora warned her he wasn't taking to being a vampire as well as she would have liked.

"No, it's not right without Lucca," Maddie finally answered. Plus she didn't feel like spending time with Jo, anyone else, but not Jo.

"Well happy birthday any way, Maddie." Jo leaned forward and pressed her lips onto Maddie's cheek. Jo wouldn't accept that Maddie had meant it when she said it was over.

Maddie still couldn't get past the scene they made at Lucca's memorial. Even though Maddie knew the truth now, she still couldn't believe that's when her friends had decided to drop such a giant bomb on her.

Jo went back inside, throwing a glance over her shoulder. Maddie pretended to ignore it.

She'd called her mom and knew she couldn't tell her everything, but she could tell her about part of the hurt. She could tell her about Jo and the book. Her mom furiously told her to break up with Jo. She and Dad couldn't believe Jo had been so callous and manipulative. Maddie agreed, but since her own actions were not without reproach, she didn't want to totally condemn her.

They'd only been back to Clear Lake for a few days, but Maddie knew her own drama was something better for them to dwell on. She was lucky they didn't pull her from school. What would she have done back at her parents' house? Wandered around looking at old photos and become a cat lady?

Plopping down on a wicker chair, broken pieces digging into her butt through her denim skirt, Maddie slouched down. She watched cars drive pass, glad the porch railing hid most of her. She got looks of sympathy and pity from everyone right now, even people she didn't know. She didn't want anyone to see her outside, alone, they might try and talk to her.

A buzz from her pocket startled her, she fished her phone out and saw a text message. It was an unknown number.

Walk down to the east corner as fast as you can.

"What the hell?" Maddie read it again to make sure she hadn't imagined it. She responded quickly, they probably just had the wrong number.

Her phone went off again, that was quick.

Madeline, walk down to the corner...now.

"Valora." Maddie's head whipped around to double check she was alone. If Jo or one of the girls knew who she was texting, she'd never hear the end of it.

Quietly, she walked over to the front door and opened it, praying no one was in the living room or coming down the stairs, but she tried to act normal just in case someone was.

She took a step into the foyer and grabbed her purse off the coat rack by the door, it was a coral colored leather bag, big enough to fit a hardback book in. Her mother gave it to her right before they left, an early birthday present. She also gave her Lucca's two tickets to a Sacramento Kings game. Maddie hated basketball but promised her mother she'd find someone deserving to give them to. They lay in a crisp envelope at the bottom of her new, shiny purse.

Making her way back to the porch, she shut the door and winced at the loud noise it made connecting with the door frame. Her white sandals made a repetitive clacking sound as she hurried down the sidewalk toward the corner and meeting place.

Heart thumping in her chest, cheeks flushed with excitement and trepidation, she rushed to the corner and stood on the lip where the sidewalk met the pavement. She teetered on the little ledge swaying back and forth, one hand gripping her phone, the other resting on her purse.

She hoped they were doing something casual, or the jean skirt and gold peasant's blouse would not fit in. She could always take her hair out of the braid and put on lipstick to dress the outfit up, if needed.

Wait, what if we aren't doing something outside the house? Looking around, she tried to nonchalantly sniff herself to make sure that the deodorant and perfume she'd put on after her shower this morning were still working and then tried to recall what underwear and bra she had on. She had several lovely bra and panty sets she would have worn instead if this were a plan.

A sleek, black car pulled up next to her, she could smell the exhaust and see her pretty but slightly frazzled appearance in the shine. It wasn't a limo, not long enough. One of the back doors opened and Mircalla stepped out.

Silver sunglasses incased her eyes, she faced the setting sun, blonde hair swirling down around her shoulders. She wore a tight black capped sleeve dress.

"Thank God," she muttered, voice crisp like the first bite of an apple. A manicured hand moved to her face and took the glasses off, so that eyes so blue green they were like staring at the Caribbean Sea, could focus on Maddie. Her mouth was a shimmering rose gold color.

"Madeline, Valora is waiting to see you, please get in." She motioned toward the darkness through the portal the open door made.

Not saying anything, Maddie got in and scooted all the way to the other door. The inside smelled of leather polish and the seats matched the exterior, black leather and very roomy. There was a partition up between them and the driver.

Mircalla got in next to her, leaving the middle seat empty. She crossed long bare legs that had very high heels the color of sunshine on their feet.

"What kind of car is this?" Maddie asked to fill the silence.

"A town car, the Dulcaras own several."

"Where are we going?"

Mircalla smiled and it was pleasant. Maddie never spent any time with her before so she wasn't sure what to expect. She looked like she'd be as stuck up as they came, but maybe that was Maddie being judgmental.

"It's a surprise, for your birthday."

"Will the others be joining us?" Maddie asked, referring to Byron and Vaughn.

"Of course not, it's a private celebration."

"And you don't mind?" Maddie and Jo had only ever been monogamous so she didn't know the protocol when dating...was it actually dating? For lack of a better word, when dating someone who also dated other people.

"No, why would..." Mircalla trailed off and it was just like in a cartoon as the light went off in her head, her eyebrows went as far up as they could go and her perfectly painted lips gave a crooked smile.

"Madeline, it's not like that. Byron, Vaughn, and I are not Valora's lovers." She reached out and patted Madeline's knee.

"You're not... I'm confused." Confused and realizing this might be a great time to get some questions answered.

"Valora doesn't speak as often as she should. In vampire terms, we are her blood kin, a part of her nest. She chooses only those she sees as bright and full of promise, which she nurtures and extracts in a most delicate fashion."

"So, you three are all..." She swallowed and took a deep breath. "Vampires?"

"No. We may become vampires at any point if we wish, and we do share some of the similarities and traits, but it's only because of a basic blood exchange." Mircalla squeezed Maddie's knee and then took her hand away. It seemed as if that was the end of the conversation.

"You don't drink blood?"

"Oh that...we do hunger for it, but we don't need it. It takes time to learn to control the urges. It's why most of us choose the dark gift after a few years. Though I've met other blood kin who have chosen to grow old and die." She leaned forward and knocked on the partition, it slowly sank down, and Maddie couldn't see the driver. If she had to guess she'd say the car drove by itself, but that was impossible.

"Please hurry, she'll be upset if we're late."

"Are there many of you?" Maddie asked.

"She takes a new bride every few years, we help feed her and in exchange are granted many gifts."

"Bride?"

Mircalla showed some panic just around her eyes. "Please don't say that in front of her, she hates it. It's personal slang between the blood kin and blood kin only."

"I won't say anything, I promise."

Mircalla's expression showed slight disbelief, she made a humming noise and glanced out the window.

"So, have you lived in Arcata long?" Maddie asked, trying for small talk.

"Sometimes it seems like forever, other days not so much."

"That's a bit cryptic. What about Valora, why is she in Arcata?"

"The Dulcaras own property here, in England and in Romania. Every twenty or thirty years she leaves an area, dies and reinvents herself, usually as her own niece or granddaughter."

"Okay, but why here? Why isn't she and all of you in a bigger city, like San Francisco or Los Angeles?"

Mircalla furrowed her brow at Maddie and then spoke slowly, "Arcata was nonexistent when she came here, wanting privacy and a new beginning. She helped it grow, now she basically owns this place. She goes where she wants and does what she wants. This town owes her."

Maddie sat back, thinking, would it be wonderful or strange to have that kind of power over one place? She opened her mouth to ask another question.

"If you want more details, you'll have to ask Valora."

"Just one more?" Maddie asked, shyly.

Mircalla made a groaning noise, pinched the bridge of her nose, and closed her eyes. "Yes, one more."

"Has she always been a teacher?"

Mircalla's face held something that looked like relief. "She's been a teacher for a few decades now. She loves teaching about her history and culture."

They rode for a few more minutes in silence. Then Mircalla cleared her throat.

"We're here."

Excitement coursed through Maddie, where were they? What should she expect? The car smoothly stopped, engine still on, purring quietly in the background.

"Well, are you going or not?" Mircalla asked, after a few moments of awkward silence.

"What?" Maddie felt out of place and stupid.

"Go. Like I said before, I am not coming with you. Valora will see you home."

"Yes, sorry." Maddie opened the door and stepped out, a midnight blue sky streaked with red greeted her as the sun set in the distance. The air smelled fresh and clean, like laundry just out of the dryer.

She found herself standing in the middle of old town Eureka, a beautiful historic downtown featuring all sorts of shops and businesses celebrating the history of northern California.

Leaning down, she spoke into the back seat before shutting the door. "Umm, where am I going?"

Mircalla simply pointed a finger and then grabbed the door handle, slamming it shut.

Following the abrupt direction, Maddie saw that only one store front was lit up, while all others were empty and dark, closed signs hanging from doors and windows.

Dinner, dancing, maybe Valora is buying me a tattoo? What if she's sweeping me away for a romantic night? Maddie paused. *Then that would make me even more of an awful person than I already am.*

As she got closer, she realized it was a bookstore. She opened the simple glass and wood door. The jingle of a bell was the only noise as she entered. The store smelled of leather, paper, and ink, that beautiful smell that comes with sniffing old books. The front of the store had curved arches and everywhere books were crammed into nooks and crannies. A desk sat in the middle of the room with two registers and a few tables and chairs lined some of the walls, crowded in against even more novels.

Walking down the obvious path that led to even more sections of used and new books, she spotted familiar headings like, fiction, fantasy, and religion, before coming to another, larger, brick archway. Above the arch said, "Rare Manuscripts," and inside was a fairy land.

Books in glass cases lined the walls while twinkling lights in soft white and pale yellow hung down from the ceiling, a sultry low tune played almost out of earshot and the scent of lilacs filled her nose.

Standing in the middle of the room was Valora, in a deep black gown with a high slit and a low neckline; it hugged each curve of her body. Her hair curled down over her shoulders, her black eyes sparkling.

"I feel underdressed," Maddie said, and then wished she could take back the stupid words.

Valora's red painted mouth curved upward in a smile. "You are perfect, just the way you are."

"You look lovely. I can't believe this is all for me." Maddie gestured to the romantic and beautiful room.

"You are special to me, Madeline West. I want to make sure you know that." Valora came closer and ran her fingers up Maddie's bare arm, causing goosebumps to appear.

"I don't understand why I'm special to you, or why you sent me those dreams," Maddie told her.

For the first time, Valora looked confused. "What dreams?"

"Even before I got to school, I was having dreams of eyes in the dark. When I saw your portrait, I realized they were yours."

"Madeline, I did not send you any dreams, you are mistaken," Valora said. She looked concerned.

"I didn't make them up." Maddie was defensive.

"Of course, you didn't. It is simply another sign you and I were meant to meet."

"Let's change the subject." Maddie felt cold, she wrapped her arms around herself.

"We can do anything you'd like, I don't eat, but I do have some wine."

Maddie thought for a moment she wanted to fuck this amazing woman, under the fake fairy lights, amidst the books, but she figured that could wait.

"Could we drink the wine and curl up together and read?" Maddie asked. She hoped it didn't sound too lame.

"Of course, that sounds perfect." Valora took her hand and led her to a corner of the room where an overly large bean bag of black velvet sat, squished next to a book shelf.

"What would you like to read, choose any novel from the store and it is yours." Valora pushed her down onto the bag and feathered her lips across Maddie's. She smelled rich and earthy. Maddie put her hands on Valora's hips, rubbing the soft fabric of her dress in-between her fingers.

"Do you own this bookstore?"

"No, but the owner owed me a favor and has been well paid," Valora said.

"What are you reading?"

"I am in the middle of reading *Nightmare Abbey* by Thomas Peacock."

"That's great! I've read it half a dozen times. It's my favorite book." She'd thought it was Jo's too, but that turned out to be bullshit. Maddie would never forgive her for that lie.

"'The critic does his utmost to blight genius in his infancy,'" Valora quoted, brilliantly. "I quite enjoy the more obscure classics."

"I like a little of everything, but for tonight? Do they have a copy of Amy Poehler's book? It's on my to-be-read list."

"I believe they do, let me go get it."

Valora disappeared into a darkened section of the store and came back with the black and bright pink novel. Maddie was about to say something else when she heard people outside, young adults laughing and talking.

"Is there a bar near here, everything else in this area is closed already, especially since it is night."

"Yes, it will get noisier before too long, does that bother you?" Valora eased herself down next to Maddie, pressing against her, running her hands over her back and shoulders as she settled into a comfortable spooning position. Her scent and touch made Maddie feel warm inside, content and happy.

"No, does it bother you?" She fingered the pages of the book, delighting in their rough texture, a great contrast to the silky smoothness of Valora's dress and the soft coolness of her hands.

"No, I enjoy hearing their sounds. Everything sounds more beautiful at night, everything is like music."

Inspired by her words, Maddie kissed her, not caring if she came away smeared with Valora's lipstick, she had to have her mouth, to run her tongue along her lips and taste her.

"Ah, Madeline, you tempt me. There is time enough tonight for that, but for now, let us read together," Valora said, smiling, as the kissed ended.

"Yes." Maddie opened her book and snuggled deeper into Valora's embrace.

CHAPTER SIXTEEN

BLOOD BORN

"You said we cannot hold ourselves to our human morality, we must do what is best for us and those we love." Miriam is crying, blood tinged tears coursing down her face.

I stand at the harbor, hidden by the shadows, an arm around her broad shoulders. I smell the sea; salt and wildness, but underneath the rich copper of blood, the stench of death and decay.

"We are not human, not anymore. Their rules are not ours, what they consider sin we consider survival," I tell her.

I can see Mira, her blonde hair being tugged from its braid by the wind. She stands talking to the authorities, getting more information for us, trying to find out how much they know. She glances back, over her shoulder, our eyes meet. With a small shake of her head, I know they are still clueless as to what caused last night's awful events.

"Then why are you angry with me? Why are you locking me back up?" Miriam asks.

"I understand what happened. You will be punished because you lost control, not because of your actions. If we want to survive, we must protect ourselves." I am

tired of explaining this to Miriam. She is centuries old and still hasn't learned her lesson.

"I did protect us. The people on that boat figured out what we are. They would have told people." Miriam is trembling against me; her hair is matted with dried blood and her gown is still stained. I need to take her home and clean her up. She will go back to the hospital tonight, back to her cell where she will not be able to harm anyone.

Miriam has spent the past few decades in a state of in-between. She spends months or years locked in the hospital. I release her and she is fine for days or weeks, but Miriam didn't take to the change well. She cannot control her basic needs and urges. She is like an animal, acting without thinking.

Her sister thinks we should destroy her. My Mira has grown cold to the world, nothing ties her to it. We feel differently than we did before, emotions are stronger, stranger. Love, fear, hate; they are each distant and intense at the same time. I tell her she must find something to connect her to the world again.

"They only knew about us because you had to sleep with that woman's husband." Mira has rejoined us, I can sense her fury like cinnamon on my tongue.

"I wanted him." Miriam shrugs.

"That's fine, but you fed off him and didn't hide the wounds. Humans are superstitious, you can't act like this. You are a danger to mother and me!"

Miriam bares her teeth at Mira, eyes red.

"Enough." I end their fight. An idea is stirring within me.

"Mother, you need to end this. Miriam cannot control herself and this isn't going to change." Mira puts her hands on her hips.

"Don't listen to her, Mother, we are so much better than humans! You tell us all the time we are an advanced species. Why don't we take over this town? We could have our own private cattle farm." Miriam's grin is laced with insanity.

They are both right. There is appeal in both options. I would mourn Miriam, but Mira and I would be safer if she were dead. Excitement flitters through me at the prospect of not hiding what we are and having an endless supply of food.

While both ideas have merit, I have a much better option.

The girls become silent as I refuse to speak or listen to them for a time. I am watching as the authorities carry mangled bodies from the hull of the ship. Miriam slaughtered everyone on that boat, she feels no remorse or guilt. They are emotions we lose after the change.

"Miriam, you will go back into your cell for the next two years."

She begins to argue.

"You will only leave it to attend class."

This freezes both girls in their tracks.

"Class?" They ask as one, and it makes me smile to hear. They did that often as children.

"You will become a nurse. This will give you access to many of the things you like, including blood. It will also give you a purpose, a goal. You will live at the hospital for the rest of your days. After you graduate, we will reevaluate your freedom."

"And what will I do?" Mira asks. She is quiet, contemplating. Miriam looks pensive, but there is a smile on her face.

"You will come and go as you always do, but you will also help me. We shall make this town ours so that none will come against us. We shall be able to feed where and when we want, and the citizens will obey and protect us."

"Yes, Mother." Mira bows her head, slightly. She is pleased with my words.

Too long have we lived among humans, hiding and scurrying like mice. If I want my daughters to thrive in the new world, there are changes I must make.

———

*M*addie waited, anxiously, in Valora's bedroom. The room was beautiful, rich, and luscious, everything deep purple with black accents, the furniture all dark wood and antique.

A large window on one wall has the drapes pulled back, letting in moonlight, complementing the soft white light that already illuminated the room.

A portrait of two beautiful girls is hung on the opposite wall. Maddie was sure she recognized the blonde girl but couldn't quite place her. Maddie asked Valora who they were and all Valora would do was give a shake of her head and tell her it was a story for another day.

Maddie was comfortable in Valora's room, she'd been in it half a dozen times. Usually she was naked, but once she'd done homework while Valora graded papers and another time they made posters for a rally they attended together.

Tonight, however, there was a different reason she was there. Valora brought her to the house to see Lucca.

Maddie didn't know how to act, or how to handle seeing her vampire brother. She knew that he hadn't taken to the transformation the way Valora hoped.

Oh God, he's going to be like in a bad vampire movie and try to kill me. Or he'll be like an animal and not even know his own name. What if he's more of a zombie than a vampire?

A door opened and Valora came into the room, softly padding across the velvety purple carpet.

"Lucca is coming now. I hope you can reach him, if not I may have no choice but to cut his new life short," Valora said, sadly.

"You mean kill him? Again?" No, Maddie wouldn't accept that.

"He's been eating animals, like a feral thing, living in the woods. I can't risk the exposure, Madeline, I'm sorry." Valora motioned toward the door and Maddie saw Byron standing there, holding her brother's arm. He brought Lucca in and Maddie stood, silently, looking at him.

He looked like Lucca, but something much more, his skin was shinier, his eyes brighter. There was no sickness in him. On the other hand, he was filthy. He looked as if he hadn't had a bath or brushed his hair in a week. He snarled at Byron, who dropped his arm and backed out of the room like Lucca was a wild animal.

Lucca sniffed around, eyes darting to and fro. Valora walked over to him and he growled at her, hands coming up in self-defense, with torn and dirty nails.

"Lucca, you know me. It's Valora, your maker," she said calmly. Lucca put his hands down and stood up straighter, his mouth closed, and his manner seemed to calm, but still he didn't say anything.

"Oh, Valora, he looks, awful...what happened?" Maddie was choking back her tears. This was it, she was really going to lose him this time.

"Sometimes it just doesn't take, I'm sorry."

"You murdered him for nothing? I could have had a few more months with him. Anything is better than this," Maddie said, she couldn't look at him, it hurt so much. This wasn't really Lucca, not anymore. This was some savage vampire who was hollow inside.

"Maddie?"

It was the barest whisper of words, but hope soared through Maddie.

"Maddie?" Lucca looked around, and when his gaze landed on her, he paused, searching her face.

It was amazing to watch, like his soul and personality was filling up his blue eyes.

"Lucca?" Maddie took a step toward him.

"Maddie!" Lucca's lips turned into a grin, showing blood stained teeth. He rushed over to her and wrapped his arms around her. He smelled really bad, but she didn't care.

Before she could embrace him, he pulled away, trembling fiercely.

"You smell, delicious," he said, through clenched teeth. Valora came quickly to his side and put a hand on his shoulder.

"Hold your breath, you don't need the air," she said. He did as she commanded, and his posture became tranquil.

"This is very encouraging," Valora said. She kept a hand on Lucca's shoulder.

"Lucca, are you, okay?" Maddie asked, joy lighting her insides.

"Yeah," he said, shakily. "I have good days and bad. I'm hungry all the time."

"I've missed you so much," Maddie told him.

"I miss you too. I wanted to come see you as soon as I woke up, but it's like I have hours where my brain feels fuzzy, all I can think about is... well...blood." He shrugged in such a sheepishly Lucca way Maddie was reassured this was her brother.

"I believe I made the correct choice. Maddie, with your help, Lucca should be able to overcome some of the issues that occurred with his change." Valora sounded satisfied, and Maddie relaxed even more.

"I have so much to tell you, so much has happened!" Maddie exclaimed.

"Valora filled me in on a lot of it. I'm still confused but I'm sorry about you and Jo," Lucca said.

"Yeah, me too, but I feel a lot more like I've found myself now." Maddie just wanted to gush and tell him so much, but she was afraid he couldn't handle the information overload, instead, she asked, "Are you doing okay though, really?"

"I can run now, Maddie, swim, climb. I've never seen the world like this. I don't have to take medicine and I can finally breathe without wondering if I'm getting enough air because it's voluntary!" He demonstrated by taking a huge breath in.

The change was automatic, his eyes locked with Maddie's, and his grin turned into a snarl. Maddie felt like prey, she wanted to run away from her brother, but knew he would give chase.

A low sound started in his throat and his whole body quaked.

"Maddie...go..." he bit out.

"Madeline, I have him. You go home. I think this is enough for today," Valora told her as she tightened her grip on Lucca. "He will not hunt you. Once the scent of your blood is out of his system, he will be fine."

"I love you, Lucca," Maddie said.

"I...love...you...go...please." Each word seemed harder than the last for him to say. His hands were balled into fists at his side.

Maddie left as quickly as she could, and while she still felt fear at the sensation of being a food source, she was delirious with bliss. She had Lucca back! Everything was going to be all right.

CHAPTER SEVENTEEN

"*M*addie!"

Maddie jumped from her seat on the couch as the front door swung open, and with a loud thud, banged into the table in the foyer.

"What?" Eyes wide, she imagined all kinds of horrible scenarios to the door being so violently handled.

"We have something to tell you!" Queenie exclaimed as she and Allison rushed into the room. Maddie had been spending as little time with Jo and her roommates as possible since the memorial service.

Every time she saw one of them, they asked her if she'd read their proof, or wanted to discuss Valora's monster status. If they were impatient with her, they talked about how they still needed to find Lucca.

Maddie wasn't a great liar, though she was getting better at it every day. She figured sooner or later they'd realize not only did she believe them, but she knew quite a bit more than they did.

She'd gone through their research and it coincided with much of what Valora had told her, though it all painted her lover in a much darker light. Maddie still was unsure of who was telling the entire truth, but more disturbingly, she didn't really care. Her time with Valora was a beautiful miracle and she was clinging to it with both hands.

"What's going on in here?" Jo came down the stairs, she looked so weary, and Maddie had a moment of guilt. Maddie missed her. She'd spent so much time with Jo it was difficult to simply stop telling her everything and asking her opinion about, well...everything.

Their eyes met, and Maddie quickly looked away, she couldn't deal with this right now.

"We saw Lucca," Allie said, breathlessly.

"You saw who?" Maddie asked, steel in her eyes and voice. A glance toward the windows told her it was already dark outside.

"Lucca. He was drinking the blood of a cat!" Queenie's eyes were practically bulging out of her head.

"I almost threw up. He used to kiss me with that mouth!"

Maddie sat quietly; they probably had seen Lucca. She'd already seen him twice and felt like they were making progress toward helping him with his transition.

"I called out to him. Oh, Maddie, he looked horrible, so pale, eyes like rubies. I can't decide whether I am going to be sick or cry." Allison did look like either of those options were right around the corner. She was a little green, and the soft flesh around her eyes puffy and red.

"I'm sorry." Maddie couldn't think of what else to say.

"That's it? We've been showing you clippings on the animal murders for a week, Professor Heeling has told you over and over it's Lucca and all you can say is 'you're sorry?'" Jo went and shut the door, then all three of them were looking at her, accusations on their faces.

"You can't deny he's a vampire," Queenie said.

"Are you sure it was him?"

"He looked right at me!" Allison said, trembling. In fear or anger, Maddie couldn't tell.

"And if I tell you I believe you, what then? You all go medieval vampire hunter on me? You stalk and stake my brother?" Maddie's hands were clasped in her lap, and she was trying not to smile so she kept her head down. Valora knew this would happen, predicted it down to the frown and crease on Jo's face.

"I don't know what's wrong with you," Allie huffed, obviously irritated.

"I do. It's Professor Dulcara, and she's still spending time with her. I overheard her telling her parents she's accepted the TA position next year," Queenie outed her.

"Maddie, no!" Jo cried.

"Yes, and I'm going to Romania in a few weeks as well," Maddie admitted. She stayed sitting, not even looking at them.

"You're...you're...contaminated. Just like Heeling said. It's like the TAs are her 50s style brides or something and now you're just like them," Jo accused.

"You don't know her like I do." Maddie finally raised her eyes to them and knew the second they all figured it out. It was as if she could see the environmentally friendly light bulbs over all their heads switch on.

"You're in love with her." It wasn't a question, but Jo looked devastated.

"I don't know." It was a truthful answer, Maddie didn't know if the word love accurately described how she felt for Valora; hungered might have been better.

"Then it's over between us."

"Maybe we should leave them alone," Queenie whispered behind her hand to Allison.

"As if, I am enjoying this," Allison said back, but they both moved away so they weren't as involved in the conversation.

"It's been over for a while, ever since you refused to come to Lucca's memorial," Maddie said. "I'm sorry, Jo." She was, deeply. She never wanted to hurt Jo, and she knew Jo never wanted to hurt her either.

"I love you," Jo said.

"You did, once. I will always love you, Jo, you're still my best friend." Maddie felt like she was sinking into the couch, as if it wanted to swallow her whole and she would let it. This was not only the worst feeling in the world but not where or when this conversation should have taken place.

"I can't be friends with you if you're with her. She's not even a person, Maddie, she's a thing! A monster!" Jo stomped away, furious.

"She isn't a monster, Jo! You don't know her like I do!" Maddie called after her, still refusing to get up as a point of pride.

"But she is a monster, Maddie," Queenie said hesitantly.

"You don't know what you're talking about."

"She does. Professor Dulcara is a murderer or have you forgotten she killed your brother and probably the Ceres family?" Allison asked.

"She didn't murder Lucca. It's you who wants to do that, and it's a leap to think she killed that family."

"Ask her. I bet she'll even admit she killed them," Queenie said, then they left Maddie and she'd never felt more alone in her life. How had everything become so topsy turvy so quickly? Of late, she felt like a baby bird kicked out of the nest too soon. Would she fly or would she spiral down and become smashed upon the pavement?

"You guys, stay away from Lucca," Maddie warned.

"He's a monster and needs to be destroyed. If you really loved him you'd agree with us," Queenie argued.

"Come on, Maddie, he's killing family pets. There's so much wrong with this situation," Allison said.

"If you hurt Lucca I'll never forgive you."

I mean it, you guys, see it in my face. I will hurt you. I will be the fierce big sister and hurt you.

Putting her book down, Maddie went up to her room, each step heavier than the last. She couldn't wait to get the hell out of school and out into the world. She had plans, she wanted to make a difference! She felt like a pariah in her home and had never wanted to run away so badly before.

Her bedroom door shut quietly behind her and she breathed easier, outside of her bedroom she felt as if someone were always watching her. They critiqued her every move, every word and action, it got tiresome.

Maddie sat on her bed and leaned back. She never hit the bed as strong, smooth, white arms snaked around her waist and pulled her against a firm and solid form. Maddie gave a tiny shriek and then bit her lip.

"Valora, what are you doing here?"

"I couldn't stay away a moment longer." Valora's black hair slithered over her shoulders as her lips connected with the sensitive skin at Maddie's neck.

Maddie shivered when Valora's tongue licked a light path under her ear and almost to her collarbone. She felt her nipples tighten at the sensation and moaned quietly under her breath. It wouldn't do for anyone to know Valora was in her room.

"You shouldn't be here."

"I know. Come to the mansion instead."

"Not tonight."

Valora pulled away and swung Maddie around so she was straddling her waist. Valora's black eyes held a feverish brightness, her cheeks were flushed and her lips almost a cherry red; she'd recently fed.

"Valora, do you want to turn me into a vampire?" Maddie asked, shyly. She was jealous Valora had chosen to feed from someone else. The past few weeks she'd been sating her hunger mainly with Maddie's blood. Valora told her she was so old she didn't need much to sustain her.

"Yes, but only if it is what you want. You could simply be blood kin like Byron and Vaughn, most of the abilities without all the hindrances," Valora said.

Maddie thought about it. She enjoyed her time with Valora, and was growing to care for her more each day. How did she want this to end? Did she want to become a vampire?

"I'll have to think about it."

"I know, dear girl. I will not pressure you." Valora kissed her forehead.

Maddie caressed Valora's arms, linking their fingers together, she took a deep breath, enjoying the flower and coppery fragrance that came off her lover's skin and clothes.

"How is Lucca?"

"Doing better, but once he smells blood, he has a hard time controlling himself. I'm worried he'll move on from animals to small children. If he does, I won't have a choice. He'll have to be taken care of."

An ache formed in Maddie's chest, and it was like losing him all over again. She'd had such high hopes that in his new form they could be as they were before.

"Allison and Queenie saw him tonight. They want to destroy him."

"I know, and if it comes to that I will take care of him myself. I wouldn't wish what Heeling would do to your brother on my worst enemy." Valora hated Heeling, every time she said his name it was if she were cursing.

"He really is a thorn in your side, isn't he?" Maddie asked. The two of them leaned forward, foreheads touching. Valora's hands began to roam, it was hard for Maddie to concentrate.

"Yes, for years he has been hounding me. It didn't take him long to find the information he craved. He is a smart man, though he has only figured out the tip of the iceberg," Valora explained.

"I need to ask you something." Maddie pulled away, knowing it was so much easier to speak, to think clearly if she wasn't touching Valora. She scooted to the edge of her bed and felt badly as Valora's face registered confusion and loneliness. Queenie and Allison have placed doubts in her mind, doubts she had to voice.

After all these weeks there was one thing Maddie knew for sure about Valora; she had spent most of her life by herself. The TAs were special to her, but not companions, not like Maddie hoped she was.

"Ask me anything," Valora said, she ran hands down her violet silk dress, smoothing the wrinkles.

Maddie took a deep breath. "Did you kill the Ceres' family?"

"I may as well have."

Maddie didn't expect those words, she expected a denial or a reasonable explanation, but there Valora sat, giving a confusing response.

"What?"

"I did not do the actual killing, no, but I did not prevent it," Valora said. She stared at Maddie, as if daring her to comment, a hardness took over her features.

"Then who killed them?" Maddie asked.

"Someone I must protect."

"That's not an answer!" Maddie exclaimed. She stood up and paced; this wasn't right. Were Jo and the girls right about Valora after all? Had she made a horrible mistake?

"The Ceres are a new family to Arcata, but they have created many ties and one of them is Austin Heeling. They were all digging into an area they should not have been," Valora said.

"So, because they were prying, they earned death?" Maddie was appalled.

"No, when they found the information, they were looking for they were taken care of before they could tell Heeling."

"I don't understand. Why did they need to die over this?"

"This town is my home. I have worked hard to have a life here and given much of myself to it—time and money. I have shared many things with this town. My daughters are not one of them."

"Your daughters?" Maddie couldn't breathe, weren't her daughters dead? This was spiraling out of control so fast; everything was perfect only a few moments before. Why had she opened her mouth? She could have lived without this knowledge, but wouldn't that make her just as bad as Valora? If she were willing to believe the lie and live the fantasy? Wasn't it always better to know the truth?

"Yes, in the story they died, but it is not the case. They lived, just as I did. I will protect them against anyone, including you, Madeline, I'm sorry." The passion behind Valora's words made Maddie's heart swell; was this truly just a woman protecting her children? Could she live with murder in this way?

"If you didn't kill them, who did?" Maddie asked. Only silence answered her. They stared at each other for a few moments before it dawned on Maddie.

The portrait! The one in her room, oh how could she be so stupid. Of course, the painting was of her daughters!

"One of your daughters is here, isn't she? When they found out about her, she killed them?"

Valora slowly nodded, she seemed hesitant. "For all anyone knows, I am the only Dulcara and it needs to stay that way. The Ceres confronted her before coming to me, they threatened to ruin my reputation. I cannot mourn them as their actions were foolish," Valora said, her mouth in a macabre grimace.

"But she killed children." Maddie felt sick to her stomach.

"I know. I have kept control of my daughter for a long while. Sometimes it does not work, and she has been...punished."

"If this has all been about keeping your daughters a secret what were Lucca and Jo doing? Wasn't that all a project for the historical society because they're mad about the annual Halloween bash?" Maddie asked. She was very confused.

"I had them going through all the records in my personal collection for any reference of the girls so I could burn it as if it never was. I also wanted to appease the rest of the city so I had them finding any references to some of the founding families, some of which are still around."

"So not entirely a lie then."

"No. I do what I have to do, Madeline. I always have and I cannot change that for you."

"I don't know if I can be okay with that, Valora. Murder is wrong, even if you didn't kill them you know who did and you're okay with it."

"If you accept me, you must accept all of me, Madeline. I am not the monster your friends think I am, but I am not human. I do what I must."

"Would you have killed them if she hadn't?" The question was a whisper, the barest hint of words and breathe.

"Yes." It was the scariest word Maddie had ever heard and the tone it was said in even worse.

"And what of Jo? Did you do something to her, did something happen to her while she was working with you?" If she was going to ask the hard questions, she may as well ask them all.

"There were a few incidents. I almost fed on her once and my TAs, well with their connection to me comes a small price. There was an incident and I stopped it, no actual harm came to her. I had to take some of her memories from her as well. I am not surprised she associates fear and pain with me. I wish this were not so."

"She says she wrote down what happened as well."

"I took her journal. I thought it better for Jolene that she not remember."

"And you think that's all right? To poke around in her mind like that. To steal her property?" Maddie's chest felt tight, as if she couldn't breathe.

"Yes." Again, that three letter word sounded horrible to her ears. "Though with her strong mind, it is not permanent."

"I think you should go." It pained her to say it; she wanted Valora to stay. Their relationship was scorching flames and ecstasy, she didn't want to lose it, but didn't know if she could keep it. Maddie gave Valora her back.

"No. You will not push me away, and I will not leave."

Maddie spun around, angry. "I can't handle this. I can't be with you. I've hurt too many people and now I know not only do you condone murder you have manipulated people I love and for all I know, me."

"Professor Heeling is a killer. He and your friends will try and kill Lucca. If they succeed, will you defend them?" Valora stood, beautiful in her anger, eyes flashing. Maddie felt fear trickle down her spine.

"You killed Lucca." There, she said the words, said them to hurt her and make her leave. Valora flinched.

"I have explained that. He was going to die, as a vampire he could be young and healthy forever. I was trying to give you a present."

"And what kind of a present is it? I might have to deal with his death all over again. No, Valora, it has to be over. You don't feel things like humans do."

Valora crossed the distance between them, grabbing Maddie by the arms, their faces inches away.

"And how is that wrong? I feel love and passion deeper than I did as a human, I feel hurt and anguish, and my heart has bled for centuries. I can see colors and touch sensations you can only dream of. I hear music and song in a way no human will ever know. Yes, it comes at a price, I must be ruthless and cruel. I must think pragmatically to protect myself and those I cherish. You cannot hold me to a human's standards, as you said, I am not human."

"I don't think I can be like you. I know, at least right now, I can't be with you." Maddie was crying now, weeping, chin to her chest.

Valora let go, she took a step back.

"I will go, but if you need me, I will be there. If you want me, I will come. You are mine, Madeline, and I will not let you go forever."

When Maddie looked up, Valora was gone, not even a hint of her perfume or indent on the bed proved she had ever been there.

A knock sounded at the door, a quick, tempered thudding.

Maddie answered. She didn't feel like crying, she felt like screaming, like tearing out her hair and running wild through the streets.

It was Queenie.

"Queenie, I think I need your help, you...and your uncle."

But you will stay away from Lucca.

CHAPTER EIGHTEEN

Diary of one Miss Allison Hastings

I don't usually think keeping a diary is a good idea, however, Professor Heeling has asked us all to document this bizarre turn of events. If this ever comes to public light, I shall simply deny every word as a laughable, and yet a fun, strange work of fiction.

My boyfriend is, or was, a vampire. The words are surreal and perhaps the most absurd I have ever written. I'm not surprised Maddie looked at us like we all belonged in a cell, at first.

She has looked at us less like a bunch of loons since she stopped seeing Valora, since Jo's missing journal arrived on our doorstep. Jo wouldn't read it, but we all did. It's not as dreadful as I imagined, but it's not good either. Poor Maddie, Jo said some awful things about her in there, and poor Jo. Being cheated on is never fun. Honestly, they're both kind of pathetic.

I know Maddie saw Lucca several times since he became a vampire, and honestly? I don't know how to feel about that.

I do feel like I'm betraying Maddie and Lucca, in a way. After she decided we were right, she made us promise to leave Lucca alone, and we all agreed. The lie stuck in my throat.

Back to Lucca, I'm sick of writing and talking about Maddie and Jo. It's all anyone wants to discuss, how Maddie's under Valora's power and can't be trusted and how Jo is a victim—not sure if I agree on either of these accounts.

Lucca was a sweet, smart, charming boy who treated me the way I deserved— like a princess. He may not have been the perfect man, but for a time he meant more to me than I have words to describe. His sudden death has left an ache in my heart. I don't know where our relationship was going, but it was something sweet and good.

When he died, I thought I'll never see him again or hear his laugh, he'll never call me princess or hold my hand. How sentimental and ridiculous those thoughts were. Thoughts like those are what got me kicked out of my old school. Maybe I am too much like my mother, a romantic as my father would say. Still, for weeks all I could think about was that I would never see Lucca again and I missed him.

Then Queenie and I saw him, crouched down low, a dead cat gripped in his hands, blood dripping from his mouth onto the poor thing's fur. I called his name in amazement and in the desire to see him again. He turned his red glowing eyes on me and gave a look that chilled me to the bone. I'm not sure he even knew who I was. He hissed, dropped the creature, and fled down the street, so fast I couldn't tell where he'd gone. It was like losing him all over again. I will never forgive that wretched woman for what she has done. I will see her destroyed.

Even after Maddie made us promise not to hurt him, I knew...I knew it was a promise we would break. Lucca became an unnatural thing, a wicked pet killer. I felt bad lying to Maddie's face, and I can't believe she thought we'd just over look Lucca being a vampire. Even before she came around to our side, we had a plan in place.

Onto more gruesome matters...

Last night was one of the most horrific and grisly moments of my life and I have seen all the Saw movies. Professor Heeling finally figured out where Lucca was spending his day time rest. Not in the Dulcara Cemetery like we all thought but in a hidden set of unmarked graves outside of town.

Jo and I went during the day just to scope the place out. It is off the road a way and everything is brown and dull, completely unworthy of notice. You follow a little path through some sad trees that empty into a clearing full of nothing but rotting, wood headstones, the smell of dust, despair, and brown weeds.

In the middle of the graves, we noticed one that looked disturbed, as if it had been recently dug up, multiple times. We dusted off the top layer of dirt and found a fancy, new, metal coffin just underneath the surface. I knew Lucca was inside the moment I put my hands on it. Though honestly it was so damn dirty I didn't want to touch it.

We couldn't open it by ourselves so we went to tell Heeling and the others.

The next day we went back, an hour or so before dawn. I can't tell you how afraid I was, how much I just wanted to turn back. This was a gross event, something I couldn't believe we were doing. But we did.

We went to the circle and uncovered the coffin. Heeling pried it open with a sickening jolt of metal on metal. The coffin was empty, pale blue satin lined the inside, and it looked as if someone had been sleeping in it. He insisted we wait until Lucca came back. Once Lucca rested in his space, we could set his spirit free.

I've never given much thought to the spirit, I mean my family goes to church, what good Christians don't? But I never gave any thought to the soul or the devil or even where we go when we die. Heeling is certain the real Lucca is trapped somewhere in his shell, screaming to be released. I don't know if I believe that or if I believe that Valora Dulcara's "magic" corrupted his good nature.

Heeling sprayed us with some herb smelling concoction he said made young vampires unable to sense humans. I swear my hair still stinks like it.

We waited, in the shadows of the trees. The night was still and calm. Sky black, a smattering of stars, barely a sound. A small light at the horizon, the only sign daylight was approaching. All five of us waited; we waited until Lucca came.

It was almost as if I still wasn't prepared to see him. I mean I had already seen him, I knew what he was. But seeing him slink into the black, gray, and white of the clearing, moon shining down on all that death was not something I was prepared for.

He was as handsome as the day we met, brown hair, blue eyes. Perfect skin. But his eyes gleamed with a hellish light and his lips curled in a demonic smile around sharp, white teeth.

I wanted to dart out, to go to him, but Scarlet's fingers on my arm dug in and stopped me. He sniffed like a dog, looking around and we moved deeper into the woods so he couldn't see us.

Until the day I saw him eating the cat, part of me thought the other girls were crazy freaks and Maddie and I should run as far away from them as we possibly could, but then I saw Lucca, an undead Lucca. I knew, I knew it was all true.

He uncovered the coffin, brushing the dust and weeds away like they were pristine scraps of silk, and opened the lid. With a self-satisfied smile, tinged in blood, he lay down and shut the lid. Like magic, the thin layer of dirt and weeds were blown, by invisible wind, back over the lid, hiding it from view.

An hour passed, until the sun began to rise, rays of light streaming into the clearing.

"He must be in his death like sleep, or all is for naught," Heeling said. I almost hated him in that moment.

"Valora doesn't sleep during the day," Scarlet mentioned.

"It is a very new vampire," Heeling explained.

"He's still Lucca," I protested, stomach sick. Maddie is never going to forgive us. I don't know if I forgive us.

"No, he's not, he's an undead monster. A prey of Valora's," Jo said. I don't completely care for Jo. She doesn't treat Maddie very well and her focus on Valora is almost all-consuming.

"Okay, so how do we do this?" Scarlet asked. She seemed the most reasonable, besides myself, of course.

"Now that we have proof, we wait for the sun to fully rise and strike," Heeling said.

It took another hour. An hour standing in the cooling air. My expensive, pink sweater was warm but not warm enough against the November chill. I moved from foot to foot in my brown, leather boots as we waited.

Finally, Heeling made a motion with his hand and I knew it was time to move. We entered the clearing, and Jo began to shove the inch of dirt from the lid of the coffin. Using the crow bar, again, Heeling opened it.

I gasped, Lucca lay inside so peaceful, his cheeks flush with color, blond eyelashes against pale skin, hands clasped over a bulging stomach, like a boy who has just enjoyed a good meal.

"He's so beautiful," I murmured. I wanted to reach down and wake him, stroke my fingers across his soft cheeks, but I didn't. What if he woke up and attacked me?

"And evil," Queenie said.

"So again, how do we do this?" Scarlet asked.

"Take this, Miss Hastings." Heeling gave me a long piece of wood, pointed like the end of a sharp pencil. "Place it over his heart, in-between the ribs is best."

I held the stake, hands trembling. Were we really doing this?

"Then, Queenie, you take this." A large, rubber headed mallet appeared from his dark carpet bag.

"You two will drive that through his chest while Scarlet and I cut off his head and fill his mouth with garlic. Jo shall stand watch, holding the cross."

"Why do I have to do thi,s and Jo gets the clean and safe part?" I asked.

"Out of us all, you loved him the best."

I sucked in a sob at his words. Had it been love? Truly? I may never know.

"Is this really necessary?" Scarlet asked.

"I wouldn't suggest it if it were not."

I think that may have been the best response.

I won't go into too much detail, as I don't think I can write it down without vomiting. I will only write this:

My pink sweater, in fact my whole outfit is ruined. It is in a bag at the bottom of my closet. Jo promised to take it and burn it along with everyone else's clothes.

His eyes blazed open the second the mallet hit the wood, his hands tried to grab me, to claw his way out of the box and away from us.

He whispered, "Princess, no." And I almost lost my nerve.

I will never forget the surprise and anguish in his eyes when the mallet pounded down again, and Professor Heeling's knife sliced into his throat. I didn't think he would be so...so...Lucca, as if being a vampire would make it so he didn't know me, didn't recognize me.

Finally, we reached his heart and his head came away with a sickening wet Velcro and crunching sound. His eyes shut and his mouth fell open, gaping.

I fell on my knees next to the coffin and threw up. It was quite undignified and made me never want to eat chicken noodle soup again. Scarlet looked queasy on the ride home and Queenie was quieter than she ever has been. Only Jo seemed unmoved and all she could talk about was when we could do the same treatment to Valora.

The stench of blood and death is like so much rotten meat and decaying flowers with a spicy undertone and it permeates everything, my clothes, skin, and hair. It may be days before I can stop smelling it.

It was hard work, harder than my hot yoga or Pilates classes ever have been. Queenie says her arms will ache for at least a week.

Maddie knew what we were up to the moment we came home. She hasn't left her room in twenty-four hours. She won't even look at us.

Heeling thinks Valora will be harder to kill, she's older and more powerful. I agree, but I don't know if I want to delve any further into this madness. Maybe I shouldn't have transferred to this school after all.

CHAPTER NINETEEN

Psychology Term Paper
Interview a psychiatric patient part three—transcribed from recording.
Mr. R.M. Rainier by Scarlet Jones.
The Last Pages—in two parts
November 21st

RM: It's good to see you again.

SJ: You too. I'm sorry I've been gone so long.

RM: It's understandable.

SJ: What is?

RM: That you've been gone, death is hardest on the young.

SJ: Who said anything about death?

RM: (Slight laugh) I did, she did, we all did. Your friend died, did he not?

SJ: Ummm, well yes, I did have a friend who died. Did you read about it in the paper?

RM: I am not allowed newspapers. I was told by my mistress. He will consume lives now.

SJ: I don't think we should be discussing this, your care staff told me death is a bad topic, let's change the subject.

RM: (Gripping the sides of his chair, a large grin on his face) To another of your friends perhaps?

SJ: No, how about we talk about your daily routine, are you still taking your medications?

RM: That's so boring! Of course, I am, but as time of my release grows nearer, I am becoming much more...me again!

SJ: Your release? Are they letting you out of here? I hadn't heard. You must be so excited.

RM: They are not letting me out of anywhere. My mistress is coming, the dark queen will give me the lives I need to escape with her. Yule is almost upon us. She promised.

SJ: I think you should stay put for the holidays, I hear they make a lovely steamed pudding for all the patients.

RM: I know you think you can destroy her, I want to help.

SJ: Why would you help us?

RM: I wouldn't!! But I want lives and she doesn't let me have enough. If I help you, will YOU get me lives?

SJ: Uh...sure...if you help us. What kind of lives?

RM: Bugs or perhaps a mouse or a bird. I know a kitten is too much to hope for.

SJ: Fine.

RM: The boxes, you must destroy the earth and then my mistress.

SJ: Let's change the subject.

RM: She's out, my mistress allowed her out.

SJ: Who's out?

RM: The other, the dangerous one, her bad kin.

SJ: Why would she be allowed out?

RM: My mistress wants to protect her, thinks she's better, but I know...I remember her screams in the night.

SJ: Why would the staff allow someone like that to go free?

RM: They don't know about her. She's hidden and special.

(Door opens and a nurse comes in. She smiles at R and me then leans down into my ear. She needs to speak to me.)

SJ: I'll be right back, okay?

R: Yes, of course, feel free.

(We leave the room.)

N: We don't usually go along with his bits or indulge his delusions; the doctors don't think it's good for him.

SJ: I'm sorry, I just thought it would keep him calm.

N: It may, or it may provoke him. He's been having more bad days of late. If you're to continue coming here, I need to insist you stop pandering to him. Ask him about who he is or was, what he does during the day, how he feels, that sort of thing or the doctor says these interviews must stop.

SJ: Of course, no problem.

(I reenter the room. Subject is sitting quite still, looking out the barred window.)

SJ: Sorry about that, now, where were we?

RM: Nowhere, nothing important.

SJ: Why don't you talk about your family?

RM: (In a low whisper eyes stuck on the window, it's gotten dark) You should warn your friend, the dark queen's eyes are upon her, she will never let her go. Nothing satisfies the hunger like another bride! (Eyes wide, even quieter, frantically.) Oh no, I've said too much! You must save her!

SJ: What are you talking about?

RM: She is in her power now. You have lost! (He suddenly lurches from his chair and two guards rush in.)

RM: The blood is the life!!

December 1st

I can no longer continue my interview with the patient R.M Rainier. When I went for my next scheduled time, it was to be informed by the staff that Mr. Rainier had been found dead, neck broken, on the floor of his bedroom the night before. It is a mystery as the door was locked and the tamper proof glass on his window intact. I have decided to turn in what I have and not continue with a new patient.

Follow up thoughts:

Either a) Mr. Rainier's medication was starting to wear off or needed to be dosed differently, b) he wasn't taking his medication and the staff will find a hidden horde, or c) something very sinister is at play. I may never know. I did find out that the Dulcara Foundation is paying for funeral and internment arrangements. This is not out of place as the foundation also paid for all his care.

Research:

Based on what information Mr. Rainier did give me, I was able to piece together some of his life.

His family still lives in town, in a house owned by Valora Dulcara. His wife and son refused to speak to me. She works as a house keeper at the Dulcara Mansion, the boy is in middle school. It felt wrong to intrude upon them anymore.

His family has lived in Arcata for five generations. I am surprised I didn't know them. They arrived by boat and then wagon train with some of the original Dulcaras from England. What records the archives held state they worked for the Dulcaras in England as well.

Insanity seemed to run in the family. I found several newspaper articles and public records about family members that seemed to suggest Mr. Rainier was not the first to be sent to a sanatorium or die young, including one suicide and one account of a husband murdering his wife and then being hung.

Those I found who knew Mr. Rainier before he became a resident at Sempervirens Psychiatric Hospital had nothing but pleasant memories of a handsome, charismatic young man that used to swallow gold fish at parties to gross out young women and never hesitated to try new things, including food.

Valora Dulcara declined to be interviewed about Mr. Rainier, his family or his death. I have included pictures of tombstones from the Dulcara Cemetery of some of Mr. Rainier's ancestors and a head shot from his days as a Real Estate Agent.

"She killed him, Maddie, I just know it," Scarlet said. She sounded so distraught over the death of her psych ward friend.

"I have no idea. I told you all I haven't seen Valora in weeks, and it's over between us." Maddie couldn't help the sadness that tinged her words, even though she'd been the one to tell her to leave. She put on a smile and a brave face for her friends, they at least needed to think it was behind her, but Maddie wasn't sure.

She missed her, missed their conversations, her touch, just how she felt in Valora's presence. She couldn't deny that her mind felt clearer now that she wasn't spending as much time with Valora. She wanted to believe her feelings had all just been Valora's powers, but she worried that wasn't completely true.

Worse of all was that cutting off Valora had meant cutting off Lucca as well. The rationale was that if Valora was an evil monster, then Lucca must be too. Maddie didn't know if she believed that, but she was trying to do the right thing, to make good choices.

Scarlet and Maddie were sitting in Maddie's room, on the floor, both cross legged in a patch of sunshine that warmed the slightly faded carpet and gave the room a gold tinge.

They didn't like Maddie to leave her room very often. They all felt she was in danger from Valora. Garlic and crosses hung around every entrance to the house, double around Maddie's room.

Maddie wanted to leave the house, she wanted to see Valora, but she couldn't do either of those things, not right now.

What she'd settle for was Scarlet to leave her alone. It was becoming harder, with each day, to pretend like everything was fine. When really, she hated each of them, just a little, for what they did to her brother.

They never came out and told her, but she knew. The moment it happened. They had made it so Lucca was permanently dead, and she didn't think she could forgive them for that. She had begged them to leave Lucca out of their plan for vengeance against Valora. Instead, they snuck out and cut off her brother's head.

"It stinks in here," Maddie commented, leaning back on her arms, weight on her wrists.

"Heeling says it's for your own good."

"I don't know why. I told you all I made her leave."

"You've invited her in once, the garlic and the crosses make sure she can't get back in and can't compel you to come out," Scarlet tried to explain.

"She never compelled me, she would never do that," Maddie said, defensively.

"So you think."

"Am I going to be locked in here forever? Escorted to class by someone until I die?"

"No, Heeling says if we destroy her then you'll be free," Scarlet said.

"His plan is taking too long!" Maddie was going stir crazy and it didn't help that every inch of her wanted to run out of the house and into Valora's arms. Maybe they were right. Maybe she really did need the protection, protection from her own thoughts and feelings.

"Have you spoken to Jo?"

"No, why would I?" Maddie asked. She still felt badly about how their relationship ended. She felt worse after reading the missing journal entries.

Valora had almost fed off Jo twice. Jo wrote that she thought she saw her climb out a second-floor window and scale down the wall like a spider. She'd seen Valora turn into mist and almost had sex with two of the TAs. Maddie was sure Valora originally wanted Jo as her next TA and changed her mind when Jo proved to be skittish and unreliable. It made her jealous, the thought that maybe she wasn't Valora's first choice.

She wondered if Valora could turn into a bird or a bat and fly away. She'd like to be able to become a raven, big and black and take off whenever she wanted.

"I think she'd forgive you, take you back, if you talked to her," Scarlet's voice broke through Maddie's musings.

"I don't know why this is hard for you guys to understand. I already apologized, but I don't want her back." Maddie felt a slight tingling sensation begin to creep over her skin, slightly painful, almost burning and knew she'd been in the sun too long.

She'd also found out by reading Jo's journal that she'd kissed another girl over the summer, and she'd written more about re-reading Sparks Notes so she could maintain the fiction she loved *Nightmare Abbey*. Jo's words were in fact "that insufferable book." Maddie also found comments that while Jo loved her, she didn't think she was very smart.

Maddie knew she hadn't done the right or good thing by sleeping with Valora before officially breaking up with Jo, but Jo had no right to act like she was the innocent party either. They both were horrible.

Trying for casual, she stretched, stood up and yawned, then sat down, out of the sun's direct path. Of late being in the sun too long was painful. She had her suspicions as to why but wouldn't worry the others. She was also growing concerned about an empty ache in the pit of her stomach, a hunger she couldn't sate, no matter what food or drink she ingested. She still ate, just not as often.

Maddie felt anxiety starting to claim her thoughts and actions, like a thousand poisonous butterflies invaded her veins.

Breathe, is there anything you can do about this right now? No, I just need to wait it out. What good is it doing you to panic? It's not, I'm okay, and I'm going to be okay.

Taking a deep, calming breath didn't work as the reek of garlic flowers went straight up her nose and made her stomach flip flop. She pressed a hand to her sick belly and pursed her lips.

"That bad?" Scarlet asked. She gave a tentative sniff, wrinkled her nose, and smiled. "It's not great but could be worse."

"You can go to your room and escape it. I can't."

"Not true, it's outside my window."

"Yes, outside your window."

"Okay, okay. I get it, the garlic is stinky," Scarlet said, laughing, her face looked relaxed. Maddie wished she had such an option. Nothing was relaxing anymore. She couldn't even enjoy her classes.

"Is Jo even going to Valora's class?"

"No, she dropped it, is taking an F, and planning to make it up over summer. Her dad is not happy."

"I bet." Maddie's guilt doubled. Was this her fault too? She glanced at the calendar. In two weeks, she should be on a plane with Valora, going to Romania, instead she was planning on celebrating the holidays here, stinking of garlic. She wasn't even seeing her mom and dad. They wanted her to come home and she wanted them to come here, but neither option was going to work out. Since all three of them were grief stricken. They made the collective decision not to wallow.

Maddie convinced them to take a cruise and they thought she and Jo were going for a romantic getaway to Disneyland. Maddie wished she were going to Disneyland; eating ice cream shaped like a cartoon character and trying to find her favorite princess to take a picture with.

Instead, she'd be cooped up in this house. She'd have to buy some souvenirs online somewhere and take a picture in a mouse hat, but the deception was worth not worrying them.

"Maybe we really should go to Disneyland."

"What?" Scarlet said and slowly blinked a few times.

"I told my parents that's where we were spending the holidays. Maybe we should get away from here and go." Maddie knew her request would be met with a denial, but the illusion felt nice to dwell in.

"I don't think so, Maddie, but if we can take care of Professor Dulcara before Christmas we'll try to find something really fun to do. Anyway, I gotta go, homework awaits." Scarlet stood up, gave one more concerned glance over her shoulder before leaving Maddie's room.

Sadness enveloped Maddie as she sat by herself, longing and grief filling her up like pouring water into a bowl.

Do you want me to come to you, dear girl? The thought whispered through Maddie's mind.

"What the hell?" Maddie asked, out loud. Had she just heard Valora's voice in her head? Was she truly cracking up now?

You are not insane. This is one of my gifts. I can sense how unhappy you are.

"I can't talk to you Valora, this isn't right." But oh, she wanted to.

I miss you, and you miss me, what is not right about this? Let me come to you. I shall fix everything.

"There's garlic everywhere. They think you're dangerous to me. I'm not sure what I believe." Maddie began to pace around the room.

If you remove the garlic, I can come, take down the crucifixes, only in your room. I will come to you and take you away from all of this.

"I want to. I'm so confused by everything, Valora. I don't know what to do or who to have faith in!" Maddie exclaimed, slapping a hand over her mouth, eyes fixed on the door. She didn't want anyone to hear her.

Believe me, I would never harm you. I gave you back Jolene's journal. I have always told you the truth. Did they ever admit what they did to your brother?

Pain, there it was, more pain. When had her life become so fraught with hurt?

"No. I know they killed him, but no, they haven't told me. I figure they cut off his head. Isn't that how you kill a vampire?" Just another few feet in the void between her and them.

Oh yes, a bitter laugh filled her mind, *they took care of him. Desecrated him, I will spare you the details.*

"Why didn't you stop them?" Valora had to have known what they were about to do.

By the time I realized it, it was too late. I was not even in town that night.

"You wanted Jo first, didn't you?" She changed the subject, she had to, it was too excruciating to think how close she came to having Lucca back.

All talking about it did was make the tiny bit of hate grow larger, soon she'd be living off it. If she wasn't careful.

I thought she may have what I crave in a new blood kin, but I never wanted or cherished her as I do you. There is something lacking in Jolene.

It shouldn't make her feel better, but it did.

"Professor Heeling says you're a monster." Weak argument, but she was losing this battle against herself. She wanted Valora.

I have known men like Heeling before. Even if you never trust me again, dear girl, do not trust him. Was Lucca a monster?

"I don't trust him, but they don't trust me either. I'm so confused. Oh, Valora, I miss you and I hate myself for it!" Maddie sank down to her knees, fist in her mouth, biting the pale, tender skin along her knuckles. She pondered her question, had Lucca been a monster too?

I love you, dear girl. You are mine. I won't let you go, but I only want you if it is willingly. Come to me, let me come to you.

Releasing her knuckle, she said, "I'm not sure how I feel. I need more time I—"

The door to her room swung open and a furious and panicked looking Jo stood in the doorway.

"Who's in here? Who are you talking to?"

Maddie stayed where she was and rubbed her fist along her flowered skater dress, hiding the bite marks from Jo.

"I'm the only one in here, Jo."

"Liar. I heard you talking to someone."

"To myself."

Jo came in, forcibly, and began to search the room.

"What are you doing? This is my room, get out." Jo's actions were just too much. Was she to have no privacy now either?

"Someone was in here!" Jo exclaimed, opening the closet and rooting around.

"No one was in here but me, now get out." Maddie came to her feet, hands on her hips.

"What's going on?" Allison asked. She was standing in the doorway, astonishment and concern in her perfect features.

"Maddie was talking to someone in here," Jo accused. She was just so angry. Maddie couldn't blame her, but she wouldn't let her own guilt let Jo get away with treating her badly.

"Maddie?" Allison questioned.

"No one was in here. I was talking to myself, it's something people do you know, especially when one has lost the person she used to speak to the most," Maddie said, eyes lowered.

"Whose fault is that?" Jo barked.

"I meant Lucca." It was cruel to play the dead brother card, but she really wanted to be left alone. She heard Allison sigh and come further into the room.

"We did you a favor. Lucca wasn't human, he was simply something disgusting that should never have existed."

"I saw him, I spoke to him! He was Lucca and you murdered him!" Maddie yelled.

"You spoke to him?" Allison said. There was a tone in her voice, like anguish.

"Yes, and he was simply Lucca and he needed my help." Maddie took pleasure in watching Allison's face fall.

"He was a vampire. He stopped being Lucca when he died and awoke a bloodthirsty monster," Jo said.

"Agree to disagree, now get out." Maddie pointed her finger at the door.

"Come on, Jo, you can't just barge in here and go through Maddie's things. Leave her alone."

"Valora was in here with her, I swear!"

Maddie watched as Allison put a gentle hand on Jo and led her from the room, waving at the windows and door.

"No, she wasn't. Look the garlic is still up." Allison pushed Jo out into the hall, talking to her in low tones. She shut the door behind her, and Maddie stayed silent and still as she heard their muffled conversation get further and further away.

"Valora?" Maddie whispered.

I am always with you.

The relief she felt at hearing those words spoke volumes. She went to the window and began tearing down the garlic. She fucking hated it.

CHAPTER TWENTY

Transcript of Social Media Conversations

Jolene Harper
Hey you up?
Allison Hastings
Yeah. Finishing a project for class. What's up?
Jolene Harper
Can't sleep. Keeping thinking about what Scarlet and Heeling told us. You know about the boxes of earth Valora must keep from her homeland?
Allison Hastings
It's a weird concept, for sure. Do we really have to find them and destroy them? It's a little far-fetched.
Jolene Harper
Do you not believe? After everything we've seen?
Allison Hastings
It's not that I don't believe it. It's that I'm not sure how involved with all this I want to be.
Jolene Harper
It's a little late for that. You helped with Lucca. Do you think Valora will just let you get away with killing one of her "children?"
Allison Hastings

I didn't think of that. I do know I want her to pay for what she did to Lucca. He wouldn't have died if she hadn't been feeding on him. BTW your broken heart profile pic is weird, what's up?

Jolene Harper

We will make her pay. For Lucca, me and for Maddie. For all of us. We should be having a good time and not worrying about vampires.

Allison Hastings

Just going to ignore my question? Don't think I don't know it's about Maddie.

Allison Hastings

Jo?? C'mon, you can talk to me. I may be a stuck-up bitch but I still care.

Jolene Harper

Maddie hurt me and I'm making a statement. Now I am going to bed.

Allison Hastings

Good night. Though one more thing. You may want to consider that you hurt Maddie too. Just saying.

Scarlet Jones
@thescarletter

If you were 13 boxes filled with dirt. Where would you hide?

Queenie Myles
Yesterday at 8:55am

Does anyone know if that abandoned house on Pear Street has an owner? I can't find the information anywhere.

Comments:
Scarlet Jones

Ummmm, not the best place to put something like this hun. At least make it friends only.

Jolene Harper

Are you sure it's not whoever took over from that insane guy Scarlet interviewed?

Madeline West

What are you doing near Pear Street? Is this about those boxes of dirt again? I told you that's all nonsense.

Jolene Harper

@madelinewest Why do you want to know? So, you can go tell your new girlfriend what we're up to?

Madeline West

@joleneharper She's not my girlfriend. I'm sorry if you don't believe me. Don't think I didn't notice your very pointed profile pic.

Allison Hastings

Ok, that's enough. Let's not air our dirty laundry for the whole world to see.

"You want me to come with you to do what?" Maddie asked.

"To destroy boxes of earth," Queenie said, simply.

"These are boxes full of dirt you think Valora is sleeping in?" Maddie knew she sounded unconvinced, but the whole thing sounded just stupid really.

"Yes. My uncle believes that to destroy Valora first we must make it so she cannot rest here in Arcata," Queenie explained, speaking slowly, as if you would to a child.

"So, this centuries old vampire keeps boxes filled with dirt just laying around in case she needs a nap?" Maddie couldn't help the questions.

That is laughable, dear girl, but it does not matter.

Maddie turned her head so Queenie couldn't see her smile.

"Yes, once she can't rest, she will be easier to kill and then you can rest too! I know these past few weeks have been tough." Queenie placed a hand on Maddie's shoulder. They were standing outside the house on the porch, it was early afternoon, a December chill in the air, the light of day dimmed by clouds.

The sky was a melancholy color somewhere between heather and slate. The partly cloudy skies the only reason Maddie could be out of the house at all. Everyone noticed that Maddie was changing, she barely ate real food anymore and could only be in direct sunlight for a few hours at a time.

Maddie gripped the wood railing of the porch, mindful of splinters, and leaned against it. The feel of the rough wood against her soft skin was the kind of distraction she needed. If she didn't concentrate, she would lapse into conversation with the woman in her head and Queenie would notice something was wrong.

As the days passed, it became more and more of a task to deny Valora. Every night she took the garlic and the crosses down but managed not to invite her. Every day she put them back up and acted like her life had not become a horror movie. She wanted to be normal again, but she also wanted to be with Valora.

What part in the movie am I? The villain, the victim? Am I the sidekick in my own life? I guess it doesn't matter. I'm not a virgin so I still die in the end.

So many people were telling her Valora was evil so it must be true, right? The woman in her head kept telling her they were wrong, serenading her with poems, stories and such strong emotions...how could such a creature be evil?

On the other hand, Maddie finally got Allie to tell her what exactly they did to her brother. Who was the real monster? The argument that it was Valora was getting flimsier every day. Maddie could barely look at or talk to her so-called friends. They had brutally desecrated Lucca. It made her sick to even think about what they did to him. It was their fault she would never speak to him again.

Feeling the rage churning under her skin, Maddie took a deep, calming breath. If they ever had a hint of her true feelings for them, they really wouldn't trust her.

Maddie had never considered herself an actress, but it seemed liked she was learning new things about herself every day.

"How do you know where she put them all?" Maddie asked.

Queenie was in the process of re-braiding her blonde hair; she wore a multi-colored striped sweater and black leggings and the fuzziest boots Maddie had ever seen in her life.

"Research," Queenie said mysteriously.

"Ah, you don't trust me."

"Sorry, Maddie."

I myself wonder how they found them and what they plan to do when they get to them.

Maddie snorted which earned her a worried glance from Queenie.

"It's not that cold, are you getting sick?" Maddie tried to change the subject, Queenie didn't usually wear so many clothes.

"My meds are late, I'm having a flare up." Queenie started to scratch her upper arm, stopped herself, and bit her lip, self-conscious.

"You know we don't care about that," Maddie said. It was sad that Queenie felt like she needed to cover up the patches of her psoriasis.

"So, there are thirteen boxes we will find and get rid of," Queenie told her, putting the conversation back on course.

Well perhaps not boxes.

Scarlet's little car pulled up in front of the house with a screech. She jumped out of the car, hair flying in every direction, curly and large. Jo followed her, but at a slower pace. They had an afternoon class at the same time.

"Is that my dress?" Queenie asked as Scarlet bounded up the stairs.

"Like I would fit in anything your scrawny ass wore. We did buy it together." The dress in question was a bright blue sweater dress with a black belt.

"Oh, I forgot." Queenie's eyes took on a cloudy absent look, one Maddie was familiar with after the last four months living together. Queenie truly was a strange girl.

"You can borrow it, but it won't fit you," Scarlet said, laughing.

"How was class?" Maddie asked.

"Boring, but that's not the news I wanted to share."

"Tell us." Queenie's eyes focused on her friend.

"Valora and all three of her TAs were not in school today and have upped their trip to Romania for Friday, earlier than expected! It's over, we don't have to worry about the boxes or anything, she'll be gone in few days." Scarlet was excited.

"That's not true," Queenie said, sadly.

"What do you mean? No Valora, no vampire, no worries," Scarlet said.

"I agree, now things can go back to normal," Maddie quickly added.

"No, she'll be back, eventually. My uncle will agree, we need to take care of things now. She always comes back." Queenie gave a deep sigh.

"Heeling also says you won't be normal again unless she's dead. You do want to be normal, right?" It was a dare from Jo, and not a subtle one.

"Fine, where are these boxes? Let's get it over with," Maddie said. Not only was she not going to be in Romania with Valora, now it looked like the TA position was disappearing too.

"We're splitting up. Jo and I are heading over to Pear Street and the boiler room at the college," Queenie explained.

"We thought you should go with Professor Heeling," Jo said, a hint of malice in her words.

"I don't think that's a good idea." Maddie wanted to refuse out right, but she walked on egg shells around Jo enough of late. Did she want to crush them beneath her feet now?

"He's going to take care of the one in the Cemetery behind the Dulcara Mansion," Scarlet mentioned.

"Is that safe?" Maddie asked.

"It's daylight, why wouldn't it be?"

"Valora can come out during the day." Maddie thought her argument was sound. The whole dirt thing didn't make sense anyway. It probably wasn't even true.

It is, but only just. I do have dirt from my homeland scattered around the city. It allows for Arcata to feel like home to me, should they desecrate it I would become very uncomfortable here. I will still be able to be awake during the day, but the sun, it will begin to sting. I am too old for much more than that.

"Then why?" Maddie pursed her lips, she hadn't meant to say that out loud.

"Then why what?" Queenie asked, confusion on her face.

"Ummm, then why does it matter when we go?"

"Daylight will still be safer."

Because I can always ship more dirt in or go home and bring the Earth back with me. It is a minor inconvenience. I am more concerned with you being alone with Austin Heeling.

"All right, when do we go?" Maddie hoped her words didn't sound as resentful as she felt.

"Allison is picking me up in about an hour to do ours," Scarlet told her. "Heeling said he'd meet you at the cemetery around the same time."

Maddie didn't say more, she simply got up and went inside to get dressed. She'd need jeans and a sweater if a romp through a cemetery was on her agenda.

By the time she got to the cemetery, the sun hid behind dark clouds and the day looked about how she imagined her emotions to be. Dark, swirling puffs of gray misery.

A glance at the Dulcara Mansion informed her that a large tour was taking place. She could even hear people as she strolled through the back garden and all its crisp fall colors and smells. Winding her way through the worn dirt path, leaves crunching beneath her boots, she came upon the entrance to the Dulcara Cemetery.

The graveyard was old and well kept, a new black iron fence surrounded it, and a large gate looming above her held a copy of the Dulcara family crest, a black dragon with two glowing red stone eyes.

The green lawn was short and thick, the perfect grass, dotted with tiny headstones and statutes. Several mausoleums added a macabre back ground to the idealistic image of the whole space.

As if the graveyard was in a perpetual twilight, everything but the grass and flowers seemed to be made of either grey or a blue green stone and the shadows seemed to move, blocking out the remaining sunlight.

Maddie moved further into the cemetery, noting the place of several old fashion lamp posts which added illumination and chased some of the darkness away. She would not want to be in this place at night.

"Ms. West! Thank you for coming." Professor Heeling stepped out from behind a medium size mausoleum near the back. He brushed his hands on his pants, leaving smears of dirt.

"So, what do we do now?" Maddie asked, already uncomfortable. This was the man who instigated and planned Lucca's second death.

"I believe the box we are looking for is in this particular crypt." He placed a hand on the side of the marble vault.

Maddie thought it was a good guess as this was the plainest crypt in the cemetery. Nothing was carved in the marble but the Dulcara name, no pictures or epitaphs. The door was simple, iron and metal, nothing adorned it like some of the others, no tiny window or flowers decorated the sides, it simply existed in the space, unassuming.

"How do you know?"

"Deduction, history, and common sense," Heeling answered. His statement made no sense, but Maddie let it go.

"Let's do this," Maddie said.

Heeling turned to the door, it opened with ease, surprising Maddie. No lock, no key?

He must have seen her surprise, Heeling stopped half in and out of the door way, nothing but murky darkness behind him.

"The historical society has keys to all the tombs here. It was easy enough to obtain." Then the darkness swallowed him as he went inside. "Coming, Ms. West?"

Maddie followed, noting how musty and stale the air smelled. Her eyes adjusted to the dark as Heeling turned on a flashlight. Turning in a circle, she looked at the tiny room. There were shelves on the walls, a few empty stone vases, and nothing else. No coffins or urns, nothing to suggest this was used for its true purpose.

"There's nothing here," she said.

"There has to be!" Heeling exclaimed, the yellow glow of his flashlight searching every inch, every corner. She could see his face in the light, he looked angry.

"What were you expecting?"

"A box full of dirt, a casket filled with Romanian earth."

"Maybe we're in the wrong one?"

"You!" He spun to face her, pointing an accusing finger. "You must know where she's hidden it. You've been in her thrall long enough. Tell me! Let me save you, save Arcata!"

Maddie took a step back from the crazy man in the mausoleum.

"I didn't have a clue about this until you all started talking about it."

"Liar!"

"Maybe it wasn't a box?" Maddie hoped her suggestion was helpful since she was seconds away from bolting from this weird man and the strange environment.

"That must be it!" He smiled and then began furiously searching the room.

Maddie stood still, inching her way closer and closer to the door, wanting to leave.

"Ah ha!" Finally, Heeling knelt, hands disappearing into a corner of the room. He bounced back into standing position, the excitement on his face resembling a child on Christmas.

"What is it?" Maddie asked. It had to be something amazing, right? Or else Heeling got a kick out of odd stuff.

He held out his hand, clutched in his grip was a blue, velvet satchel.

"A fancy lady's purse?"

"No, child...it's what is inside it." With shaking hands, he opened the bag. Inside was a zip lock filled with rich, deep brown soil. Ripping open the zip lock, he spread the dirt all over the ground, happily stamping on it.

"Ok, we found it, what next? Can we leave?"

"No, we must make sure she cannot use it." He pulled out what looked like thin, white crackers.

"Seriously? The host? Isn't that some Catholic communion shit? Where did you even get that?" Maddie asked.

"That's not important, here, crumple these and spread them all over the dirt, then the vampire won't be able to use it." He held out the host to her.

Desperate to get this strange task over with, Maddie took the host. They burned, hissing. She dropped them to the ground and gripped her hand to her chest, what had he done to them? Put acid on them?

"What the fuck?"

"As I suspected, Valora has already begun to make you into one like her, you cannot bare the touch of a holy object." Heeling said, a smug expression filling his features.

"Impossible, you must have laced them with something." The denial felt stupid; she knew he was correct.

"Laced with something that burns you and not me? Please, Ms. West, you are getting an A in my class. I know you're smarter than that." Leaning down, he took the host and began to break it into pieces, leaving little shards in the dirt.

"Do not worry, we shall kill Valora and you will be free. I'm sorry I caused you pain, but we had to know how deep her poison went. Deeper than I thought, which is unfortunate." Straightening, he made eye contact with Maddie.

"You said if you kill her that will change, right?" It felt like such a betrayal to Valora to even utter those words.

"Yes, but for now you can't be trusted. I'm sorry, Ms. West. My research has shown that the vampire can use you against us." Heeling brushed past her.

The jolt of disbelief she felt was like a brand searing into her skin as he slammed the door of the mausoleum. She darted to the metal and pounded on it, the flesh on her fist turning a light shade of pink as it encountered the cooling, hard obstruction.

"Are you kidding me?" she screamed, hand going to her pocket and pulling out her phone.

"I'm sorry Ms. West. I can't have Valora Dulcara aware of our plans. I'll send someone for you in a few hours."

"I'll freeze before then or starve!" The sentence was a gross exaggeration; she probably wouldn't do either, but fear was filling her veins and her phone registered no signal.

A pause and then a chuckle. "You will not, such dramatics from a Women's Studies major. Not surprising."

"My friends will not be okay with this. I will go to the school board or the police." She tried to hold back her tears but knew he could hear her fright and anger. She wouldn't cry, she'd spent too many of the past weeks crying.

"If you do, I will have no choice but to let them know about your intimate relationship with Valora Dulcara. Your friends may not be happy about this incident, but they and you will understand. It's for your own good."

She heard his footsteps move away from the door. It was dark, the only was light from her phone.

"You're a nutter!" she screamed at the receding sounds, knowing Professor Heeling was getting further and further away.

"This can't be helping. Oh, Lucca, what have I gotten myself into?" Maddie sank down to the floor, back against the icy door. She shivered until it warmed from her body heat. It wasn't super cold, but if he left her in here long enough it would become so. Jo and the girls wouldn't be okay with this, right?

Arms tight around herself, she thought about Lucca and how much she missed him. She wished he was there with her, or at least still alive. Even if her so called friends thought Heeling's behavior was explainable, Lucca would never condone him shutting her up anywhere, especially a tomb.

Madeline? Are you hurt? What's going on?

Relief surged through her, Valora! She'd forgotten their amazing and impossible connection.

"No! Heeling shut me up in a mausoleum so I wouldn't follow him to the other dirt sites and tell you!" The ridiculousness of saying it out loud when the voice lived in her mind did not escape her.

He did what? Ah, he must suspect our connection. Sly old fox. I really should have done something about him a long time ago. How long did he say he was keeping you in there?

"I don't know. He said eventually he'd send someone for me. When they were done with all their...plotting...I guess." Why wasn't she offering to come get her?

Do you need help? Would you like me to come to you? Be aware, if I do this, you cannot leave me again. I will not rescue you to have you scorn me again.

Maddie opened her mouth to shout yes and then snapped it closed as the weight of Valora's words hung around her thoughts. Was she okay with this? Is this what she wanted? Her phone locked again, and she pressed it hard, comforted as it lit up and she wasn't surrounded by blackness.

Was it her imagination or was the inside of the mausoleum getting even darker?

Pulling her knees to her chest, she opened the flashlight app on her phone and shone it into the corners, but the light couldn't pierce the all-consuming darkness. It was unnatural and certainly hadn't been there before, the shadows seemed to be moving.

"Are you afraid?" a voice from the dark asked. It wasn't male or female and the sound grated on her nerves. Of course, she was afraid, she knew nothing had been in there a minute ago.

This is it, I'm going to die in here.

"I asked you a question, and no, you're not." Whatever it was chuckled.

"Yes." *Shit.*

"You don't need to be. I just wanted a better look at you. Such profanity from a young lady. I wish I could say I am surprised."

Those words did not comfort her.

"Why?" It took her two tries to get the word out. Fear was filling her up, eventually it would spill out all over the marble.

"I am not here to harm you...today."

"What or who are you?" If she didn't keep talking, she might pass out.

"Too complicated a question for our short time."

Maddie didn't know what else to say.

"Did you enjoy the dreams I sent you?"

"You sent the dreams? Were they your eyes?" Maddie asked.

"Do they look like mine?"

Suddenly two glowing, fiery eyes appeared in the dark, inhuman and frightening.

Maddie swallowed the scream trying to force its way from her mouth. She pushed her back against the door, wishing she could get further away. She shook her head no and the thing occupying the shadows laughed again.

The eyes blinked and were gone.

"They were Valora's eyes," it said.

"Why?" Again, it took her longer than she wanted to admit saying the simple word.

"I can only tell you three things. Would you like to hear them?"

"Yes." It was here for a reason, as frightened as Maddie was, she had to know why.

"You were meant for Valora. Ask her whatever stupid questions your fragile mortal mind wants but know it won't matter." Its voice seemed to get harder to listen to with every word, her ears hurt.

"You may not tell Valora you spoke to me, or I will come back for you."

Maddie had no doubt that was true.

"Embrace your new life, Madeline West. It has been forever changed. You have amused me up until this point. Take your own darkness and dive into it."

The darkness lifted and again it was simply the murkiness of the mausoleum. With shaking hands, she aimed her phone's light at the back of the room, it lit up every nook and cranny, yet there was nothing there but dust and age.

Madeline?

Maddie wanted to answer right away, but she needed to know something first.

"Did you kill that guy, the one at the hospital?" She felt stupid talking to herself.

Yes, he long outlived his usefulness. I did not like doing it. He was a...friend.

Maddie could feel Valora's sorrow.

"So, you're not why he went insane?"

No, his family has a history of it. It is possible that keeping Dulcara family secrets does not help, but they are not the cause.

Maddie didn't know what to think or say. It bothered her that Valora could speak so easily of killing, but not as much as it should.

So, do I come for you or not? An answer quickly please, dear girl. I do not have all day. I have my own preparations.

"Yes! Please come get me! I miss you! I want you!" The words tumbled out of Maddie's mouth before she could stop them, and she didn't want to.

A large cracking noise sounded behind her, the door shuddered, and she tumbled back into empty air. Her head and back connected to the ground with a thud and a dull ache radiated through her body. Laying there, she stared straight up into Valora's glowing red eyes.

CHAPTER TWENTY-ONE

Texts between Austin Heeling and Queenie Myles

Niece- I was right. I've left your friend in the cemetery. Collect her when you are done

Oh. I didn't want to think so. I'm on the other side of town. I'll send one of the girls

We may have to dispose of her. If she gets in the way

Like Dead? Like dead dead Maddie? IDK Also- mom says you shouldn't talk like you're prim and proper. You're from SOCAL! LOL

Texts between Queenie Myles and Scarlet Jones

My uncle left Maddie at the cemetery. Can you go get her?

?????He just left her there? Why?

Says Valora's put the vamp mojo on her.

We told her to go with him. We didn't tell her it was a damn test. He's not a doctor.

It's getting cold. Go get her. I bet she's sad. We'll buy her pizza to make it up. Vegetarian pizza.

Yeah, I'm so sure THAT will make her feel better after being ditched. BTW tell Jo to hurry up with the tickets to Romania.

Pizza makes EVERYONE feel better. I'll tell Jo.

Texts between Jolene Harper and Allison Hastings

I think we can use Maddie's connection to Valora to help us.

How so?

Heeling says she's acting vampire like because they are mentally and emotionally connected. I bet we could reverse it.

IDK that sounds like using her. Unless it's for something serious like political gain I don't like the idea of using anyone.

It's a good idea.

Hey, I thought Queenie said Maddie was here in a crypt somewhere? BTW why aren't we pissed he locked her in with dead people? That's not ok.

That's what he said. No, it isn't cool but what else was he supposed to do?

Well she's not here now...Shit, the door to the mausoleum's been ripped off the hinges!

We better get back to the house! Meet you there!

*V*alora's half naked body pressed against Maddie, no sweat or signs of chill, even though the window was wide open, letting in the cool air.

No space lay between them in Maddie's bed, just flesh and feeling, fabric and fascination. Maddie trembled under Valora's hands, nestling deeper into her embrace as the aftershock of her last orgasm faded away.

Maddie's hair was plastered against her face with drying sweat, large breasts swelling against Valora's smaller bosoms.

Maddie touched the spot on her neck where Valora's fangs had just been. The wound was still there, two tiny pin pricks. Normally Valora would lick them afterward and they would vanish. Some sort of weird vampire magic, but she hadn't, not yet.

"Do they hurt?" Valora asked.

"No, just not used to them."

"They match your birth mark. I want to leave them on you forever."

"Why am I naked and you're not?" Maddie teased, reaching up and tracing Valora's lips with a warm finger. The light in the room faded around them, shadows grew along the walls.

"Because I wanted you to be. We will have plenty of time for me to be naked in the nights ahead," Valora said. She kissed Maddie's finger and slowly pulled away from her, sitting up, no embarrassment showing. Valora studied Maddie as she wound her long, black hair into a knot on the top of her head.

"What are we going to do?" Maddie asked. Gripping the purple sheet, she sat up, though not as gracefully as Valora.

"I need you to do something for me."

"What?"

"Something that insures you can't leave me again."

"I won't, I promise." Maddie knew that leaving Valora was no longer an option, whether it would be healthier for her or not. She wanted to be with her forever, even if that meant giving up her humanity.

"Heeling and your friends have become too big of a problem, I cannot deal with them here in Arcata, it must be in my homeland," Valora told her. Reaching out a hand she took Maddie's and interlaced their fingers.

"You're leaving soon, isn't that enough?" She didn't like the thought of Valora going without her.

"No, they will come after me and you must help them to do so." The expression on her lover's face was stern and serious.

"I can do that. I just don't understand. Is the situation really that grim?" The idea of getting revenge on Lucca's murderers was appealing.

"Heeling would destroy me, those I care about and everything I have worked for. I got sloppy and it is partially my fault. Hopefully if I go away for a time I can come back to Arcata in a few years and reinvent myself... with you at my side." Valora tugged Maddie's hand and she went to her, inches from her face and all-knowing eyes, so intense.

"I still don't know if I want to be a vampire."

"You will love being with me forever, Madeline. Together we will change the world. You can use your new abilities to fight against misogyny and I have the funds to back any quest you undertake."

"Why did you choose me? I'm not so special." *At least I know why her eyes were in my dreams now.*

Valora touched the red birth marks. "Long ago, someone told me I wouldn't find love again until I met the person who bared my mark without my bite. I know this is you. Have known it since I laid eyes on you. I can feel it, we are the same, you and I."

"Are we evil?" Maddie asked, in a hushed whisper.

"We are beyond good and evil, Madeline. Now will you do something for me? Bind yourself to me and my life force, for eternity?"

"Yes," Maddie whispered, it could only ever have been yes.

"To do what I want there is a special ritual you must take part in." Valora raised a hand to her chest and before Maddie could blink, she used a nail to cut into her skin, a razor fine line that quickly filled with crimson.

A sudden desire rushed through Maddie, a craving. Like when you turn on the AC or heater after it's been off a long while and the scent rushes through your nose and into the back of your mouth; an ozone flavor you will never be able to satisfy. Maddie stared at the blood, mesmerized.

Valora put a hand behind Maddie's head and pushed her until her lips touched the wound, connecting with electricity. Valora sucked in a breath as Maddie began to drink, using her tongue to extract as much blood as she could. Valora made a painful and yet erotic sound and Maddie found herself enraptured in bliss, thinking, this is what it's like if you could lick the pavement after it rains, if you could have the satisfaction of tasting petrichor.

"And you, their best beloved one, are now to me, flesh of my flesh, blood of my blood, kin of my kin, my bountiful wine-press for a while and shall later be my companion and my helper." With Valora's words, Maddie lifted her head, lips stained red and received a heartfelt and tender kiss.

A knock at the door interrupted their peace filled moment. Maddie looked, with panic on her face, to the closed and yet unlocked door.

"Maddie are you in there?" It was Scarlet.

"What do we do?" Maddie asked, afraid.

"You pretend that I am a monster," Valora said. She stood, almost violent and fast.

"Maddie!" Allison; an urgent sounding Allison.

The door slammed opened, the sound of wood on wood, an awful brash thud. Valora growled and shoved Maddie back on the bed, teeth growing, showing pure, white fangs, she snarled at the intruders and dashed to the window. Before the girls could process what they were seeing, Valora was gone, mist in the night.

Maddie frantically clasped a hand to her chest and did something she'd never thought to do, not in a million years. She pretended to faint. Eyes rolling back in her head, she dropped onto the bed, limbs loose, eyes still, face smashed into the bedding, she softened her breathing and tried to calm her heart rate.

"Oh, shit!"

Maddie felt hands on her and smelled dove soap, she knew it was Scarlet. The girl took her pulse and checked her breathing.

"I think she just fainted," Allison's voice sounded from near her feet.

"She's got blood on her mouth and bite marks, it may be more than simple shock, she may have lost too much blood," Scarlet said, worry plain in her voice.

"Go downstairs and tell the others what happened. I'll wake her up and make sure she's not really sick." Scarlet smoothed Maddie's hair away from her face, fingers pressing against the bite mark, trying to stop the minimal bleeding. Maddie wanted to smack her hands away, didn't want her touching a private moment between Valora and herself.

"Jo is going to be angry."

"Jo is always angry."

When Maddie assumed Scarlet was the only one in the room, she fluttered her eyes and slowly opened them. "What...what happened?" she asked, groggy and unsure.

"Valora was in here with you." Scarlet helped her sit up and then made herself busy finding Maddie clothing.

"I don't remember anything after the door being torn away from the mausoleum," Maddie lied. "Oh, the mausoleum! Do I have a few choice words for Professor Heeling?"

"Yeah, none of us are happy about that." Scarlet handed her a deep blue peasants' blouse and a white skirt as well as appropriate under garments.

"Look, Maddie, I don't want to freak you out...but some weird shit was going down in this room. There's blood on your face, and Valora, she looked flat out creepy," Scarlet said.

"She's a monster, I don't know what she's done to me, but I can feel her, in my mind," Maddie cried, mustering up tears.

"See, we want to prevent her from hurting anyone else. Can you, will you help us? Heeling and Jo think they can use this connection to find out where she's going and what she's up to."

"I think I can," Maddie whispered, bowing her head, shamefully. "I'd like to try."

"Then come downstairs with me. We'll figure all this out, I promise. We have a plan."

"Can I take a shower first?"

Scarlet seemed to release a breath she'd been holding, her entire posture relaxed. "You're not a prisoner, you're our friend. Go shower and change. We'll be downstairs when you're ready."

An hour or so later, Maddie descended the stairs and walked into the living room. She hunched a bit, trying to project embarrassment and depression. Her toes, nail polish glittery, peeked out from under her skirt and she dug them into the carpet in the living room, pale little piggys against the sea.

"Maddie, come sit with me." Queenie's delicate yet rough skinned hand encased her wrist and gave a small tug. Maddie allowed herself to be led and sank down next to Queenie on a couch, she finally looked up.

Allison had an expression that was a mix between annoyance and concern, while Scarlet seemed thoughtful. Maddie had known Jo long enough to see the anger and hurt written across her features and had to hide her disgust at the look of anticipation on Professor Heeling's face.

"We need to do a test, Maddie, I'm sorry," Scarlet said from her perch on the opposite couch.

"Another test, didn't he already do one?" Maddie asked.

"I want them to see for themselves," Heeling explained.

"Fine, do what you need to."

Scarlet came over to her and took a crucifix out of her jeans, it was tiny, no bigger than a post it note, silver. She held it up, Maddie flinched as it got closer and closer, when it touched her lower arm she screamed, a real emotion. Searing, burning hot pain and a sick hissing noise.

"Oh, shit!" Scarlet cried, taking the offensive object away from Maddie's skin as tears leaked down Maddie's face.

"That was not good," Queenie commented.

"It is as we feared," Heeling said.

"Didn't we already know this? The host and she barely goes out into the sun," Allison said.

"I'm unclean," Maddie sobbed, drawing on the pain to help force emotion into her words.

"Don't worry, we'll fix it," Queenie said, but her eyes were focused on the burn, and she made no move to get up or help. Scarlet left the room for a moment and came back with burn salve and gauze. She knelt in front of Maddie. The white cotton was awkward to have taped to her arm, but the salve helped with the pain.

"We can't fix it as she's connected to that monster now," Jo's words were filled with bitterness.

"Really, Jo, what have we been talking about if it's not to save and help Maddie?" Allison asked, finally moving her eyes from Maddie to Jo.

"We are going to kill a monster and it just so happens to help Miss West as well," Heeling put in.

"She's a victim too, Jo. Get over your own pain and focus," Allison said.

"You are being soft on her because she's Lucca's sister."

"And you're not even though until a few weeks ago you proclaimed to love her, think on that Jo."

"Enough of this," Heeling said, stopping their argument.

"Yes, I don't like being talked about as if I'm not here," Maddie agreed, trying hard not to appear frustrated and bothered by all of them.

"We've also discussed an additional plan as Valora has fled to her homeland," Heeling said.

"We're going to Romania!" Queenie gushed, even as her uncle frowned at her. "I'm so excited. Mom told me if I take enough pictures, I can put together a photo book and she'll send it to a publisher friend."

"Romania? How are we going to afford that?" Maddie asked. No way were her parents going to cough up the money, especially when they thought she would be in Disneyland over the holiday break.

"Let's just say we pooled our resources," Allison said, which must have been code for Allison and Jo's rich daddies gave them money.

"And passports?" Maddie asked. She had hers from her trip with Lucca over the summer, but surely not everyone did.

"Covered," Scarlet said. "But there's one more thing."

"Isn't there always?" Maddie asked.

"Maddie, my uncle thinks that if we try hypnosis it might allow you to connect with Valora, so that we can find out where she is and what she's doing," Queenie said, softly, patting Maddie's arm like you would a small child's head.

"Hypnosis?" Maddie asked, skeptical.

"I thought the same thing, but it's worth a go, yeah?" Scarlet placed both her hands on Maddie's knees and looked her straight in the face, eager.

"If you think it will help, I'll do it, under one condition."

"And what's that?" Jo barked out her question.

Maddie took a deep breath and lied, it didn't feel as awful as she thought it would. "That if I turn into a vampire you all promise to kill me."

I guess now is the time to see if my lying skills are any good.

CHAPTER TWENTY-TWO

Madeline—

I have asked Orson to deliver this message for me as I am worried you are being monitored. He has been instructed to approach you only if you are alone. Don't worry about his safety, he is much older than some of my other blood kin and Heeling will not recognize him. Orson was one of the first vampires I made after coming to America.

Mircalla, Byron, Vaughn, and I took a late night flight into Bucharest, in fact I am probably still in the air as you read this. It is a twenty hour flight with several stops. If you need to, you can contact me at the Époque Hotel. Leave a message, we will be staying one night.

I own a home in Brasov which is about two hours away from Bucharest. It is called the Villa Curajos, it is easy to find. My blood kin will be staying there while I go on to the ruins of my family's castle. It is hard to find, and I have kept it that way for a reason. They are located past Apata Romania within the Persani Mountains near Paduera Bogatii. It is a dense and rich forest, I wish I could be with you to see your face the first time you see my homeland, it is truly beautiful. I have enclosed a map.

I am already missing you terribly and hope to be with you soon. Do not feel bad about deceiving your friends. Perhaps they should have gotten to know me or treated you with more respect before turning to Heeling and his conspiracy theories. By now, he has told you about how he killed one of my blood kin and his mate—a peace filled couple who never harmed anyone and instead brought joy through their artwork.

Most of my blood kin are harmless, and they look to me to protect them, I am the one who gets my hands dirty. I hope for you to meet more of them in the future.

I love you, dear girl.

Valora.

*M*addie folded the note and put it in her pocket. She'd have to hide it and the map somewhere no one would look. She might just memorize the letter's contents and burn it. She leaned against the door frame, bare toes getting cold from the outside temperate while her back side relished in the warmth from the heater.

"Is there anything else?" she asked the man standing in front of her. He was a very pale, balding man with dark eyes. He wore a black trench coat and matching slacks. With the black night sky behind him, only his white skin made him noticeable.

"Yes," he said, voice deep and soft. He handed her a brown package. She tore into it to find a novel.

It looked old, a hardback with a simple black cover. In gold, it read *Blood Born* by Bethany Stratton. She'd never heard of it, tucking it under one arm she decided to look at it after Orson left.

"Where'd you drive up from?" She assumed drive, though she didn't see a car anywhere, maybe he took the bus?

"I didn't drive up from anywhere, but I am from Reno," Orson said; the smile on his face implied a joke in there somewhere and gave Maddie the creeps.

"Ah, what do you do in Reno?" There had to be a reason Valora chose him, right?

"I am a biochemist."

That actually made sense.

"Well you better go, I'm sure my roommates will be back soon." Plus, she wanted him to leave. She imagined that he must be the kind of vampire who slept in a crypt and used cobwebs as blankets.

"Yes."

She blinked and he was gone, as in disappeared. Maddie gaped at the empty spot in front of the door for several seconds before she closed her mouth and the door.

Jo had gone to get Heeling for their first hypnosis session. They were planning to leave for Romania tomorrow afternoon and wanted as much information as they could get.

Scarlet and Queenie were with her mom and Allison said she needed new clothes for the trip. It surprised Maddie that they left her alone.

Not knowing when they would be back, she darted up the stairs and into her room, her suitcase for the trip was already packed and sitting in the middle of her bed. That would be the best place to put the letter and map, for now. No reason for anyone to go snooping through her things this close to departure time.

A slam downstairs along with the fall of footsteps alerted her to people being home. She just wanted to finish reading her book, eat a few cookies, and go to bed, but instead she had to deal with Jo and Heeling.

"Maddie?"

Her name radiated up the stairs and through the door—Jo.

Opening the door, she frowned and called back, "Coming!"

She made them wait a bit longer than necessary, so all of them were frowning when she finally walked into the living room.

"Are you ready?" Heeling asked.

"Yes, where do you want me?"

"Just lay down on the couch."

Maddie did as instructed trying not to show how irritated she was by all of this. Jo had her arms crossed and stood a few feet away, frowning.

"Are you going to just stare at me the whole time?" Maddie asked.

"Is there something else I should be doing?" Jo asked and Maddie could hear the bitterness leaking into her voice.

"Yes, recording for me." Heeling passed a small recording device to Jo and then focused his attention on Maddie. He kneeled next to her smelling of pine, blue eyes intense.

"I really don't like you." Maddie couldn't stop the words.

"Maddie!" Jo scolded.

Heeling's lips turned up ever so slightly. "I know, but I promise after we free you from Valora, you will find me quite charming."

Laughter rang through Maddie's mind, not her own, but Valora's throaty tones.

"Okay, let's do this." Maddie closed her eyes and took a deep breath.

He won't be able to hypnotize you, dear girl. Just reach toward me with your mind and you will catch thoughts, feelings, and even glimpses of where I am.

Heeling took her hand in his and she wanted to jerk it back, instead she made herself relax. This was going to be just like when she meditated.

"Alright, Maddie, I want you to relax, let all the tension and anxiety flow out of your muscles."

Easier said than done. Taking another deep breath, she thought about how the couch felt and easing the tension from her muscles, letting go of any anxiety. Heeling needed to believe this was working.

"I want you to control your breathing, deep breaths in and out, in through your nose and out through your mouth, feel each breath flow through you."

Maddie did as she was told and started thinking about Valora, what did it mean, reach toward her with her mind, how was that even possible?

A clock began to tick in the background, weird, there wasn't a clock in the living room. She wished Heeling would move farther away, she could smell his orange tic tac breath and didn't like it.

"Focus your attention on the sound of the clock, the tone of each tick. Let your mind become distracted."

She did like the sound it made, very rhythmic. She could still feel her connection with Valora, and with each sound of the clock, it was as if the connection widened, like she could step through it and simply be with her.

"Feel yourself relax even further, in fact you find yourself quite tired, you want to sleep, but you should not."

A nap sounded like such a good idea, could she get up, go back to her room, and have some peace and quiet? No, if she did that now they'd know this was never going to work.

Rumbling sounds of an engine.

"You are relaxing even further, getting to a stage of optimal relaxation."

How many times was he going to use the word relax?

Smells of recycled air and many warm bodies.

"Try and open your eyes," Heeling commanded.

Don't! Don't do or say anything, Valora instructed. Maddie kept her eyes closed, wondering if she started snoring, they would leave her alone.

"Think about Valora Dulcara, imagine her person and her connection to you. Can you see her clearly in your mind, smell her perfume, hear her voice?"

"Yes."

Nothing but land outside the window, feelings that it will be good to be home.

"What do you see? What can you feel? Take it all in."

Feel of soft leather seats.

"I'm so glad I can afford first class, I miss the days of boats and trains," were Valorie's thoughts in Maddie's mind.

"Is it really working?" Jo asked, in a whisper.

Heeling shushed Jo. "Yes, now don't interrupt." He squeezed her hand, a little too tight and she kept herself lax in his grip.

"Do you know where she is?" The eagerness gave a tremble to his voice.

"Yes, I know."

"I am going to count to four and snap my fingers, at the sound you will awaken refreshed and willing to help us."

"One."

Maddie did not want to do this any longer.

"Two."

She really wished she was with Valora.

"Three."

After all the time she and Jo spent together, how could Jo be okay with Heeling treating her like a science experiment. The man had locked her in a mausoleum!

"Four." The sound of a snap and Maddie opened her eyes, blinking against the light.

"Did I do it?"

"I believe so. Tell me what you felt, what you saw," Heeling said.

"Please, Maddie, we need to know if this worked, so we can use it once we are in Romania," Jo said.

"She's in an airplane and is close to landing in Romania. She has a home in Brasov she's looking forward to seeing again," Maddie told them.

"Anything else?" Jo asked.

"What else could there be? It was cold, and I think she's in first class."

"It's enough for now, good job, Miss West." Heeling let go of her hand, standing he stretched, and Maddie heard his back pop, God she didn't want to get old.

Jo came near and offered her a hand up, Maddie considered rejecting it, but didn't. She allowed Jo to help her up off the couch.

"I'll leave you girls to it then, I have some things to wrap up before we leave tomorrow." Heeling packed up a little brown bag Maddie hadn't noticed before. In went a small clock and the room seemed emptier without its noise. Maybe they should invest in one themselves? An old-fashioned coo coo clock with a tiny little bird living in it, or heavy silver one with roman numerals.

"Maddie, I want to talk to you," Jo said before Maddie could slip from the room.

"About?"

"Us."

Maddie inwardly groaned, this wasn't a conversation she wanted to have.

"So, talk."

Jo's frown was a perfect combo of pout and irritation, the creases in her forehead like tiny roads. "Why are you being like this? You were never like this before."

Maddie sighed. Digging her feet into the rug, she played with the edge of her dark green tank top, trying to decide how to tell Jo how she was feeling.

Everything was different now. After drinking Valora's blood, it was like they were one person and there could never be room for anyone else. Maddie knew it should frighten her, but she didn't care. All she could think about was Valora.

"What do you mean before?" Maddie stalled for time, she really didn't know what to say. When Valora was drinking from her, there was a connection, one she never had with Jo and now...now it was like there was an invisible cord between them pulsing with deep and rich emotions.

Jo walked over to the window. "You know, before Valora Dulcara came into our lives."

The windows of the room were dark, the occasional beam of light from a passing car splashed against the wall. Maddie followed its pattern, sad when it winked out.

"That was before Lucca died and I found out we based our relationship on a lie." She finally decided on a partial truth, even though saying Lucca's name still hurt. Lifting her head, she could tell Jo was upset by her words. It seemed like all they did lately was hurt each other. What did she expect?

"I loved Lucca too, Maddie, I know how much he meant to you. I know I should have told you about the book much sooner, but I didn't know how."

"You weren't at his memorial service."

"I was there, at the end." Jo's thin lips flattened even further, and Maddie hoped the emotion in her eyes was guilt, but Jo didn't believe in regret.

"Yes, with Professor Heeling to ambush me, and then I found out our whole relationship was a lie."

"And you ran off to be with Valora Dulcara. You should be grateful I can even look at you, knowing you've been with that thing."

"You killed him, or did you forget that detail."

"I didn't kill Lucca, I helped kill a monster."

"Then why did you want to talk?" Maddie shut down. Why did Jo think Maddie owed her even a second of her time? A sound in the distance caused a flare of anxiety inside her breast.

They needed to speed this up. She'd heard a car and really didn't want an audience for their drama.

"I miss you."

Maddie could give her this, at least. "I miss you too." It was true, Jo and she had been together long enough that this separation was no longer about being romantically entangled as it was losing a friend.

"Do you think we could try again?"

Maddie heard footsteps on the porch. She froze, was it unusual she could or was this a side effect of her relationship with Valora? Jo wasn't acting like she knew anyone was outside.

"Face it, Jo, we were falling apart long before any of this craziness went down. I'm not the same girl you fell in love with. I want to be friends, let's start with that." Two truths and a lie.

Key in the front door.

The door opened, and the sound of Allison's voice greeting them rang through the room.

"You'll think differently once we break this hold Valora has on you." Jo huffed and stormed from the room.

"Did I interrupt something?" Allison asked, looking perfect as always, but sincerely concerned.

"No, we've been done for a while."

CHAPTER TWENTY-THREE

Mom—'Cause you asked, here's our info for the trip—Love Scarlet
P.S. Don't worry, I'll stop and try to buy medical journals in Bucharest.

Travel Itinerary
Teacher: Austin Heeling
Students: Queenie Myles, Scarlet Jones, Jolene Harper, Madeline West
Depart: December 10th
Delta Airlines SFO – CDG 3:10:00 p.m.- 10:10 p.m.
Lay over in Paris 1 hr 40 mins
Depart: CDG- OTP 12:30 a.m.- 4:20 p.m.
Arrive in Bucharest 4:20 p.m. December 12th
Train to Brasov, Romania 2 hr 45 min
Check in Hotel Decebal around 8:00 p.m. December 12
December 14th
Drive to Apata, Romania- Planning to arrive around 8:00 a.m. and be back in Brasov by midnight
December 16th
Same basic flight just in reverse- I've included copies of all flight number and phone numbers just in case.
Departing 6:50 a.m. arriving in San Francisco 12:35 am on December 17th

"*Y*ou think we should split up? Is that wise?" Scarlet asked. They were huddled into one of the two hotel rooms they checked into only nine hours prior.

They were staying at a small hotel in Brasov, Romania. It was a narrow multi storied hotel, white on the outside and looked old, but nice. The rooms were brown and red, clean, pleasant, and basic. The room Maddie was in had a red tiled bathroom, a balcony, and large windows. A small box TV sat in one corner and a tall green plant in another.

There were two queen size beds and a roll out. Heeling had his own room, lucky bastard, while they were packed in like sardines.

"Isn't it bad enough I'm forced to share a bed, let alone not get enough sleep?" Allison huffed, she sat on the edge of the bed she was forced to share with Jo.

Maddie rubbed the grit from her eyes. She was suffering jet lag and simply wanted a hot shower, a good meal, and more sleep. Instead, she'd been woken up at 5:00 a.m. after only being asleep five hours, to be told more craziness. A crick in her back made its presence known as she stretched. Queenie did volunteer to sleep on the roll out, but Maddie took it instead; she thought Queenie and Scarlet would be more comfortable sleeping together. Everyone was giving her side-eye since they got to Romania.

It didn't help that in the last "hypnosis" session she'd given them near to nothing but let a laugh slip at something Valora told her. In retrospect, she probably should have paid more attention to what was going on around her, not inside her.

"Yes, from what Miss West told us, Valora owns a home here in Brasov, and the trances have provided us with an address. Some of us should go there, while the rest head to Apata and try to figure out the location of the castle," Heeling explained.

"This is the time in horror movies where I usually say, 'No! Bad idea!'" Allison told them.

"Why would going to her house here matter?" Queenie asked. She was covered from head to toe, only her eyes visible from the amount of winter clothes she had on. It was much colder than she could have even imagined.

"Even though Maddie's been helpful, I am worried that Valora could be using the connection to gain insight to our actions as well. When I tried to hypnotize her just now, it didn't work as well as it has, this causes me great concern," Heeling clarified.

"We don't even know where we're going," Scarlet pointed out.

"Maddie has a map," Jo announced. Everyone turned to look at her and the room fell dead silent. She held the rolled map in her left hand, squeezing it hard enough it was wrinkled.

Maddie didn't even move, she stayed still, anger pooling in her belly, how like Jo to decide to go through her things. Thankfully she'd destroyed the letter.

"Maddie?" Queenie's word held a bit of betrayal.

"I've had it for a while now." Not a total lie. "Valora gave it to me." Complete truth. "I thought it might be helpful, I was going to give it to you if you guys gave me a chance." Flat out lie.

"Why did you go through her things?" Allison asked, accusatorily.

"She's been in league with the enemy before, probably still is." Jo shrugged; she met Maddie's eyes and flinched.

"Let me see that." Heeling snatched it from Jo's hand, spread it open on the bed, and began to study it, making soft little mmm hmmm noises every few seconds.

Finally, he stopped, and a sinister smile crept over his features. "Yes, this will work." Standing, he began conducting them like an orchestra.

"Maddie and I will go the house, the rest of you will take the train and travel to the location on this map. We will meet you there if nothing is at the house."

"Now?" Maddie asked.

"Now."

They weren't planning to check out of the hotel, so each of them packed a small bag. The goal was to be back at the hotel before the morning, if all went as planned.

Aside from some eccentricities, they all were dressed similar. There was snow on the ground, and the high for the day was said to be ten degrees. They all wore lace up waterproof boots with good traction, warm socks, and jeans. Most of them had on some sort of thermal underwear as well.

Allison bought them all varying shades and textures of parkas as early

Christmas presents. Maddie's was blood red with faux black fur trim along the hood, while Jo's was army green. Allison's idea had been so good the rest of the girls followed.

Queenie bought them all handmade scarves to "match" their personality, so while Maddie's was red and black, Queenie herself had a scarf of gold and bronze. Maddie's contribution? Black flip top fingerless gloves while Jo purchased ear muffs, sunscreen, and sunglasses for the troop and made them each a list of what needed to go in their packs for winter hiking.

Scarlet insisted they each have chapstick, lotion, and hand warmers for their packs and gave a lecture from her mom on what could happen to them if they got frostbite.

Finishing off her look, Maddie pulled on a thick silver sweater and she was ready to go. She didn't want to be alone with Professor Heeling after last time but didn't think she had much of a choice.

When they got done dressing and making sure they wouldn't freeze to death or starve in the outdoors, Maddie asked the question that had been bothering her.

"Aren't we worried about the vampires being awake?"

"Don't worry, we will wait until the sun comes up," Heeling said.

"But at home they are out and about in the daylight," Maddie argued.

"Yeah, we think they can be awake, but their powers are diminished by the sun. However, without their native earth they will be even more helpless, hopefully asleep," Queenie explained.

"Wouldn't it be better to wait until the sun has risen, I checked, it won't rise until after 7:30 am," Scarlet said.

"We don't have the time. I want to get to them the moment they head to their daytime rest," Heeling said.

"Even though they don't act like normal vampires?" Maddie was confused, his logic didn't follow normal paths. What if they'd simply brought their native earth with them? His need for revenge against Valora made him reckless, which would work in their favor, in the end.

He knows too much, I should have killed him years ago. You should know, when he makes it into the house during the day, he will be correct, they will be asleep. They are not fully turned, which means they cannot yet use the earth as I can. I can carry it with me, theirs must be always be beneath their feet. Valora whispered into her mind.

Maddie didn't understand. Didn't Valora realize that Heeling would come here, and they wouldn't be safe? Why had she left them unprotected?

I didn't, do not worry.

"But not Valora, right? She won't have these same rules?" Allison asked.

"She's too damn ancient, it's why we came here so fast, we destroyed her supply of soil back home," Jo answered.

"That's not entirely true, Jo," Heeling said, the smile on his face unpleasant. "I left something out of my research, something I didn't want documented."

"Uncle?" Queenie seemed as confused as the rest of them felt.

"I'm sorry, Queenie, but it was safer this way. Remember the tale I told you, the one you frightened them with when you went camping?"

They all nodded, it had been a good story.

"What I left out was that in the tale the mother makes a bargain with the devil and in it a rule is made. She must return to her home once every six years and sleep for one whole night, without protection from elements or people. This is on top of the other restrictions I've already mentioned. Inconvenient, but a small price for immortality and eternal youth." Heeling was like a proud papa, boasting over his child's accomplishments.

"Is that really true?" Maddie asked. She wasn't speaking to them, but they need not know that.

Yes, in a few hours I will sleep in the place my children were born, do not fret so. My life is long, and I have many powers, but they are not without rules, like anything else.

How could she not fret? This meant their ridiculous plan may actually work!

"Yes, it is, don't doubt me now, Miss West. Let's get to it, shall we?" Heeling's answer held bite, like he couldn't believe she was second guessing him.

While the girls went to procure tickets to the local train, Heeling and Maddie took the rental car to find Villa Curajos.

The car they rented was small and Maddie figured would barely fit all of them when they met up and Heeling seemed to sweat at the idea of driving on the wrong side of the road.

Speaking only a few words of the local dialect, Maddie was of no help trying to locate Valora's home. Eventually, with only an hour lost going down wrong streets they finally found the house. It was about ten minutes outside Brasov proper and down a long lane so that the house could not be seen from the main road way.

The house was beautiful, a perfect two-story villa with porches that wrapped around the first and second floor. Maddie was surprised by the amount and size of the windows and that it was a buttercup yellow siding that met stone. The entry way curved, and the roof came to several points, one that looked like a small tower.

Heeling didn't try to mask their arrival. He pulled the car into the front yard, parked, and slammed the door when he got out.

He sprayed them both with his herbal concoction, it made Maddie sneeze.

Maddie followed him, her eyes never leaving the house, she knew Valora wasn't in there, but she was sure her "brides" were.

"Stand here. I'm sorry, Miss West, but I can't trust you," Heeling said, he pulled out a bottle of water and began to sprinkle it in a circle around her, then he broke up tiny pieces of the host and placed them on top of the circle.

"Is that holy water?" Maddie asked, the water combined with the host made her uncomfortable, her skin itched, and when she tried to step over it, tiny pinpricks of pain seemed to run across her skin.

"Stay in the circle as it will protect all of us." He put out a hand stopping her and crossed in himself. "I know it's uncomfortable for you, but trust me, it will keep us safe."

"Coming here at night was stupid," Maddie said.

"It was a tactical choice. They will go back to their beds as the sun rises and I shall destroy them." He pulled out a small tarp from his vampire hunting bag and put it on the ground, motioning for Maddie to sit.

Maddie figured he had ideas about coffins and crypts, but she was sure they slept in beds like regular people. She also found the excitement in his voice disgusting and disturbing.

"Do you want them to come out here and try to kill us?"

"They can try, but they won't succeed." Light sparkled in his eyes.

"You're enjoying this too much." Maddie sat on the ground, shivering, curling her legs underneath her. It was still an hour to sunrise.

"Did Queenie tell you about my ex-wife?"

Maddie simply nodded.

"It was an exhilarating kill, gave my life even more purpose. This is going to be a great day." It was as if Heeling thought he'd already succeeded.

"Maddie."

Her voice came softly to them and Maddie felt the strong urge to answer it.

"Maddie." This time louder. She swiveled around trying to find the source, it didn't sound like Mircalla or Byron.

"Maddie." The call again and the urge deep in her stomach to stand and step over the holy water circle got stronger.

It is Vaughn. They are drawn to you now that my blood flows in you. I will have cause to regret this later, but I can do nothing about it now. I should have left them in California. They would have more strength there.

Maddie found him coming from behind the house, he practically floated, gliding across the snow almost colorless in the moonlight. The only color brief splashes of sun in the distance adding to the deepness of the shadows and the ominous appearance of the area.

"They come. I knew they would," Heeling muttered. He had a stake in one hand and a gun in the other. Had he confused them with werewolves all of the sudden?

Maddie turned to face him. "You knew?" Oh, that made much more sense. She was the lure to make sure he could fulfill his sick fantasy of killing more vampires.

Just another reason her connection to Valora made her happy, He couldn't truly use her to hurt Vaughn and the others, not when she'd been playing him as well.

"What are you doing with this old man, Maddie? Come inside with me." Vaughn was closer now, his skin pale and his hair a stark contrast black and curling down over his shoulders. His eyes were black holes in his face surrounded by a thin rim of white. He wore a white shirt and black slacks, his feet bare.

"Don't answer him," Heeling commanded.

Maddie wanted to but knew to obey Heeling.

"Come inside where it's warm and be with family, your true family,"

Vaughn insisted. He sneered at Heeling. "We can kill him together, I know you have found a taste for blood."

Maddie glanced at Heeling and the pulse pounding in his neck. Is this what taking blood from Valora had done to her? Was she really craving the red riches found beneath his skin?

It is a side effect, dear girl, but one you don't yet need act on. Just ignore it, I am sorry, this was...unforeseen. I thought he had more control, or I never would have brought him. It seems even after all these years I am not infallible.

"Don't listen to him, Miss West, you are stronger than the hold that vampire bitch has over you."

"Where are the others?" Maddie asked, more to herself than anyone else. She worried about Valora but seeing her make an active mistake made her fall in love with her a little more. She'd worried Valora was too perfect, but she wasn't.

"They are cowardly, they stay inside, but I could feel your flame, the life force in your veins that echoes my own," Vaughn said, his feet were just an inch away from the circle, she could smell his cologne and see the puffs of air his breath made.

"Go back inside, Vaughn, please." Maddie couldn't help it. With Heeling looking at him like he wanted to take his head and mount it on a wall somewhere and Valora sounding miserable in her head, she was suddenly very worried for him.

"Don't speak to him, Miss West!" Heeling thrust out the stake, showing a silver crucifix was attached. Vaughn smirked, but it did cause him to back up a few steps, his eyes never leaving Maddie's face.

Maddie noticed new colors coming into view as the sun began to rise in the distance. Against the black came a cold blue, a deep purple and a fiery red. The darkness and shadows on the ground fled from the warmth, slipping away against the house and plants.

"The sun, Vaughn." She had to warn him, he seemed so focused on her. If he was still out here when it came up would it burn him? Would Heeling pounce on him and shove the stake in his chest?

He will not burn, but it will be like a very bad sunburn and he will struggle to keep awake. I must break off contact now, dear girl. I am sorry.

Vaughn cried out, not in anguish or surprise but in longing. "Please come with me, you feel like my mistress and you should not be out here, especially with him," he begged, one hand out.

She shook her head and Vaughn fled, back the way he came, disappearing, she assumed, into the house.

"We shall give it a few moments, then I will go inside. You will stay out here, if I am not back in one hour, find the others, and leave this place," Heeling said, looking upon her with disappointment.

"They know you're coming, they will kill you," Maddie told him, one last attempt to save his life.

"They will be weak and asleep. You just saw it. He could not be out here with the daylight. My predictions were correct. Without native soil these three are helpless," Heeling argued. He crossed the circle and walked away.

"You don't know that!" Maddie screamed after him, certain she was watching a man walk to his death.

CHAPTER TWENTY-FOUR

Transcript from Professor Austin Heeling's Digital Voice Recorder

Static.

    Footsteps.

    A cough, low and muffled.

    Metal against metal, clicks and clanks.

    HUSHED WHISPERS: Personal log of AH—not using my full name in case this comes into the hands of someone in authority, even though they may not believe any of it.

    I am going into the Villa Curajos and had used a standard lock pick to get through the back door. My goal? To confront and kill three vampire suspects. MW is waiting outside in a circle of holy water and host.

    A door opening.

    AH: The house is dark, not empty or abandoned, but like the entire house is asleep. I am using a low watt flashlight. I don't want to announce my presence, though if they are awake, they will have already heard me. My handy spray, however, prevents the monsters from sensing or smelling me.

    Breathing.

    AH: I believe I will be able to find and destroy all three without much fuss. If I act fast enough. My hypothesis has been proven, these young vampires are weak

weakest. He could not protect himself and so he perished. I, however, am stronger." Mircalla had a feral smile on her face.

"Byron?"

"In the basement, cowering."

"Basement?"

"More like a storm cellar. It's not attached to the house."

Confusion flooded Maddie. Hadn't Heeling bragged about killing other vampires? Mircalla could kill him easily enough. Why was Mircalla awake and powerful enough to kill him? Is this what Valora meant when she said she hadn't left them without defenses?

"Your thoughts are in your eyes." Mircalla sighed in a resigned and annoyed way as she glanced at the rising sun and put her hands on her hips.

"Your Professor Heeling was a fool. Because he killed young and inexperienced vampires in the past, he thought we would be easy prey as well."

"Why didn't you save Vaughn? If he was asleep and defenseless how could you let Heeling murder him?" The poor boy, Maddie wished she could have saved him, though Mircalla seemed to have a survival of the fittest mentality.

"To lure Heeling into complicity I had to give him something, Valora will understand," Mircalla explained, her tone becoming increasingly more exasperated.

Maddie wondered if Valora would understand. Couldn't she mourn his passing? Would there be some sort of celebration of his life or funeral for his death? What was the protocol for vampire funerals? Had she used Maddie to kill Heeling? Could Maddie live with herself if she had? Mircalla didn't seem upset about her blood kin's death. Did Valora have similar feelings, and if she didn't care about Vaughn's death what did that mean for their relationship?

"You are strong and passionate, Madeline West, a good choice for Valora to make. I do not hate you as you believe, but you are too soft hearted and too human." Mircalla leaned forward and placed her hands on both sides of Maddie's head. Instantly, calmness and serenity filled her as did understanding. Heeling had been threatening Valora and her people, it was only right he die. Vaughn's death was sad, but as Mircalla said, sometimes sacrifices must be made for the good of the many. None of this meant Valora was a chaotic evil or that her feelings for Maddie were disingenuous.

"I must go now," Mircalla said, glancing at the sky again. "If I have answered enough of your questions? Why this has been left up to me I'll never know."

"You said the sun doesn't bother you."

"It doesn't because only those blood kin without their native soil, or the very young, have that particular weakness. I would, however, like to sleep before the others wake up."

"So, you're not..."

"Young, nor am I human. Now I want to have a bath and clean up after the professor's visit."

Maddie's mind reeled for a moment at the information, Mircalla was a vampire...pretending to be blood kin? What?

"Have you not figured it out yet?" Mircalla asked.

If a lightbulb could form over one's head and go off, Maddie imagined that it would have happened there and then. In her mind, she saw the portrait in Valora's room.

"It's you. You're her daughter," Maddie breathed.

"And lucky for you not the crazy one."

Maddie had nothing to say. She was too busy taking in this new piece of information.

"You should find your friends and Valora," Mircalla said, actively trying to get rid of her.

"Will she really be asleep?" Maddie asked, trying to keep up with the conversation.

"Yes, and alone. I will kill you should your friends succeed in harming her, know that, Madeline West." Mircalla gave a head tilt and turned to go back inside.

Fear bled into Maddie as she watched her go; she didn't doubt for a second Mircalla would keep her word.

"Oh, and Madeline?" Mircalla didn't even turn around, she stood in the doorway, mostly inside, ready to shut out the daylight.

"Yes."

"If you haven't yet, I'd read that book, especially chapter twenty-two."

The door slammed shut without Mircalla touching it, and Maddie jumped at the noise.

Maddie got into the small rental car and started the engine, the feel of the heater coming on was a Godsend and she spent a few seconds soaking up the heat before sending a quick text to her friends. Then she took out the map and placed it on the dashboard.

Grabbing her bag from the back seat, she dug out the novel. She hadn't read it yet, but she'd done some research. Blood Born was printed in the early 1900s and was very unpopular. Most copies were lost in a fire, and it was now a collector's item for rare manuscripts.

She flipped through to chapter twenty-two; if Mircalla wanted her to read it, it must be important.

CHAPTER TWENTY-FIVE

Blood Born

Chapter 22

"You should have called for me when she got out of control," I say, looking at my youngest daughter, my Mira.

"I thought I could handle her," Mira says; she is pouting, over three-hundred years old and she still pouts like I found her coloring on her bedroom walls.

"Obviously not." I take in the carnage. It is an entire wagon train, women, men, children...all slaughtered. A waste. I could not drink this much blood if I wanted to. Instead, most of it stains the green grass and is sprayed upon trees.

Cows and oxen are restless a few feet from us, they know what we are, but they are not afraid, only wary.

"Where is she? Where is Miriam?" I walk through the death, it reeks like rotten meat, rusted iron, and feces. I don't know what I'm going to do. I'll have to clean this up, cover it up somehow, my mind reels with options.

"I locked her up. She's in our wagon. Rainier is standing guard," Mira admits.

"You left her alone, with Rainier? What made you think this was a good idea?" When I told them to leave our home, I hoped for better outcomes than this. They both have so much potential, they are brilliant and strong blessed with immortality and strength.

They are flawed, however. Mira is too optimistic and greedy, Miriam is weak and lacks self-control.

"California is the new frontier, there is money to be made and a new life to live! We wanted an adventure, we've become bored," Mira explains.

"You brought Miriam all this way, surrounded by humans and isolated. Of course, this was the outcome." We are closer to their wagon and I can hear my eldest daughter's shrieks.

"We could make this place ours, Mama. You've been wanting a change, stay here with us," Mira says. Her idea has merit, but she cannot stay, she cannot be linked to this and her sister, she cannot continue unchecked.

"That's not a bad idea, but you must go. I have your mess to clean up and you cannot be here."

"You would send us from you again?" Pain radiates in her words. Her blue eyes are filled with confusion and hurt.

———

Bethany Stratton

"Just you. Miriam must stay with me. She cannot be left on her own." I approach the wagon and Rainier, who is sitting on the ground, tips his hat at me. He is a good man and his family has served us for years.

I lift the back flap, my daughter, my spitting image, sits tied up with ropes laced with holy water. I can see the burns in her flesh and hear the hissing as the holy liquid touches her flesh, it has weakened her.

She gazes up at me through half closed eyes, covered in blood, hair and clothes matted with it. Shame flickers over her features and she begins to cry.

"I'm so sorry, Mama," she whispers.

"Don't fret so, I will take care of it, of you." It is not like I have anything else to do. "I will help build a town here and I will hide you in it."

I turn to Mira. "In a century or so, you will return to me as well." I tuck a strand of blonde hair behind one of her ears, she has a smudge of blood on her nose.

"What will happen to me?" Miriam asks.

"I am going to lock you up, so you can't hurt anyone."

Her cries echo well into the night.

———

*M*addie pulled into a gravel parking lot, though the word parking lot might be too generous. The building in front of her looked more like someone's home than a restaurant. Apata was a tiny town, nothing more than a village in Transylvania that was near the Persani Mountains and the wildlife refuge Padurea Bogatii. Apata consisted of more than a dozen stone houses with thatched roofs and farms all centered on a church. People looked at her, not suspiciously, but in curiosity, as she drove by.

Her thoughts were still on what she read. Was it the story of Valora and her daughters? The chapter talked about how the mother helps build a town in California, founds a hospital, and locks her crazy daughter away. Was Miriam real? Was she still locked away in one of the hospitals, on which Valora was on the board? Was this the daughter that killed the Ceres? Or was it Mircalla?

Rubbing her temples, she stilled her thoughts and cleared her mind. Now was not the time. She had to deal with her friends and Heeling's death.

She parked and opened the door, rubbing her eyes. What she really wanted was a cup of coffee and a bed, not to be hunting down an ancient vampire. She also did not want to be the bearer of bad news. Queenie's reaction to her uncle's death was bound to be bad. They were close.

So much death, her thoughts strayed to Lucca; he'd laugh at her if he knew what she was doing right now. She wished she could ask his advice.

He would laugh, Lucca was always in such good spirits. He would find this all ridiculous.

At least the drive to Apata was nice. While the road was narrow and twisted, it was beautiful. Mountains loomed against the horizon and dark trees and other foliage crowded the road. She imagined during warmer months it was prettier with more colors, but it didn't matter. Even the naked trees gave the area its own unique splendor. There was snow on the ground, but the roads were clear, the snow fall hadn't been recent.

Stepping from the car, she took a deep breath, filling her lungs with biting cold fresh air; it stung her cheeks, but felt good. Gravel mixed with snow crunched under her boots as she went up to the tiny white building, looking for the entrance. The sunshine hit her, and a prickly stinging inched across her hands and face. she needed to get out of the daylight.

A brown, wooden door that seemed to see better days had the establishment's name and hours posted. How the girls even knew to come here to get something to eat was beyond her. She turned an old, brass doorknob and walked in. The room was dim, the walls russet stone meeting hardwood floors that no longer had any shine to them. Several tables were scattered around the room, none of them vacant. Many of the patrons looked up when she opened the door, but quickly went back to their business.

Maddie's stomach growled at the scent of food in the air.

A bar in one corner had a woman standing behind it. She was robust with large, dark eyes and black hair streaked with gray tied in a braid. She smiled and came bustling forward.

"You are with the Americans, yes?" she asked, her English halting.

"Yes."

"This way."

Maddie followed her as they weaved in between tables, making their way to the back of the room next to a curtained doorway where Maddie could hear cooking.

"Maddie!" Queenie exclaimed, standing when she saw her.

"Thank you," Maddie told the woman, before being embraced by the blonde girl.

"I will bring you food," the woman said and left them alone.

"She will?" Maddie asked as Queenie pointed out an empty chair.

"Whether you want her to or not," Scarlet said, laughing. They all had plates of half eaten food and cups of coffee. Allison took an empty red mug and poured the hot, black liquid from a pot in the middle of the table, the bitter aroma flooded Maddie's nose and she wanted to drool.

"Where's my uncle?" Queenie asked.

Maddie burned her tongue on the hot liquid, taking a quick sip as she considered what to say. Turning somber eyes on Queenie she told the truth.

"He underestimated Valora's TAs. I think he killed one, but, I'm so sorry, Queenie... He didn't make it." Digging into her purse, she took out the digital recorder and placed it on the table.

"What? No, that's not possible." Queenie slumped in her chair and tears filled her eyes. She reached out a shaking hand and gripped the recorder.

Now for the partial lie. "I was so scared. Mircalla brought this out to me, I didn't think she was going to let me go, but I was still in the holy water circle. When the sun rose too high, she fled back into the house, and I escaped."

"Here, eat something." Allison passed a pastry that seemed to be filled with cheese and raisins. Maddie gratefully took a bite; she was starving. Though the food was good, it wasn't fulfilling the sensation of craving.

"I can't believe it, what am I going to tell my mother?" Queenie asked, clutching the recorder to her chest looking pale and in disbelief.

"We'll think of something," Jo said as she leaned over and squeezed her shoulder. "We all knew that this was a dangerous mission."

The woman came back and put a bowl of yellow porridge and a plate full of eggs and black sausage in front of Maddie.

"Thank you," she said again. The woman took the coffee carafe with her as it was empty now.

"Please, I so did not think someone would die. Maybe we should go home," Allison suggested.

"You'd give up so easily? I thought you loved Lucca. Valora murdered him and you would let her go. Heeling knew this could be dangerous and we're so close," Jo argued.

"Yes, Uncle Austin would want us to continue," Queenie said, sniffling.

"We're really going to go find her and kill her?" Allison asked.

"We did come all this way, and if we don't then what will happen to Maddie?" Scarlet pointed out.

"I may not be safe, but all of you would be. I'm willing to take that risk," Maddie said, picking up a fork and digging into the food, it smelled beyond delightful.

"No, Jo's right. I read Lucca's journal and Jo's. Valora is a monster and needs to be stopped. If we don't do it, who will?" Allison said, taking a deep breath and putting a look of determination on her face.

"We did all the leg work, and we drove her here on purpose. It wasn't as if Heeling did it all by himself," Scarlet said.

"You really want to go through with this?" Maddie asked in between bites, she'd really hoped they would change their minds.

"Yes, but I think we need to look at this logically," Scarlet said.

"Logically? We are hunting vampires!" Queenie exclaimed and was instantly hushed by her friends. Who knew how much the other people were eavesdropping and understanding?

"That if we follow the map and we don't find Valora by tonight, we return to Brasov and go home," Scarlet continued.

"And what, try and go back to our normal lives? Valora will return to school and take out her vengeance on us," Jo said.

"I don't think so. She won't risk it. She might eventually come back, but it will be after we've all graduated," Scarlet countered, ever logical.

"And Maddie?" Allison asked.

"I will handle my own problems. I'd rather stay connected to Valora than see any of you hurt," Maddie told them. She was trying so hard to mix truth with lies. She really did want them to give up this mission and go home, but she also wanted them punished for her brother's death.

"What if you can't control it anymore? My uncle was sure you'd get worse and eventually Valora would turn you," Queenie said, eyes large, dried tracks of tears on her cheeks.

"Then you all will do as you promised." Maddie ended the conversation.

The woman came back with a full carafe of coffee.

"What are all you young women doing in this part of Transylvania?" she asked as she filled all their cups and began clearing away empty dishes. Her accent was thick and difficult to understand.

"We are doing a project for school," Scarlet answered after a few tense seconds as they tried to decide what to tell her.

"We do not get many Americans through here."

"We're headed toward Padurea Bogatii," Maddie said, hoping she wasn't butchering their language.

The woman froze, then slowly straightened, dark eyes bright. She made the sign of the cross. "That is a bad idea, that area is cursed."

"Cursed?" Jo asked.

"Yes, I'm sorry, we do not like to speak of it. Most believe the entire area to be haunted. Please do not go there."

Queenie opened her mouth, but Allison squeezed her thigh in warning.

"Fine, we won't, we'll head back to Brasov. Thanks for the warning," she said. The woman looked relieved and left them alone.

"Well that's interesting," Scarlet said.

"But not surprising," Jo said, an uneasy silence filled the table.

They finished eating and paid, leaving a substantial tip. By the time they piled into the little car, it was almost noon.

They drove into the Persani Mountains and followed the map Valora gave Maddie. The snow on the ground glittered like diamonds and the trees were bare, some holding snow, others, like the beech still held orange and brown remnants of their fall leaves. They left the main road for a smaller, but well-maintained side road that got narrower and became snake like as it wound up into the mountains until it simply ended.

Pulling off to the side of the road, they parked the car and got out.

"Everyone, check your packs," Jo instructed. "I don't want anyone getting frostbite or dehydrated."

"We're not worried. We have you, the great outdoors woman," Maddie teased, and Jo gave her a grin that felt just like the old days.

It couldn't have been more than fifteen degrees outside and even dressed as warmly as they were it was still freezing. The sun shone down through the trees offering a bit more warmth. Thankfully the day was clear, and the weather was supposed to stay sunny.

"Everyone got their gear on? Sunscreen applied? Sunglasses on?" Jo asked. Her pack was the biggest as she was the most fit and used to these sorts of conditions. She carried water, matches, and snacks; each girl had a thermal blanket.

We probably look like freaks. If anyone saw us, they would think we were crazy. Are we a cult? Fanatic ice campers? Perhaps a mirage and when they look back, we would disappear.

"Yup," Scarlet said, adjusting her pack. "Let's go."

A worn looking trail veered off to the right, toward denser forest and higher mountains.

"This is no hidden path. Someone comes here or at least pays for it to be maintained," Jo mentioned as they began their trek.

"Seems reasonable, if this is near Valora's old home she wouldn't want to cut through plants every time she came to visit," Allison responded.

"Can we not talk? I'm going to be out of breath before we get a mile if I'm expected to chat as well," Scarlet grumbled.

Normally that was Maddie's line. Jo always mentioned Maddie was softer, rounder than she was. However, Maddie was having no trouble with the rocks and hills they were hiking. She wondered if that was a side effect of Valora's blood.

The woods were quiet and as the girls got deeper into them, the time between comments became longer until the silence was almost unbearable. The snow dampened sound and it was if they were walking through a painting of a snow-covered mountain instead of the real thing. Hornbeam trees loomed above them so that only streaks of sunlight got through.

Jo left markers along the trail, just in case, and they stopped about an hour in to get water and fuel themselves. Maddie knew Jo was having fun, even Queenie seemed to keep a smile on her face, but Allison and Scarlet were looking more haggard with every step.

Maddie took the map from Jo so she could see how far they had to travel. Her feet were starting to hurt, and she worried about them getting lost or winding up not getting back to the car before dark. While she was certain Valora would find her, she didn't want her friends to freeze to death, maybe a bit of frostbite would be okay though.

Thankfully, the snow wasn't more than a few inches deep or this would have been an even more harrowing experience. Maddie read a bit about snow hiking before the trip and had all sorts of tips and warnings blazing through her mind.

Images of forest rangers finding their blue frozen corpses haunted her dreams.

"This really is too good of a path," Jo announced at 3:00 p.m. They were stopped again.

"I can't imagine what it would be like if it were a shitty path," Scarlet said.

"I know, but it does worry me. What if she's waiting for us?" Jo asked, wiping excess water from her lips, and then she passed the bottle to Queenie.

"She might be." Queenie drank deeply and soon they were off again. They may as well not have stopped that second time for as they began to descend downhill they came to a row of thick oak trees and the path stopped dead.

"What do we do now?" Allison asked.

"Keep going," Jo said. She pushed through the barren trees, so thick that almost no snow was on the ground, just rocks and dead leaves.

Branches grabbed at their clothes and snagged fabric and skin, the rocks hurt their feet and the sound of their boots against the ground hurt their ears; it was so unnatural and affronting.

Jo broke off a branch, pushing through that last bit of vegetation, she tried to stop but her momentum was too great, and she tripped, stumbling into a clearing and over a rock. She swore and hit the ground, hard.

"Jo! Are you okay?" Scarlet asked as they huddled around Jo, who was holding her ankle.

"Yeah, stupid mistake, dumb rock." Jo held out her arm and they helped her up. She tested her ankle, grimaced, and then put her weight on it.

"I don't think it's anything too serious, thankfully," Jo grumbled.

"Ummm, that's not a rock," Maddie said, throat dry. They all took a moment to look at their surroundings. Over a dozen grey and white rocks dotted the immediate area, as did a partial stone wall about a foot high, in most places it was so crumbled you couldn't even call it a wall, but enough was left to map out a specific area.

"Oh, gross!" Allison said.

"A cemetery?" Queenie asked. She knelt and brushed off snow and dirt from the headstone Jo tripped over.

"I can't read it. There is a name and date, but it's so old," Queenie said, awed.

"Can we please leave the cemetery? I don't want to stand on dead people any longer," Allison said squeamishly.

I wonder who is buried here? Members of Valora's family? Perhaps the people she killed? A motherless child, a consumption victim, or even a blind, beggar woman.

They walked until they passed a piece of the ancient wall and could be sure they no longer stood in the graveyard.

Maddie looked at the map. "I think we're here, I'm pretty sure this symbol represents the cemetery, so the castle ruins should only be half a mile in that direction." She pointed to the north and they all looked.

Sure enough, the ruins of a castle stood out against the blue sky. The mountains surrounded the whole area, creating a little valley, just like in Valora's story. She could see an overgrown dirt road leading up toward the ruins and what seemed to be the foundations of several smaller buildings near the graveyard.

From what they could see, no actual livable or useable buildings remained of the castle, simply its skeleton, gray with old black scorch marks straining against the cold, collapsing down around itself. It was one of the most depressing sights Maddie had ever seen. She didn't understand how Valora could keep coming back here and being reminded.

"Are we ready?" Scarlet asked.

"Yes," Jo answered for all of them, quickening the pace she took the lead, almost marching up the road, through the undergrowth, all cold and dead beneath their feet.

CHAPTER TWENTY-SIX

Blood Born

I stand gazing at the blood pooled beneath my feet. It washes the stone walls of our home. The stench of copper, gore, and fear permeate every inch. It will take forever to clean but clean it I must.

This is not the first time my home has been stained red and it will not be the last. The dark gift given to me assures that more blood will spill within these walls. My duty is to protect this land, its people, and my home. That is why I am alive, and my husband and sons are not.

I smell the fire licking against the logs in the parlor, I know the heat slowly claims the coldness of the room, but I no longer feel cold, so building the fire is simply a habit. A habit from a former life.

More men will come. I am leaving behind a mystery, of course they will come. It is no use, I will always be here, and they will die by my hand before I allow them to brutally savage this area again.

Too much time passed between my death and my awakening, I spent too long in the dark. Too long figuring out what I was, what I had become. I will waste no more time. I will clean this blood and I will live my life.

I put the bucket on the ground and kneel, my dress soaking up the crimson. I put my pale, soft hands in the water and grab the hard bristle brush. Out of the corner of my eye, the painting watches me, it mocks me. I close my eyes against tears, they sting. My emotions feel heightened, intense, so strong, and stronger than while my heart beats.

An ache forms in my chest as I think of them. I grip the wet brush harder, it connects with the floor, a scratching dragging sound. My husband, my sons, why are they not here with me? Why are others special, but they are not? Is it a punishment? A curse for suicide and murder?

Are my beloved boys not with me because upon the moment of their slaughter their souls were found pure and set free? I will never know.

The water in the bucket turns pink as I clean the brush and start the process again. I have several others full of clean water around me, but eventually I will need to fetch more. I do not have much time before the sun rises. Thankfully, I have new powers to help, I can move faster than I did in my old life, so much faster.

"Mother? Let us help." I hear her steps before her voice. I don't look up.

———

Bethany Stratton

"This is my mess."

"It is our mess, you did this for us, for our people, we can help."

"I don't want your hands dirty." Rocking back on my heels, I see two pairs of slippers; they are both here, both standing before me. I am at once relieved and filled with regret and sorrow. Had I known my actions would damn them as well as me I would have taken a different path, but it is too late for those regrets.

"You must go from here, you must never return," I tell them. They both look shocked at my words, hurt and angry.

"Why?" my oldest asks; she is not a month older than twenty-one and never will be. She is not brave or strong, she would hide behind my skirts as a child. Her hair as black as mine, a smaller, chubbier version of me. She should not have been here, she should have been married, home with a husband, the swell of a child within her. I was selfish, I kept her with me too long.

"No, we won't leave you. This is our home too." My youngest crosses her arms under her breasts. She is blonde, the spitting image of her father. She turned eighteen days before her death, she is too smart for her own good.

"No one can know you survived. They will see me as protector, and a monster.

More will come and try to kill me, to take this place. I cannot bear the thought of you dying...again." I plead with them, they must leave. I took their lives thinking to save them from ruin, humiliation, and pain. Now they have the chance to go and live, outside these walls, some place new, fresh, and exciting.

"You would cast us off, after all this? Send us from you?" My oldest begins to cry.

"You will see me again, when I am no longer needed here, but I must protect you. Please think of your father, your brothers." I will not cry, I have spent too long in the company of grief. I will miss them, but they must leave.

"You are sure this is what you want?" My youngest asks. She wants to protect me, to help me. She forgave me faster than her sister did.

"Yes, please, tomorrow night." I have a few hours left with them. I wish I wasn't spending it cleaning up a villain's blood. This is not how I wish for them to remember me.

"But Mother..." my eldest starts again, but her sister nudges her with an elbow.

"We will still help you clean," my youngest says, she reaches for a bucket.

———

They reached the crest of the hill and the entire valley stood in clear view below them, brown and weathered by the elements and time of year. Maddie could imagine how beautiful and fertile it would be in the spring. Some plants still held tints of green, struggling against the cold.

"This place would have been a decent size castle," Scarlet says as they view the remains of Valora's home. The jagged edges and decaying walls held the hint of room shapes, most half buried by vegetation.

"They say the flames burned all through the night. I'm surprised there's anything left," Queenie said.

"Who says that?" Maddie asked.

"My uncle," Queenie answered, her smile watered down, eyes sad.

Guilt climbed up through Maddie's throat and coated her tongue. She hadn't liked Professor Heeling, but she wasn't quite okay with his death either. Why couldn't he have just left well enough alone?

"Well, isn't Professor Dulcara supposed to be here? Where is she?" Allison asked, peering all around her, trying to find some secret area.

"In a hurry, are you?" Scarlet raised one eyebrow at her.

"Yes, what she did to my Lucca is unforgiveable. Let's destroy her, and then leave. I want to go home." Allison wrapped arms around herself, she shivered in the sunlight.

"Aren't you guys afraid? She's an ancient vampire. You don't think we're just all going to wind up dead?" Maybe she could still dissuade them.

"There's more of us than of her, plus she'll be vulnerable, like the professor said," Jo said. "Split up, we've got to find where she is sleeping."

Maddie had a feeling she knew where Valora was; she debated between leading them astray or getting it over with, eventually one of her friends would figure it out. Making her way back behind the castle remains, she found a path leading downward, scorched stone littered the path and she had to step over and around many obstacles, and what she assumed was a left-over set of stairs. She could smell age, dust and slight decay all around her and it wasn't unpleasant.

Finally, she came upon an entryway, most of the wall surrounding it lay in piles at her feet, but it was wide enough to get through and led down into the ground. Maddie stuck her head in, using her phone as a flashlight, she swiped at a cobweb, grateful there wasn't a spider attached.

An intact set of stairs led down deeper into the earth. There was no light, just the smell of damp dirt and campfires. This must be the catacombs of the old castle, the one where Valora and her daughters died.

"I found it!" she called.

"Woah, that is seriously creepy," Scarlet said, joining her.

"Are you sure she's down there?" Allison asked, nervously.

"Where else could she be? Good find, Maddie," Jo complimented her and Maddie felt a bit like a puppy who'd proven house training worked.

"Let's do this. You don't think there are rats though, right?" Queenie said.

"I doubt it, too cold." Scarlet put an arm around her friend.

One by one, they squeezed in through the entrance, all using flashlights, as they carefully went down. Most of the stairs were undamaged, but a few were chipped. The steps were stone, but also wood, so they had to move slowly, testing each step before any weight could be placed.

Maddie thought about all the people who had walked these steps before her, scurrying maids, solemn mourners, perhaps a wine cellar or food pantry had also lay this way and not just the dead.

Their noises echoed inside, causing each girl to flinch, but no one spoke. It was as if they were acting under an unspoken rule to be as silent as they could.

Finally, they reached the bottom and gazed upon a large, dome-like chamber; one wall held stacked tombs of granite with names and dates on each of them.

"These are too new to have been here when the fire happened," Scarlet said. She walked over, shining the flash light's yellow beam onto one panel.

"They must have been replaced." Allison swept her own light around the room and made a pleasant noise, pointing out a series of torches to Jo.

As the room filled with soft firelight and the smell of burning oil, they could see a faint smattering of dead leaves on the ground as well as several doors leading from the main room. The walls and roof were a combination of rotting wood, packed dirt, and rock.

"Everyone, try a door," Jo instructed.

Maddie simply stood in the middle of the room with her as there were not enough doors for everyone.

Scarlet's door held nothing but debris and would be impossible to get through let alone guess the conditions of the rooms on the other side. There may not even be anything if there was a cave in over the years, or if the fire had gotten to it somehow.

Allison's door opened on empty space, stairs that went down a few feet and ended in a black hole, even shining a light one couldn't see the bottom, just hear air as it moved around the great empty space.

"I've found something," Queenie said, holding her door wide open; it led into a room that was the twin of the one they currently stood in, just half its size.

"What?" Jo asked. She dropped her pack and pulled out a large machete.

"There's a box in here," Queenie whispered, digging through her own bag she took out a bowie knife.

"Get ready," Jo said. "Maddie, you stay back here, I don't want you in the way."

"But..."

"No, Maddie, do what I say, please." Jo placed a hand on her and gave her a light shove.

"You can't all go in there," Maddie said. "There's not enough room."

Allison took a cross and holy water from her bag, face like steel, actions smooth.

"Are you sure about this? We can still leave," Maddie said.

"We've come this far, I have to see this through. The rest of you can leave if you'd like," Jo said.

"No, for Lucca."

Maddie wanted to slap Allison for invoking Lucca's name. If not for them, he might be with her now and not in the afterlife. How dare they use Lucca for their crusade?

"For Uncle Austin."

"Being a doctor is about helping people, how many has this monster hurt? If I can do something about it I will," Scarlet said.

"You stay out here with Maddie, okay?" Jo asked.

"Are you sure?"

"Yes, she needs...protection."

Maddie was positive that wasn't what Jo meant, probably more along the lines of Maddie needs watching.

"I still think this is a bad idea," Maddie tried one last time and all she got for her trouble was looks of suspicion and pity.

"I'll stay out here with you, Maddie. Trust them, they can do this," Scarlet said. Did she have confidence in them or was it all for show?

The three of them made eye contact and then went in the room and shut the door.

Maddie tensed; she took a step toward the door, but Scarlet stopped her.

Maddie heard a growl and sounds of flesh hitting flesh, like in a fight. Something hard hit the wall causing both girls to jump. They heard Jo swear and Allison scream.

"We have to help!" Maddie strained against Scarlet's hold.

"No, there's nothing we can do." She didn't sound so sure, but her grip was firm.

Sinister laughter leaked out from under the door, then water splashing and a hissing noise. Another scream and disgustingly unrecognizable noises and then silence.

The smell of rich iron filled blood penetrated the room, causing Maddie's mouth to water and then the door swung open.

Jo and Allison stood side by side, covered in blood, Queenie lay on the ground next to them, unconscious, but breathing. Maddie, feeling anxiety like she never had before, rushed forward, and pushed past her friends. Heart in her throat, fear boiling in her stomach, her eyes frantically searched the room. The box was open, purple silks inside as a bedding, but nothing else, nothing else but pools and pools of blood.

Maddie fell to her knees, and then there was nothing but blackness.

CHAPTER TWENTY-SEVEN

Personal Journal of Jolene Harper
Entry # 227

Now that things are a little quieter, I can record what happened in the catacombs, though by quiet I simply mean we are home and we are safe, well most of us are, but I'm getting ahead of myself. I'm writing this on my laptop from outside Maddie's hospital room. They say she'll be waking up soon.

Allison, Queenie, and I went into that room, and I shut the door. I didn't want Maddie to see, or more likely interfere. Allison opened the box, and Valora lay there, looking peaceful and asleep. It didn't last long. Her eyes flew open, red as garnets, and she growled at us, sitting up, fast as lightning.

I have never been so afraid. I'm embarrassed to say that I froze. Queenie rushed her and thrust her bowie knife into Valora's chest, blood came flooding out, fast and there was so much. Valora staggered and Allison advanced. She got a black eye for her trouble and then Valora turned on Queenie.

Before Allison or I could react, she picked up Queenie by the throat and threw her at the door. Queenie hit with a sickening smack and didn't get back up.

At this point, Valora gave a laugh, but looked like she was weakening. Her fangs were like pointed pieces of porcelain and I knew if she got them into me, she'd never let go and I would die there.

Allison doused Valora with holy water and shoved the cross at her, the combination of that and the blood loss allowed me my chance, and I thrust the machete through her throat. Eyes wide, she gasped and gurgled. She dropped to the floor, hand reaching for the door and then she was still, her black hair spread across the floor mingling with her blood.

I didn't have a chance to use any of the other precautions Heeling told us about. Her body began to wither, cracking and flaking off. She turned to dust and an abnormal wind swept through the tiny room, whisking her ashes away.

When Maddie saw the empty coffin, she collapsed, and we couldn't wake her. It took hours to get her and Queenie back to the car.

Thankfully, we are all still here to tell the tale. Queenie got a pretty bad concussion, but at least she is alive. Scarlet patched her up on the way back to the car.

Maddie awoke long enough for us to travel back to the United States and then slipped into what they are calling a fugue state due to trauma or shock. They think she might kill herself and have had to put her in a medically induced coma.

I truly believe her actions leading up to Valora's death were all caused by being mesmerized by that awful creature. I cannot blame her. She wasn't in control of herself. When she's better, I'll help her figure that out.

I still don't know what to tell her parents and have simply feigned ignorance. They think it's just Lucca's death catching up with her. They were angry with me when they realized we'd been in Romania and not Disneyland. Lucky for me my dad didn't seem to care much.

All of that aside, I feel so much happier and lighter. Dulcara Mansion is closed right now while they try to figure out who's in charge since Valora Dulcara is still on "sabbatical" and her class has been taken over by a visiting professor.

As for Professor Heeling, Queenie's parents have put out missing persons reports for him. The tale we spun was that he slipped off in Romania and never returned to the hotel. I don't know if his body will ever show up, and I feel rotten most of his family may not get the closure they need.

I feel like I should take up Heeling's work and go after the rest of Valora's students. After all, Byron and Mircalla are still out there. Queenie agrees with me, but it will have to wait. When Maddie wakes, things will be different, and I want her to know that.

Oh, here comes the nurse.

*M*addie opened her eyes and it felt like they were crusted over, and she'd been asleep for months. She lay in a hospital gown in a white room in a bed with railings and buttons all over it. An IV rested in her hand, and her throat felt parched and raw.

The lights overhead were bright, almost too bright, and she could hear not only the machines in her room but those in the room next door as well.

The sickening smell of disease, bodily fluids, cleaning products, and antiseptic drifted up her nose, causing her to grimace.

"You're awake." A voice from a person she couldn't see.

"What happened?" Maddie asked, after a few false starts, her voice sounded alien.

"They say when you got home from Romania you purposely drank yourself sick. They think it's an attempted suicide."

She still couldn't see who was talking.

"I don't remember anything, not even getting home," Maddie said.

"Pretty common after trauma or shock. I'll go let your family and the doctor know you're awake."

Maddie watched as the back of a black-haired nurse left the room.

She tried to sit up but couldn't so instead she worked cold and weak fingers to the railing and pushed a button. The bed slowly moved her into sitting position.

"Hey, you're awake!" Allison and Scarlet were the first in the room.

"Where are Mom and Dad?" Maddie asked. She was suddenly very uncomfortable, her throat felt like it was on fire. She swallowed a few times and used her anxiety coping skills. The sensation finally lessoned so she didn't feel like ripping out her IV and darting from the room.

"They were actually at the house taking a break. They'll be here in a bit," Scarlet said. There were shadows under her eyes.

"I'm glad to see you're doing okay, you had us worried," Allison accused.

"Where's Queenie? She's okay, right?" Maddie said the words, but they were meaningless; she didn't care if Queenie was okay or not. She wanted to know about Valora.

"Queenie won't come see you. I think she blames you for Heeling's death, a little," Scarlet said.

"Me too, I'm so sorry, I didn't want that," Maddie stated; it wasn't a lie, she was sorry Queenie blamed her for Heeling's death.

"We told them he left us at the hotel and didn't come back," Allison filled in. It took Maddie a moment to understand they were giving her a cover story.

"Do you think she'll get over it?" Maddie asked.

"Eventually. Queenie is a pretty forgiving and forgetting kind of person." Scarlet's brown eyes held hope. "Well, unless you like to kill innocent animals."

"You never told me, how'd you two meet?" Maddie asked, hoping to lighten the tone of the room, but she didn't feel jovial.

"She tried to liberate some fish we were dissecting in a science class."

"Classic Queenie," Maddie commented.

"We just wanted to see you, once you're out of here we'll throw a party to celebrate. I even bought you a present." Allison held a cream-colored box in one hand and a vase full of white roses in the other.

"That's more than one." Maddie felt it a superficial gesture, for when they first met she'd given Allison the benefit of the doubt, Lucca had loved her so much. That privilege was revoked the moment Allison told her the details of her brother's second death.

"These were actually left outside your door, probably from your family or Jo. The box is from me."

Maddie opened the box to find a yellow, cashmere scarf, not really her style, but Allison didn't know Maddie, at least, not the real Maddie.

"Thanks, Allison, you didn't have to."

Her gaze strayed to the flowers. Was this another attempt by Jo for reconciliation? She hoped not.

"Oh, I know, but when you're in the hospital, you get gifts. When I had my tonsils out, Daddy bought me a diamond bracelet." She held her wrist out to show off the gold, sparkling jewelry that hung daintily off her thin wrist. She placed the flowers on the table next to her.

"We'll leave you alone. We know Jo wanted to talk to you before your parents got here," Allison said.

"I'm glad we were able to destroy Valora before her hold on you got any more serious. We were all really concerned," Scarlet said. "Don't blame yourself for Heeling's death, okay? He knew it was dangerous going in."

"I know, thanks," Maddie responded, a bit distracted: what else could she say? That she'd been planning to ditch them all for Valora? That she hadn't thought their plan would work and the woman she was falling in love with was now dead? That of course it wasn't her fault Austin Heeling was dead, it was his?

Maddie questioned if she'd really been falling in love with Valora. She knew that they all thought she'd tried to kill herself, but she didn't remember any of it. She felt a little empty without Valora, but she also felt cold inside, distant. Had her death broken their blood ties? Had her feelings never quite been her own and always been Valora?

"I just wish Lucca was here, he'd be so proud of all of us," Allison said weakly as they walked out the door.

"Yes, I wish Lucca was here too." This time her words were sincere. If she could change just one thing, it would be to have Lucca be there, especially if it meant he was there instead of them.

Jo came in right after them, giving Maddie no time to process anything else. Jo looked how she always did, though there were new wrinkles on her face.

Her hair was mussed, like she'd been running her fingers through it and her clothes looked slept in.

"You're awake," Jo said.

"Interesting opening statement, counselor," Maddie replied, a teasing smile on her face. Jo paused, eyes wide, and then cracked a grin.

"Yeah, dumb statement more like." She pulled a chair up next to the bed, the sound it made on the floor grated on Maddie's nerves.

"How have you been? I'm sorry if I worried you," Maddie said, a pit in her stomach. It was so hard to talk to Jo now. She wasn't in love with her anymore, but she missed her friend and she worried Jo had never really been her friend.

It was harder to hate Jo for Lucca's death than the rest, simply because she'd been in love with her for so long first.

"I've been okay, I feel a lot better now that Professor Dulcara is dead. I was anxious for you. I didn't think her death would physically affect you. Heeling never mentioned that." She reached out and linked her hand with Maddie's.

Maddie gave it a squeeze and then pulled away, tucking her hand beneath the blue blanket.

"Did you send the flowers?" Maddie asked, trying to fill the tense air between them.

Jo looked at the flowers and shrugged. "Wish I could say yes, but no. Though you've had a ton of family send stuff and call to check on you."

They lapsed again into more uncomfortable silence, heavy with unspoken words.

"What's up, Jo?" Maddie asked; she knew her, there was something on her mind.

"You really hurt me, Maddie, and I know I hurt you, too. We made such a mess of things, but I'm ready to forgive and forget. We can put it all behind us, the vampires, and the darkness. We can start anew. This was supposed to be our time together." Jo made eye contact, she seemed so earnest, but Maddie could taste a hint of dishonesty in her words.

Wait, had she just tasted Jo's dishonesty?

"Ms. West, your parents are here, shall I show them in?" The nurse was back at the door. This time Maddie could see her face, recognition hit her like a ton of bricks. She stilled, trying not to show the shock on her face, just in case Jo was paying close attention.

The nurse was a beautiful woman, and she looked so much like Valora it hurt for Maddie to keep eyes on her, just a curvy version of her lover. Maddie was surprised Jo hadn't seen the resemblance. Were the cosmos punishing her?

"Yes, you can show them in," Maddie finally answered.

The nurse came in and checked a few things, helped Maddie sit up, and fussed with a few of the monitors.

"She'll have to leave when they come in, two-person maximum," the nurse said and left the room again.

"Has she been my nurse this whole time?" Maddie asked, a weird anxiety in her belly. What did this mean?

"Yes, she's very attentive, has taken care to make sure all your tests and paperwork are complete. They have such a great staff here. Something was up with one of your blood tests early on, but she fixed it," Jo said, a bit absentmindedly. "Now on to my question?"

"What's her name?" Maddie asked.

"Miriam. She's great. Do you need me to get her to come back? Are you feeling all right?" Jo asked, unease in her face, and she looked at Maddie's monitors, suspecting a problem.

Maddie wasn't paying attention to Jo because two of the fresh, white roses were now black and withered, and in between them sat a card she was sure hadn't been there before.

"Valora," Maddie whispered, a secret smile on her face. Jo jerked back like she'd been slapped.

"I guess it's not the nurse you want after all. You'll change your mind about us, Maddie. We belong together. You and I both know it." Jo got up and left the room, slamming the door behind her.

Emotions surged through Maddie, hunger and want, like she was being filled to the brim by a pitcher full of desire. Her skin came alive and her senses soared.

Maddie didn't acknowledge Jo leaving, she grabbed the card and opened it. Inside was a single sentence:

I told you, sweet girl, you're mine—for eternity.
—V

Don't miss your next favorite book!
Join the Fire & Ice YA Books newsletter today!
www.fireandiceya.com/mail.html

THANK YOU FOR READING

Did you enjoy this book?

We invite you to leave a review at the website of your choice, such as Goodreads, Amazon, Barnes & Noble, etc.

DID YOU KNOW THAT LEAVING A REVIEW...

- Helps other readers find books they may enjoy.
- Gives you a chance to let your voice be heard.
- Gives authors recognition for their hard work.
- Doesn't have to be long. A sentence or two about why you liked the book will do.

ABOUT THE AUTHOR

Renee Lake is a mother of four from Utah. She loves bats and is passionate about women's reproductive rights. Her lame super hero power is being able to sing any song after only hearing it once. This is quite problematic when her husband listens to French pop music.

Her favorite book is Jurassic Park and her favorite movie is any version of Sense and Sensibility she can get her hands on.

She has eight books published. When she's not taming her crazy kids or writing, you can find her exploring the wilds of Thedas or shopping at the Citadel.

www.thehauntedgravebooks.com

f facebook.com/authorreneetravis

🐦 twitter.com/damianarose

www.ingramcontent.com/pod-product-compliance
Lightning Source LLC
Chambersburg PA
CBHW050516260626
47157CB00004B/1355